ENTER THE DREAMER

S. A. BASTEDO

For Kris.
Thanks for going on this journey with me.
I couldn't have done it without you.

Our truest life
is when we are in dreams awake.

— *Henry David Thoreau*

CONTENTS

WHAT HAPPENED BEFORE

Seven Years Ago

The worst things happen on the most beautiful days. Ten year old Cash stood on his front porch and stared at the perfectly blue sky and cotton candy clouds. A warm breeze ruffled his blond hair as he braced himself to face his approaching neighbor, Mrs. Davies. He knew he shouldn't have run across her yard but he couldn't wait to show his dad his new comic book. Must have trampled her precious begonias. Cash bunched his hands into fists and turned slowly. His septuagenarian neighbor stormed toward him with a grim look on her face. Nothing could have prepared him—

"Your parents are dead," she stated with an emphatic full stop.

An involuntary sound escaped from his throat somewhere between a choke and a laugh. Before he could say anything she continued in her forced tone, "Your mother went to sell her vegetables on Islenook Island and your father accompanied her. The ferry they were on collided with a ship and no one on the ferry survived." The lines on her face relaxed slightly. She continued, "I'm sorry, Cash, this must be a lot to take in."

He didn't feel right. He was either going to fall over or float off into the air. His head was swimming. Was everything getting darker? Turning his head, his body followed and took a couple of steps toward the door. After several tries, he found the handle and pushed. The door creaked open revealing shadows and silence. He stepped in and closed the door behind him. When Mrs. Davies knocked he slid the deadbolt into place

"Cash, don't worry. I've called the police. They'll be here soon and will know what to do. I have to pop home and take a roast out of the oven. Of course, it's half-cooked. But no matter… I'll be right back and will wait with you. Alright? Cash?"

The only response she heard was Cash's head thumping quietly against the door. Clarity suddenly pierced the fog.

"Police…" he murmured, "I can't stay here!"

At his school, the older boys told horror stories about the orphanage just outside of town where kids with no family ended up. He dashed up the stairs to his room. Ripping the bookbag from his back, he flipped it over and dumped out the contents, then threw open the drawers of his dresser. Pants, sweaters, two shirts, and underwear all went into the bag. Then he grabbed a comb and his toothbrush which he also shoved in the sack. Back downstairs he hurried. He knew that if anyone showed up, his chance to get away would disappear.

The next stop was the living room. He passed by their new cathedral-style radio proudly sitting on a cabinet across from the sofa. It was still a novelty to listen to the BBC after dinner. Their family portrait from last fall sat on a side table next to his father's favorite chair. Cash plucked the photo frame and paused only long enough for a pang to hit his stomach at the sight of his and his parents' smiling faces. As he took the photo, he knocked a book on the floor. It was the book his father had been reading to him. The bright orange cover held stories about daring feats at the circus. On the cover, an illustrated bear and lion posed in front of a big top. With a half-pained grin, Cash placed the photo and book at the top of his bag and closed it. There was only one thought in his determined young mind. He was going to find the circus.

CHAPTER 1

THE DISCOVERY

Present Day

Muck faster, boy!" called Barnaby as he pounded on the sliding door of the train compartment. Cash used his upper arm to adjust the bandana covering his mouth and nose and tried to keep the pitchfork piled with elephant excrement balanced. At 17, he was tall, lean, and strong. His face had finally shed the roundness of youth, and he had noticed some of the younger tumblers giggling and waving at him over the last few months. Cash walked to the open car door and flung the poop into the wheelbarrow below. He quickly followed it with more muck from the elephants' train car, nearly missing Barnaby as he approached. Ignoring the flying feces, the head animal handler peeked his head into the compartment and aggressively waved him out.

"Better get back to your car. We're fixin' to pull out at six." Cash glanced at his bare wrists and back to Barnaby quizzically. Just then, the warning whistle blared. "Five minutes! Get goin'!" Barnaby yelled right before he turned away to load up.

Cash recklessly threw out loads of the remaining muck, not even trying to get it in the wheelbarrow. Then he attached the pitchfork to the bracket on the wall and hopped out of the car. He started to push the wheelbarrow toward the forest.

"What are you doing?!" Cash heard from over his shoulder. A quick glance revealed Tony, his bunkmate, running towards him. "We're pulling out!"

Cash struggled with the wheelbarrow.

"Leave it!" Tony yelled.

Cash dropped the wheelbarrow and tried to push the big car door closed, but it wouldn't budge. He shoved against the door a few more times and began to panic at the lack of movement.

Pulling his bandana down, Cash yelled, "Help me with this door!" The train's whistle blew from the front of the train.

Tony grabbed the rear handle of the door and the boys pushed together. The door budged and slid with an unwilling squeal on its track. Cash quickly threw the padlock in place and clicked it closed. Then the boys ran toward their quarters at the back of the train together. With four more cars to go, the train started moving. Slowly at first, but it wouldn't take long for it to be chugging along too quickly to jump on.

"Hurry!" Tony shouted as he picked up his pace. Cash pushed his lean frame as fast as it would go, arms pumping by his sides. Tony reached the caboose first and hopped on the stairs to the platform behind the caboose.

The horrifying thought of being left alone in the eastern European countryside was enough to summon an almost magical reserve of energy. Cash sped up and narrowed his sight on the caboose. As he approached the back of the train, everything that had been a blur seemed to fall into slow motion. He was aware of the mechanical movement of the train, his feet on the grass mixed with gravel. After a few more powerful strides, Cash bent his left knee and jumped athletically.

He glided through the air with ease, his legs looking for a landing place. He would have made it perfectly onto the platform of the caboose had it not been for Tony standing there ready to pull him up — that and a strange jerking sensation like time was catching back up with him. Cash flew into Tony and both boys tumbled to the hard metal platform.

"That was a close one," Tony wheezed, having a hard time breathing with Cash still crushing his chest. "What were you thinking, Cash? What's the first thing they told you when you started here?"

"I know, I know," Cash gasped.

"You gotta make sure you're in your compartment when the warning whistle sounds," Tony exasperated.

"Yeah, yeah. I've never cut it that close before in the seven years I've been here," Cash rebutted.

"Exactly. You should know better and not get lazy about it," Tony chided.

"Mucking takes forever now that there are two elephants. It's impossible to keep their car clean. Barnaby doesn't care that there's twice as much work now, he'll bust me if I don't keep up," Cash added in his defense.

"You literally have the worst job in the whole circus. You've got to find something else," Tony said, picking a piece of popcorn out of his hair and tossing it into the wind.

"I know, but I don't know what to do. I'm not funny

enough to be a clown, or tall or short enough to be a side-show. Can't train animals and I'm too clumsy to juggle…" Cash closed his eyes in frustration.

"And you definitely can't cook. I was sick for three days after you made beans in our car." Tony made a vomiting sound.

"It wasn't that bad!" Cash laughed.

"OK, two days." Tony conceded.

The boys sat in lighthearted silence for a few minutes, legs through the railing, dangling off the back of the caboose. They were best friends, yet opposite in many ways. Tony was short with olive skin and dark hair that he always carefully parted. Cash stood tall and lean with wavy blonde hair that hung down to his eyes.

"Maybe you could sell tickets? Get a gig in the red wagon." Tony suggested, always the optimist.

"Yeah, maybe." Cash sighed and stared at the fading landscape. The setting sun shone golden rays on the green and yellow corn fields. "But I don't think I'm that lucky."

Cash went inside the caboose and climbed into his bed to rest while Tony folded the table out from the wall and sat down. They each had a bed on opposite ends of the car. Janky, wooden planks lined the floor, ceiling and walls. At one point, the walls had been painted a light blue, but only the occasional patch of paint remained. They built their own shelves, and Tony had come up with the idea of the fold-down table. Other cars were nicer but were packed with eight to twelve bunks. The caboose sat empty for years due to rumors that it was haunted. Before Cash arrived, Tony started sleeping in there, and they had slowly made it homey and livable.

"By the way, why weren't you on the train when the

whistle sounded?" Asked Cash, propping himself up on one arm.

"I was visiting the tumblers," he said with a sly smile. Cash didn't need to ask any more questions. Tony was ever the charmer and Cash suspected he had a crush on one of them.

———

The next morning Cash awoke to the first rays of the bright morning sunshine coming in through the window.

"Ugh. Forgot to close the curtain again."

The train had stopped moving at some point during the night. They were either at the next town or just stopping to give the animals a break. Either way, if they were stopped, he had to get to his job. He got out of bed and looked around for a pair of socks. Cash stumbled to the "kitchen" area that consisted of one small burner, a kettle, a pot, and a skillet. Since the cookhouse wouldn't be up and running yet, he dumped some oats in the pot and added water. Quietly unfolding the table from the wall, he sat down as Tony rustled in his bed.

"Those food sellers have it easy," Cash mumbled. "Sleeping in as late as they want." Tony snored in response.

Tony had started in the circus as part of the clowns' act. Not a clown, but the little kid who ran around and played tricks on the slow clown. He outgrew that job several years ago. Since then he'd been hocking popcorn and cotton candy during the show as one of the barkers who walks around the stands with a tray of popcorn.

While the oatmeal cooked, Cash stuck his head out the door and spotted the red wagon. That meant they had arrived at the next city sometime during the night. As the central hub of the whole circus, it was always the first thing erected. The red wagon had to be ready for job assignments, questions, and locals arriving way too early. Across the midway where the concessions and game booths would go, the tent master and his crew were prepping the bale ring and side poles for the big top. When the oatmeal was ready, Cash ate it plain and left to find Nina and, hopefully, a new job.

Cash nervously walked up the steps to the Red Wagon and paused. He knew it was a long shot, but it was all he had left. Hope encouraged him to raise his fist and knock gently, not sure if Nina was there yet. He shifted his weight uncomfortably as he paused and debated leaving, when he heard soft footsteps coming to the door.

Seven Years Ago

Cash sat in the drab front room of the red wagon. One pathetic ray of light played hide and seek with the curtain covering the window on the front door. Cash snapped his attention back to Ringmaster Mastiff.

"As I was saying, boy…" The ringmaster snarled the last word as he reached out an arm to support himself on the wall so he could ominously lean over Cash to make his point. Elon Mastiff wasn't a tall man, but his broad shoulders and large head blocked the sliver of light from the window as he towered over Cash seated in a chair. The ringmaster's face was so close to Cash's that he could see leftovers of the ringmaster's lunch in his teeth.

"The most important thing to remember when working for my circus is DON'T GET LEFT BEHIND!" The large man warned in his gravelly voice.

Cash gulped.

The ringmaster continued nearly at a yell."Nothing stops my train once it's rolling. The show will always go on because I refuse to be late because some nincompoop lost track of TIME!"

The ringmaster worked himself into such a frenzy that his crude black hair loosened from its pomade and stuck out straight. His top hat bounced and jiggled but somehow defied gravity and never fell off of his head. At the word "time", the Ringmaster's eyes darted above Cash's head to check the time on the dusty cuckoo clock. Without looking at Cash again, he stormed out of the room and down the hall. A door slammed.

Cash's heart rate eventually slowed and he loosened his grip on the red vinyl chair where he was perched. He wiped a bead of sweat from his forehead, mussing up his blonde hair. It seemed like the ringmaster was not coming back and he was alone in the red wagon. Unsure where to go or what to do next, he decided to wait and see if someone else would show up with instructions. Just as he became nervous that the ringmaster would return and yell at him for still being there, the front door flew open and chaos tumbled in. A clown with big, flappy red shoes tripped into the room and caught his balance. After him, a dainty woman in her mid-thirties with pink glasses pulled one of the largest men he had ever seen into the room.

A gasp escaped from Cash and he clasped his hands over his mouth. The man was wearing a boar costume.

"Bonkers! Sit!" The woman gestured toward his side

of the room. "Boris! Stop moving!" She commanded the two men. The clown strode over toward Cash, sagged into the chair next to him, and scanned him out of the corner of his eye.

"Never seen you before," the clown stated.

"No. I'm, I'm new," Cash said.

"You OK, kid? You look like you've seen a ghost."

"I had a dream about a boar last night."

"Huh, that's weird. You dream a lot?" the clown inquired.

"I don't know. Not a lot, I don't think. But they kind of stick in my memory."

The clown looked at him and grunted. "Bonkers," he said after a moment, holding out his hand.

Cash looked at the clown's hand before offering his own hand and his name. "Cash," he said.

"Ah. A smart one. Thought I had a buzzer, didn't you?"

Cash shrugged.

"Nah. Too obvious for me."

Across the room, the big man was pulling at his head.

"What is going on?" Cash whispered to Bonkers.

"Comedy," the clown replied with a mischievous grin.

A deep, muffled voice came from the animal's head. "He must have put glue on it! I can't get out of the suit with the head on! Nina, get it off!" The boar man bent over and Nina pulled at the head, but it didn't budge. She put a knee on the man's shoulder and pulled with all of her strength. Bonkers doubled over, and when he sat back up, tears of laughter ran down his painted cheeks.

"I'm going to have to cut it off. Sit down." The boar man sat on the ground. Cash watched the woman take a pair of scissors and slowly cut around the neck of the boar. When she was almost done, Bonkers got up to leave.

"I better get out of here before Boris is free of that thing," the clown whispered as he tiptoed for the door. He slipped out just as Nina pulled off the boar's head and stepped away. The man in the suit was on his feet in a moment and looking around wildly.

"Where'd he go?" Boris yelled, his eyes finally falling on Cash.

Cash pointed toward the door. Boris turned to leave.

"Boris, don't! I'll find him later and talk to him," Nina said calmly.

"Fine," the big man gritted his teeth and grabbed his boar's head from the ground.

Nina finally turned her attention to Cash. "You must be Cash. Sorry about that nonsense. Boris and Bonkers are actually good friends. Sometimes Bonkers' jokes go too far though."

Boris shook his head, then tucked the boar's head under one arm and stretched a hand out to Cash.

"I'm Boris. Welcome to the circus."

Present Day

The door of the red wagon opened slightly and the face of a sleepy, spectacled Nina appeared.

"Hey Cash," was all she got out before a big yawn overtook her. "What're you doing here so early?" she asked, opening the door all the way, inviting him in.

Cash gratefully entered the dull room. The only times he had been in the room were when he started at the circus seven years ago, and twice a month for his pay.

Aside from that he had never shown up unexpectedly. Nina leaned against her desk and reached for her steaming mug of coffee.

Cash blurted out quickly, "I want to come work for you here, at the Red Wagon. Tony said there's an opening now that the kid with the lisp went home."

"Oh, Cash, I'm so sorry. Elon filled that role right away. He gave the job to Sacha," she replied apologetically.

Any sense of hope Cash felt earlier shattered. He looked away and concentrated, trying to think of alternatives.

"Maybe I could talk to one of the other departments and help you find something," Nina offered.

"I've pretty done it all. Except for the red wagon and acrobatics.

"Oh, I see." Nina paused to think. "I can't help you with the acrobats. Lorenzo recruits them himself. Apparently, he's the only one who can recognize 'the gift' as he calls it."

Cash thought for a moment. "I can't work in other departments, but maybe Sacha can. You could transfer him to the kitchen or the clowns and I'll work here with you. I'm sure he's talented. His uncle *and* father own circuses. He probably can do loads of neat things!" The excitement on Cash's face juxtaposed the discomfort on Nina's.

"I can't do that, Cash. I'm so sorry," Nina said, actually looking very sorry.

"Are…are you sure? It would work out great…"

Nina shook her head and glanced down the hall toward the ringmaster's office.

"Elon wants to keep… an eye on Sacha. Even though Sacha is his nephew, the ringmaster thinks Sacha might be stealing money from the circus. You know how the ringmaster is about money."

Everyone knew how he was about money. His performance jacket, and the interior of his train car were both the color of money. And once he had money he kept an iron first locked around it. Cash glanced at the towering safe in the corner with interest. It seemed to look back at him.

Cash thought for a moment. Tony usually caught any whisper of turmoil and suspicion in the circus, but here he was getting the scoop. He wanted a little more information.

"So the ringmaster is spying on his nephew?" Cash dropped his voice to a conspiratorial whisper.

Nina matched his whisper and said, "Elon and his brother Louka, Sacha's father, haven't spoken in almost 20 years. Supposedly, Sacha and his father had an epic argument. Shouting and spitting, right in the big top after one of Louka's shows. They were on the verge of punching and wrestling with each other when Louka whipped off his top hat and threw it at his son in exasperation and commanded Sacha to leave right away without even getting his things and to never come back!"

"How could a father do that to his son?!" Cash thought of his own father. William Connor had never come anywhere close to yelling. Not even when Cash left the gate open and the dog got out. Not when he lost his job at the first university where he taught. Cash's father loved his son and his wife and always spoke with love, hope, and respect.

Nina continued, "I don't know. But Sacha wandered the countryside looking for our circus, hoping that his uncle would take him in. Louka's and Elon's circuses have competed for years, but it's gotten more and more intense in the last few. Elon is always trying to stay ahead of Louka.

Sacha walked a long way to find us and Elon took Sacha in and gave him a job taking tickets at the Tent of Mysteries to start. But there's something unsettling about Sacha. He's always looking over his shoulder, and jumpy. The rumor is that he's planning to steal money so he can get away from circus life altogether. Unfortunately, Cash, I can't move Sacha anywhere else."

"It's OK. Thanks for trying, Nina. I guess I'm only good for cleaning out the elephant car."

"That's not true, Cash. You're smart and you're a hard worker. You're just young and learning and you're going to find your niche. Even if you can't find anything to do at the circus - so what?! One day you'll leave us and live out in the real world and be more successful than any of us! I know it's hard now, but you're going to do great things. Something will change for you." Nina's insistence surprised Cash. He could feel the warm hints of hope growing. Not as strong as before, but it was back, and that's what he needed to keep doing his job.

———

"Well, if it isn't the boy who lost my wheelbarrow," Barnaby said with a dripping, syrupy voice.

"I didn't have time to load it…" Cash tried to look busy.

"Excuses! I wish *you* would have got left! Wudda made my life easier. But now you're the one who's gonna regret it. This town is tiny. There aren't any wheelbarrows to buy. So I found you a nice, old tarp. Have fun dragging the elephant gifts into the woods." Barnaby jabbed an old finger towards the elephant car where a blue, faded tarp sat on the ground. The old man turned to attend to the other animals. "Stop staring at my back with your mouth hanging open. GET TO WORK!" Barnaby ordered.

Cash unfolded the tarp, then shoved open the door to the elephant car and quickly covered his ears as a loud, elephant trumpet emitted from the car. After it subsided, Cash hopped in the car and pulled his bandana over his nose and mouth to try and prevent a headache.

"Good morning, Flora. Morning, Major. Looks like I'll be looking after you for a while longer. It's not that I mind you so much, just what comes out of you." He rubbed Flora's trunk and she teasingly bumped him with it.

"Feisty today, huh?" He laughed and turned to Major.

"Hey, old boy. Ready for another exciting day at the circus?" Major made a huffing sound and looked bored.

"Well, move over. Let me see what you left for me." With that, Cash firmly nudged the elephants with the elephant guide, the long pole that prompted their movements in the show, to nudge them out of the way so he could get to work with the shovel.

When his arms were cramping and he couldn't shovel anymore, Cash hopped out of the car, walked a ways away, pulled the bandana from his face, and pulled in a deep breath of fresh, clean air. Grass, flowers, sunshine, a hint of the casserole Helen was preparing in the cookhouse. "Ahhhh. Much better," Cash said out loud as he stretched his arms.

Bang! Cash jumped and turned around almost tripping over himself. Lorenzo, the performance director, stood there in his black and white striped shirt, beret, red neck scarf, and antique walking cane. The greatest acrobat trainer of all time! (So he said). Lorenzo was spry for his age. The last thing he needed was a walking stick, at least for walking. Lorenzo used it to jab at things dramatically, stamp into the ground for emphasis, and get people's attention by banging it loudly.

"So, the boy with the elephant friends has a hidden talent," Lorenzo said coyly in his indistinguishable accent that sounded a little bit French, a little bit Italian.

"You must have the wrong person. I don't have any hidden talents. I wish I did. But I'm not good at much besides taking care of Flora and Major."

"You lie! Don't hide it from me! You have 'the gift'! No one recognizes 'the gift' like Lorenzo the Great!" He approached Cash talking loudly and gesticulating violently with his arms. His eyes sparkled mysteriously.

Cash backed up slowly. "I really don't think you're talking about me. I definitely do *not* have any gifts."

"Quiet! Yesterday as we were pulling out from that last, miserable town, I stuck my head out of my window to say good riddance. We rounded a bend. What did I see but a young man running for the back of the train," Lorenzo quieted his voice and paused for a dramatic effect before continuing, "This boy ran with the grace of a gazelle over the rocks and grass. Lorenzo thought to himself, 'He will never make the train. No one can make that jump.' And then my always truthful eyes watched the boy leap onto the back of the train like a mountain lion pouncing on its prey. No one without 'the gift' could make that jump! So I went to the Ringmaster and said, 'Who is the blonde boy at the back of the train!? I must have him and train him!'

'Cash Connor,' the Ringmaster said. But he warned me. 'Be careful, Lorenzo. Every job he's had, someone has gotten sick or hurt. I can't afford to lose you or one of the other acrobats.' But Lorenzo doesn't care! And so I have found you. Tomorrow at 8 a.m.. We start your training. Good day!"

Lorenzo twirled around and walked confidently toward where the sledge gang was pounding the stakes and pins of the Big Tent.

Cash stared after the lively, older man, mouth hanging open. He moved to return to the caboose but almost choked on hope when his body tried to laugh, cry, and gasp all at once.

"Nina was right. Things are changing!" Cash exclaimed.

He walked off to the sound of Barnaby's stuttering at him, "Wait, what?! Now who's going to muck the elephants!"

Then turning, Barnaby called after Lorenzo. "How could you do this to me!?"

CHAPTER 2

LETTING GO

Cash sat on the front row of the bleachers with one other new acrobat, a sixteen-year-old girl who had recently joined the circus from a local dog and pony show. Two weeks had passed since Lorenzo "discovered" him. He had never worked so hard for anything in his life or been so sore. Every morning he conditioned with the other acrobats and then ran drills on the trampoline. The closer he got to finally getting on a trapeze, the more nervous and excited he became.

Lorenzo was pacing and lecturing in front of them. Cash had to force himself to focus on the words and block out the cacophony of practice happening behind his instructor. Fire-breathers in red and purple leotards rolled around the ring on four-foot-tall balls, spouting fire toward the bleachers. A monkey chased Bonkers around the ring and down one of the tunnels. All the while, a dozen tumblers were flipping and bouncing off springboards.

"Trapeze artists are brave, they must have courage of iron. There is no doubting that. But it is not enough. You must practice to PERFECTION. You must TRUST your partner more than you trust anyone else. You must TRAIN until you dream about your moves. You must have unbreakable CONCENTRATION. You cannot become distracted when you are up in the air!"

Lorenzo paused as Bonkers chased the monkey right behind him, then continued his monologue once the clown ran off. "Every routine is a dance with fate. One mistake, one missed beat, one glance away and you're falling, falling, falling." He paused for dramatic effect, hands suspended in the air.

The new girl raised her hand. "Have you ever had an acrobat get in a serious accident? Where they can't perform anymore?"

Lorenzo turned toward her and glared. "You dare to question me? I train the best acrobats in the world!"

An awkward silence hovered as the girl continued to look at Lorenzo questioningly while Lorenzo avoided the question.

"But have you?" She pressed insistently.

"Yes, once, but we do not speak of such things. It's bad luck to speak of failure," Lorenzo dismissed the subject and began explaining their training schedule.

Beyond Lorenzo, Bella, the star, flew through the air toward her partner. Her long-sleeved golden costume shimmered in the spotlight and contrasted beautifully with her dark skin. Hanging by his knees on his trapeze, her partner caught Bella by the wrists and they swung together. His red and gold outfit looked like tongues of fire flicking through the air.

"There are two main reasons an acrobat falls during a routine. The first reason is 'casting'. This is where you change your mind mid-air. You must know exactly what you are going to do on every single move before you make the move or let go. If you have a double mind about it, you'll end up in the net." Cash listened to Lorenzo as he watched Bella, now on her own trapeze, perfectly executing flips and twirls. Each move was purposeful and exact, never hesitant. She radiated confidence.

"The second reason is equipment failure. We check the equipment before and after each performance, but there is always a chance something will go wrong. There is a net, but it can be just as dangerous as the ground. When you fall from 25 feet, or 40 feet if you are especially brave, going as fast as you've been flipping and turning, you have to protect yourself. The only way to safely fall is to curl up in a ball as tight as you can and let the net catch you," Lorenzo finished sternly.

Cash and the new girl took turns climbing to the lowest platform and jumping off into their protective tucks. From the 10-foot practice platforms, falling wasn't that scary, but Cash looked up to the regular height and then the extra-tall platforms, and a gulp of fear formed in his throat.

After that day, their training progressed quickly. Falling changed to swinging, then flipping on trampolines, then flipping from one trampoline to another. After several more weeks, Cash realized that he wasn't failing and he was even doing much better than the new girl. Maybe Lorenzo was right and he did have a "gift". If the gift started as a seed, it was now budding. Energized by finding something he excelled at, Cash stayed late most days to perfect his new skills. His endurance grew with each practice. Even his grip which was shaky at first, held firm for trick after trick.

One evening after staying particularly late after practice, Cash entered the cookhouse and glared around the crowded, noisy room. Rows and rows of picnic-style tables and benches were full of circus folk. The clowns noisily honked and jangled and ate their dinner together. The animal handlers sat together. Two monkeys ran down their table causing havoc. The acrobats and tumblers occupied another table and the carnies another. The equestrian team sat across the room in their own secluded corner. Cash noticed Tony sitting with Boris and Bella at a table in the middle of the room. At the front of the room, on an elevated stage the ringmaster, Lorenzo, Barnaby, Nina, and Sacha sat at the head table.

On his way to the buffet, Cash passed Helen, the cook, who was carrying a tub of dirty dishes.

"Oh hey, Cash honey. Have you eaten yet? No, you haven't. The boys just started putting dinner away. Come with me. I'll make you a plate. It was shepherd's pie tonight," she offered.

Cash obediently followed Helen past the mostly-empty buffet and into the kitchen. He was met by the hustle and bustle of boys his age and younger clearing plates and flinging mashed potatoes. Around the circus, they were known as Helen's Boys. Kids who couldn't find a place anywhere else were sent here. Sickly ones and those who were injured in a clowning accident or animal incident. You wouldn't know it from the chaos in the kitchen. A couple of weeks in Helen's kitchen and they were all lively and active again.

"Grab a stool at the prep table," Helen said as she nonchalantly ducked under a stream of airborne baby carrots.

All the feelings of working in Helen's kitchen came flooding back. The fun, the excitement, the hard work, and the acceptance of everyone. Leaving the kitchen had been the worst part of Cash's circus life so far. He was thankful to finally find his place as an acrobat, but there was nothing like the camaraderie of Helen's Boys. People thought the circus was in the big top. They'd never been in the kitchen where the real antics happened day in and day out.

Cash plopped on a stool as Helen whisked around to different spots in the kitchen, dumping spoonfuls of this and that onto a plate. With a big smile, she slid the towering plate towards Cash and took the stool across from him. Cash closed his eyes and inhaled the savory scents of garlic mashed potatoes, roasted carrots and ground beef. Around them, Helen's boys clanged pots and pans as everyone cleaned the serving pans and utensils.

"How was training today, Mr. Acrobat?" Helen always had a friendly gleam in her eye and was easy to talk to.

"I didn't let go," Cash mumbled to his mashed potatoes.

"What do you mean you didn't let go?" Helen inquired.

"We were practicing on the regular performance trapezes. At first, we were practicing swinging and getting our rhythm. I got that down. I started doing that last week on my own. We've been getting used to the bar by pulling ourselves up, hanging by our legs, getting back to the platform. Once we were in sync with our partner, we were supposed to do a Backend Hocks Off. It's not fancy, you basically hang by your legs and let go for your partner to catch you," Cash paused, not able to look a Helen. "I couldn't let go."

"Why not?" She asked nonjudgmentally.

"I… I'm scared of falling. The practice platform is easy, but above that my hands freeze," he admitted.

"I'm sure everyone is scared of falling at the beginning, Cash. That's why they start you out down low where you won't get hurt. If you're going to fall, this is the time to fall," Helen encouraged him in her kind voice.

Cash continued, "Yeah. But Lorenzo went on and on about how dangerous is it and how the net can hurt you. And have you SEEN how high those platforms are?"

"But that's why he teaches you how to fall properly, so even from the top you won't get hurt. Even more than that, I've been at this circus for a long time and if there's one thing I know, it's that Lorenzo really does recognize the acrobatic gift in people. He wouldn't have picked you if he didn't believe in you. I loved having you in my kitchen, but I always knew you were meant for something bigger. And I'm sorry you had to shovel elephant mess for so long before finding this, but now you're doing it! You're an acrobat, Cash! These guys would give anything to get chosen by Lorenzo," she said, gesturing to the kids whirring in the kitchen around her. "You just have to trust yourself and let go. I know you can do it. Tomorrow will be a better day." She grabbed his hand as she made her point. Cash felt a new surge of courage as he looked into Helen's eyes.

Splat! A spoonful of mashed potatoes hit Cash right in the cheek. Laughter exploded around them.

"Billy!" Yelled Helen. "At least throw him a towel to clean up!" Helen and Cash both continued to chuckle as he caught the dishrag and wiped the mashed potatoes from his face.

CHAPTER 3

THE FORTUNE TELLER

The next morning, a sliver of sunshine sneaking through the window woke up Cash. He stretched and thought about the conversation with Helen.

"It's going to be a good day!" he said out loud.

"Not if you don't let me sleep," mumbled Tony as he grabbed an extra pillow and put it over his head.

Cash tiptoed over and lifted the pillow with two fingers. "Are you going to stop by my practice? I could use a friendly face watching."

"What did I tell you about letting me sleep?!" Tony grabbed the pillow from Cash and hit him with it. Tony closed his eyes, snuggled back into bed, and said, "Yeah. You know I'll be there."

With that extra boost of confidence, Cash crept out of the caboose and headed for the big top. He passed Boris entering the cookhouse. He was too nervous and excited to eat. Plus, his food might come back up if he was on the trapeze.

"Good morning, young man!" Lorenzo boomed as Cash walked along the ring to his seat on the bleachers. "Did you find some courage during the night?"

"I did, sir! I'm ready," Cash replied.

"Good. You're up first with aerial work. BELLA! You and the boy with the *magic courage* will begin. He's flying and starting with a Backend Hocks Off, you're catching. Acrobats, warm up!" Lorenzo announced.

Cash reluctantly peeled himself from the bleacher and began jogging around the ring with the other acrobats. He lagged to the back of the group and soon Bella was in stride next to him.

"Have you done this before?" she asked matter of factly.

"No. This is my first trick," Cash replied.

"Backend Hocks Off is a long name for a straightforward trick. I'll be hanging by my knees. You start by hanging by your hands, then pull your legs up and over the bar so you're also hanging by your knees. Once we are in sync and reach each other, let go. I'll catch you. Don't hesitate and you'll be fine." She looked towards the bleachers. "Oh! There's Boris! See you at the top!"

Boris and Bella got to know each other while performing in one of Boris' acts together and had been dating for about a year. Cash suspected that Boris had asked to use some of the acrobats in his act just to spend time with Bella. Either way, they were hard to separate. He was big and strong and she was petite and sweet. Her chocolate-colored skin and gold-tinted brown eyes contrasted beautifully with his pale skin and sharp blue eyes.

After a couple of laps around the ring, Cash heard Lorenzo proclaim, "To the boards!"

Cash headed toward the ladder to his platform as Bella climbed up to her side. At the bottom of the ladder, Cash chalked his hands so he wouldn't slip on the bar. Sweat was already accumulating on his forehead and palms. At the top of the ladder, he stepped onto the platform and looked down. He was on the regular performance platform, but it was still unnerving knowing he was about to let go of his trapeze with nothing to catch him but the net if Bella missed. Jojo, one of the prop hands, used the bar hook to catch the hanging trapeze and pull it toward Cash. Cash placed both hands firmly on the bar. He had spent lots of time hanging and swinging on the bar, but doing a trick and trusting someone to catch him was another thing altogether. Across the rigging, he saw Bella adjusting her grip on her trapeze. They both settled into position and stared at each other, waiting for the call from Lorenzo. It was hard to breathe.

From the ground came Lorenzo's proud voice, "READY!!...." Cash took a deep breath and pushed away all thoughts except for envisioning the moves he was about to make.

"HEP!!" Called Lorenzo.

That was their cue. Simultaneously, Cash and Bella hopped from their platforms and were airborne. They swung to the middle for momentum and then back to the platforms. As they headed back toward the middle, Cash prepared for his release. He shot his legs into the air with precision and wrapped them over the bar so he was hanging upside down. Then he arched his back and extended his arms over his head. As he swung closer to Bella, he saw her right there, close, arms out, ready to catch him. He briefly closed his eyes as he let go of the trapeze, not able to watch his lifeline slip away.

Their arms connected and he was swinging with her back towards her platform. She let go over the platform and Cash easily stepped onto the solid wood. He stood still, lost in thought, full of pride and…what was that? Joy. Excitement exploded in his chest. He loved it! Bella took another swing while she pulled herself up so she was hanging on by her hands. When she swung back to the platform, she hopped off, bumping into Cash and knocking him out of his reverie.

She slapped him on the back, "That was perfect! Your timing, release, the catch - everything!"

"YOU DID GREAT MY FRIEND!" Boris exploded.

Cash peeped over the platform to see Boris standing at the bottom of the ladder with a huge smile on his face. Cash scrambled down the ladder and Boris shook his hand excitedly.

"You're a natural. You have nothing to be scared of!" Boris encouraged.

"Shhh. No need to tell everyone he was scared." Bella said with a smile still on her face as she hopped down from the ladder.

"Excellent!" Called Lorenzo with his megaphone from his director's chair. "Back to your platforms! Do it again! Half-time!"

Cash jogged back to his ladder and hurried up. Jojo had the trapeze waiting for him. With confidence, he grabbed the bar and waited for the signal. Last time the few seconds before Lorenzo's call had seemed like an eternity. This time he couldn't wait.

"Ready!…HEP!" Lorenzo announced.

Cash jumped and launched into the air. There was no swing before the trick, they were going straight to the middle and doing the trick on the first swing. Again, he shot his legs into the air, gripped the bar with his leg, then let go, swung his hands over his head, connected with

Bella, and swung back to her platform.

Lorenzo had them do several more tricks, all progressively harder. Cash and Bella nailed all of them. When it was time for another team to practice, Cash and Bella climbed down from the platforms and sat on the bleachers. While the next team warmed up, Lorenzo came over.

"Well done! So the scared boy is quite the trapeze artist. It's not so hard, no? Tomorrow we will try cutaways. You can practice your flips on the trampoline," Lorenzo said approvingly.

Cash and Bella took turns flipping and coaching each other while the tumblers practiced in the ring and Lorenzo coached the other flyers. At the end of practice, the other acrobats came up to congratulate him. Wondering why he had ever been afraid, Cash, Boris and Bella headed to the cookhouse for lunch.

———

One Month Later

The first thing Cash heard was the loud sound of Tony trying to quietly get ready for the day. His roommate was average height for his age but was stockier than most. Anything he tried to do quietly had the opposite effect. If he made breakfast, he knocked into any pots and pans near the stove. Reach for something on the top shelf and he was bound to bump the rest of the shelves on the way down. Cash was used to Tony's noise, but it was unusual for Tony to be awake before him. The only exception was the opening day of the circus in a new town. They must have pulled in during the night.

Tony crept across the caboose until he was right in front of Cash's face. Cash feigned sleep, but could sense his friend's approach, and then feel his breath on his face.

"Cash, you awake?" Tony whispered.

Cash remained comatose for a moment then yelled, "YES!" The startled Tony took several jumbled steps backward, ran into the kitchen table that they had forgotten to fold up, lost his balance, flopped backward, and ended up sprawled on his back across the table.

"If you had been dead and done that, I'm sure I would have somersaulted backward over the table and dropped dead myself," Tony commented from his prone position.

Cash laughed and Tony joined in as he sat up on the table.

"Where are we?" Cash asked, peeking behind the curtain by his bed.

"Catpernicke," said Tony as he stepped to the door and looked outside. The train had stopped outside of town. An expansive field was laid out before them. In the distance, they could see a few houses, and to the right, a cluster of buildings. The houses and shops also dotted the hillside just beyond the main section of the town. At the top of the hill, Tony spied the steeple of a church. "We came here a couple years ago, remember? It was so cold Bonkers thought he got frostbite on his toes. But it looks like we got some good weather. The advance cars got here a couple days ago. They were out postering the town last night and said they were going to do 10,000 posters. Ha! There aren't enough walls in this place! I bet they did 4,000. Get dressed and let's go meet some townies!"

The canvas men had put up the Red Wagon and were now working on the tent. Town folk were already milling around, eating popcorn and looking at the animals. Barn-aby had Flora out and there was a line of children waiting to pet her trunk.

Cash could see Nina in the ticket window of the red wagon, looking flustered at all the people wanting to buy tickets for that evening's show. Sacha was nowhere to be seen. She stuck her head out the window and looked around. Shaking her head, she withdrew into the office and took money for the next ticket.

"Oh, hey! Nick is open! I bet I can score us some break-fast!" Tony directed them toward their favorite fried food stand.

A few minutes later the boys were walking again, but this time with full mouths.

"I like Helen's cooking," Cash mumbled, "but there's nothing like a candy apple for breakfast!"

"Breakfast of champions," added Tony juggling his apple, fried waffle and popcorn. "Let's stop here and eat."

They were near the perimeter of the circus and took shelter from the wind along the side of a purple tent.

Munching his apple Tony said, "You know whose tent this is, right? It's old Magda's. You ever seen her in action?"

"Yeah, it's kind of goofy," Cash replied.

Just then there was a rustling from the other side of the tent as the flap whipped open. Cash and Tony leaned around the corner stealthily to see if it was Magda. The old woman emerged from the tent and slowly walked a few paces, leaning heavily on her short, knotty cane. She wore a gray shawl over a flowing white shirt. Her full, black skirt hung to the ground and her wiry gray hair was mostly tucked into a bun. Even her eyes were gray. The only color was the purple kerchief around her neck.

The boys watched as she called to a passerby in a dusty, creaky voice.

"Fortune reading! Just a few pennies to see what the future holds. You! With the pretty lady!" Magda screeched and pointed a finger as gnarled as her cane toward a young couple. They glanced at each other, then turned and walked towards Magda.

As they approached, Magda put her cane under her arm and held her palm out face up. She waited for the man to approach and offer his hand.

"Oh!" Magda croaked with her face a few inches from the man's hand. "Your love line is strong. You must be deeply in love." She looked up from her bent-over position but directed her eyes to the young woman.

"Oh my gosh! We just got engaged. We're SO in love!" gushed the young woman. She shoved her hand with a large ring on it towards Magda, who barely noticed and turned back towards the man's palm.

"There is a shift coming soon for you," Magda said to the man.

Again the young woman jumped in, "How did you know!? We're getting married in three months! It's fast, but why wait when you're in love?"

"Uh oh," continued Magda, tracing a line on the man's palm. "Your finances are going to take a downturn." The young woman was ready to say something, but froze, mouth open, ready to speak but not sure what to say.

The young man paused, then turned to his fiancé and said, "Exactly how much have the vendors been quoting you for the wedding?!" They began to bicker. Magda put out her hand for her payment, and the young man deposited several coins in her hand without even looking at her.

The couple slowly walked off, both talking intensely at the same time. The old woman sank back into her tent, coins grasped to her chest.

"Seriously?" Cash said to Tony after watching the exchange. "That was just observation. And very basic observation at that."

"Yeah. The fortune telling is a joke, but people fall for it and expect it at the circus. Magda has other…gifts. She can freak you out. I've never seen anyone…" Right then Cash, looking over Tony's shoulder, saw Sacha emerge from behind Magda's tent looking like he didn't want anyone to spot him. Another figure dressed in black that Cash didn't recognize was leaving the scene, but that person headed towards the woods behind the circus. They looked around to see if anyone was watching and Cash caught a glimpse of the person's profile. The stranger's face was ghost-white.

CHAPTER 4

FADE TO BLACK

Cash quickly exited the caboose and shivered in the chilly morning air. The sun was out and there was the buzz of a new town, a new crowd, another wow-ing show. Having been an acrobat for several towns now, he was finally getting used to the new rhythms: arrive at a town, rehearse in the afternoon, show that night. Stay in town for a couple of days, or maybe a week, perform every night, and then move on and do it all again.

He hopped down from the caboose, shoved his hands as far into his pockets as they would go, and made a beeline for the cookhouse. Barnaby and his handlers had set up a large fence for Flora and Major. The townies were always in awe of the elephants.

"This'll help get people in the door as soon as possible," Barnaby said.

Flora was standing by the fence, scratching her side with her trunk. Cash went out of his way to say good morning to her.

"Miss me, girl?" he asked as he stroked her between the eyes. She nodded her head and waved her truck, an elephant's way of agreeing. "Yeah, I miss you too." Flora nuzzled toward Cash, then went to join Major across their makeshift ring.

Two young boys ran up and jumped on the lower rail.

"Elephants!" Cried the smaller one. Bouncy brown curls topped his head and he was missing his two front teeth.

The older boy adjusted his red baseball cap and said, "Elephants are cool, but I like the clowns best. Their jokes are funny."

"I like elephants, clowns, and acrobats!" Listed the young boy.

"Cousin Alexei said he saw this circus a couple of weeks ago and said they have a trapeze… uh… trapeze flyer a couple of years older than me who does all sorts of amazing tricks. He said he was the best trapeze person he's ever seen," the older boy informed the younger.

"Whoa… I want to be a trapeze person when I get older!"

Cash turned away before the boys noticed he was standing there. They were talking about him. In the time since his first successful tricks with Bella, Cash discovered that he had a natural talent for flying and flipping through the air. Lorenzo was overjoyed to have a star in the air and headlining the show. Being the star was grueling. His newfound stardom meant staying after the other acrobats left for extra training sessions with Lorenzo. Cash was sore most days and usually went to bed minutes after dinner. Now that he was more used to it, he loved the challenge and satisfaction of letting go of the bar mid-air, completing a trick, and nailing the finish. His confidence was growing and he always tried to be better and quicker. Lorenzo gave him new tricks to try almost every day. Tonight they were debuting a new finale to their act, a triple summersault with a catch and a double pirouette.

He ran through the trick in his mind. Start on the platform. Swing out and back for momentum. On the next swing out let go at the top and summersault three times. Bella would be there in a leg hang with her hands free to catch Cash by his hands. Grab Bella's hands and swing towards her platform. Then on the swing back let go in the middle. Pirouette twice and catch his trapeze that would still be swinging. It was the most complicated trick they had done. For the past two weeks, they had been nailing it on the lower trapezes. The lower platforms were 25 feet from the ground, which meant a 15-foot fall. Lorenzo made them practice falling from the lower platforms, and he had fallen a couple of times when they first started practicing, but falling into the net from that height didn't hurt.

The higher platforms, however, were 40 feet in the air, all the way at the top of the tent. The drop was twice that of the lower platforms. Falling more than 30 feet made him nervous and it was much more dangerous. Even with a net, if he didn't tuck into a ball perfectly, he would get hurt. The acrobats didn't even practice falling from those platforms since it was so risky. Lorenzo wanted them all the way at the top for tonight's performance. They were practicing it that afternoon for the first time on the high platforms. Cash repeated to himself that it was the same thing they had been doing, but he couldn't quite shake the nervous feeling in his stomach.

Slipping quickly into the cookhouse, Cash looked around for his friends. He couldn't miss Boris' bulking frame near the front of the food line. He quickly made his way toward Boris and gave a half smile and wave to the people who called out greetings and "good mornings". A couple of months ago half of the people in the tent knew him only as the boy who shoveled elephant poop. Now everyone knew his name. He still wasn't used to it. Boris, Bella, and Tony were all talking cheerfully when he walked up.

"There's our star!" Boris yelled as the big man crushed Cash into a side hug.

"Shhh!" said Cash embarrassed, "You don't have to announce that to everyone."

"Sorry, my friend." His other arm was around Bella who smiled warmly up at Boris, then over to Cash.

"Are you ready for the high traps, Cash?" she asked. Cash liked Bella and Boris' relationship. He had never met anyone as nice and graceful as Bella. She offered a finesse to Boris' edges and straightforward style.

"Yeah… well…" He knew his friends would know how he was feeling, no matter what he said so he might as well tell them the truth. "I'm nervous. I know we've been nailing the trick, but I've never done anything more than a summersault up top. I can't quite shake the nerves."

Bella responded first. "I was nervous my first time too, but it worked out. You're one of the most talented flyers I've seen. Your timing is always perfect. I really think you'll do great!"

"Yeah man," said Tony, swallowing a bit of toast and jam he had plucked from Bonkers' tray as he walked by. "You're going to do great! You kind of have to since you're the star of the show tonight."

"Don't pressure him, Tony!" piped in Boris. "Cash, here's what I know. You are talented. You have been doing this trick on the lower traps for two weeks without any problems. You have no reason to worry."

"Thanks, guys," said Cash, feeling better for a moment.

They stepped up to where Helen was serving up breakfast.

"Well, if it isn't my favorite people in the circus! I hope your morning is going well. Here's an extra scoop of eggs. I know how hard Lorenzo has been working you. It will give you strength and maybe some good luck," She winked as she doubled his portion.

After a fun breakfast with his best friends, Cash couldn't remember why he had even been nervous. He stayed behind for a few minutes to talk with Helen as she cleaned up, then headed for the 'boose. As he neared a bend in the tracks, he heard a man yelling from ahead of the curve. Another man responded in tone. It was Boris. But it wasn't his normal yell when he was just talking too loudly. He was angry. Angrier than Cash had ever heard him before. Cash slowed down and peeked around Barnaby's car. Boris' huge back and towering figure obscured the other man. His friend had finished yelling and Cash could barely hear what the other man was saying, he was talking at a menacingly low volume. Every muscle in Boris' back strained with tension. When the man finished talking, Boris turned and kicked the car out of frustration.

Without looking at the man again, Boris ducked between two cars, leaving the man standing by himself. He was an incongruous sort of man. Not one of their circus crew. He wore reasonably nice clothes, but they were disheveled. He was probably about Boris' age but looked much, much older. His hair had been gelled and combed at some point, but not recently and several strands stuck out in haphazard directions. The sight of the man made Cash's skin crawl. As Cash scrutinized the man from his hidden spot, the stranger ran his hands over his dark hair, turned, and walked in the direction of the village. Cash briefly thought of going after Boris to find out what had just happened, but realized he was cutting it close to practice time. He'd rather wait to find out Boris' secret than risk Lorenzo's fury.

Cash entered the big top to a flurry of activity. He could hear the chatter and feel the excitement of an opening night, but his mind reran the argument he had just witnessed. Bella sat on the floor across the tent stretching. Cash jogged over and sat down next to her, joining in the warmups.

"Have you seen Boris recently?" Cash asked Bella, diving in without any small talk.

"Not since breakfast. I came here early to coach Eleana on tumbling drills. Why?" She asked in return.

Cash quickly and quietly relayed what he had seen. They both looked around and then switched the legs they were stretching.

"That's so unlike Boris. I've only seen him really angry once," Bella said in a tone that told Cash she was thinking and trying to figure out what made him so angry.

"Do you have any idea who the man was?" Cash asked.

"Boris mentioned that his sister and niece live near here. Maybe that was his sister's husband. Boris never mentions him, but I can't think of anyone else he would know here. Especially anyone he'd be angry with," Bella wondered.

"I don't want Boris to know I was spying on him, but I'm worried. I thought they were going to hurt each other," Cash pleaded.

"I'll try to find out what's going on without him knowing you saw," Bella replied with a reassuring smile.

"Thanks," he added.

Lorenzo's voice resounded in the tent through his bullhorn.

"Cash and Bella! To your platforms for rehearsal! NOW!"

Cash hopped up and held out his hand to Bella. He helped her up and she said, "Good luck, Cash. You've got this."

"Good luck, Bella." They quickly hugged and headed in opposite directions toward their platforms.

Helen walked through the dark, quiet hallway to the main ring door. Dim bulbs provided enough light so she wouldn't trip on anything. She struggled with a large box full of bags of fresh popcorn. The size, more than the weight slowed her down as she arrived at the entrance and tried to find a gap in the black, velvet curtain. The curtain kept the townies from getting a sneak peek of the performance before showtime. Finally, the curtain parted and she carried the box over to where Tony was prepping his sales for the evening. The ring was abuzz with final practices and warm-ups. The equestrians were stretching along the edge of the ring near them, while Barnaby directed Flora, the elephant, to her stand in the center of the ring.

Tony had several carrying trays loaded with bags of popcorn so he could run back and grab another as soon as he sold out. She dropped the box on the first row of bleachers next to Tony.

"Here you go. Last batch for tonight," she said with a tired smile.

"Thanks, Helen. I would have come to get it," replied Tony.

"I had to leave the kitchen and if I'd left it there, you would have only had a few kernels left when you went back for it," she said with a laugh, knowing better than to leave popcorn unattended where her chaotic boys would be sure to discover it.

"Oh, is this Cash and Bella's new routine?" Helen asked, looking up at the two people flying through the air.

"Yeah! They're looking good too. This is their best routine by far," Tony praised.

"Oh good! Has Cash done the triple-triple yet?" Helen asked nervously.

"No, not yet. I think Lorenzo is making sure they're in sync and warm before calling that one," Tony suggested.

They stood in silence as Cash and Bella performed a simple backend whip and then an alien split. Bella flew through the air holding on to her trapeze with her legs in a split. Cash caught her when she let go, and after one swing she let go again and caught her trapeze. Then Lorenzo called, "Trip sum trip peer!" through his bullhorn.

Cash and Bella remounted their high platforms. With a bag of popcorn in one hand, Helen reached out and grabbed Tony's arm with her other hand.

"Here we go," she whispered.

This was it. Helen and Tony looked at each other with hopeful but scared glances, then glued their eyes to the top of the tent.

———

Cash heard Lorenzo's call and landed on his platform, letting the trapeze swing out as he focused and tried to calm his nerves. Jojo hooked his trapeze and brought it back to the platform. Cash wiped his forehead on his arm.

"Nervous, eh?" Jojo said as he reached out and grabbed the trapeze.

"Yeah," said Cash. "A little. I've never done this trick at this height. I really don't want to fall from here."

"No. You don't," said Jojo. "You'll be fine," he added in a carefree way like he did this every day.

Cash glanced at him and secured his hands on the trapeze with an exhale. He saw Bella line up and grab her trapeze. They looked at each other across the ring and waited for their cue. Cash's heartbeat sped up in the seemingly eternal silence. It seemed like all the activity in the tent had stopped, he wanted to look around but didn't dare take his eyes off Bella.

"Breathe," he reminded himself.

Then it began with Lorenzo's booming, "Ready!!…" Bella nodded. Cash nodded solemnly in return.

"HEP!!" At Lorenzo's command, they jumped from their platforms.

Cash and Bella took their first swing toward the middle to ramp up momentum. They seesawed back toward their platforms swinging their legs to build up speed. As she went back toward the middle, Bella pulled herself up and over her bar and into a leg hang, ready to catch Cash as he came out of his triple summersault. He felt the timing in his body and in his swing, preparing to let go for the summersaults. He saw a flash of Bella and felt the timing, then let go of his trapeze.

Just as he let go, something felt wrong. But he tucked

into his summersaults and came out to see Bella's arms reaching out for his. He was coming in at the wrong angle. Cash twisted his upper body a few degrees to the right and reached for Bella's hands. Their hands clasped tightly. They swung back towards her platform, Cash getting ready for the triple pirouette back to his trapeze. Again, Cash felt the tempo with his body as they swung out. He glanced up at Bella as he neared the release point. Her eyes were focused on his platform, but then her eyes widened and Cash saw a split second of terror. Bella couldn't process what she saw quickly enough, and Cash let go when he was supposed to.

Bella let out a scream. "CASH!"

"Noooooooo!!" Helen and Tony yelled at the same time as Bella.

Cash pirouetted perfectly through the air. He had only a fraction of a second of awareness that something was horribly wrong before everything went black.

———

Cash was aware of darkness. He turned slowly around to see if anything was visible through the murky cloud. Nothing. He could hear his breath, his heartbeat. Then he heard a whisper. It got louder. The sing-song voice of a little girl.

"Rock-a-bye baby in the tree top…" As she finished the first line of the lullaby, a spotlight switched on, illuminating a large tree, as big as a small skyscraper. Cash shielded his eyes at the sudden brightness.

"When the wind blows, the cradle will rock."

Looking towards the top of the tree, Cash noticed something on one of the bare branches. A baby's crib.

"When the bough breaks, the cradle will fall."

Cash looked to the base of the tree. A man was running back and forth along the lowest branches, eyes fixed on the crib up at the top. The man turned. It was Boris. There was a loud cracking sound and the crib started to fall.

"And down will come baby, cradle and all."

———

Cash's friends huddled around him as Dr. Johan Keller listened to his heartbeat and peeked under his eyelids.

"He's unconscious. I can't assess the full damage until he wakes up," the doctor announced without emotion.

"How long will that be?" Asked Bella, very worried.

"I couldn't tell you. Could be a couple of hours or a couple of days. That was quite a fall he took." The doctor gingerly picked up Cash's right arm. "I'd say there are several broken places in the arm. I'll wrap it until the swelling goes down and we can set it."

"How long until he can fly again?" asked Lorenzo. Everyone turned to look at him with exasperated expressions. "I mean... I hope him the best. Full recovery. He'll take his time. But what do you think, doctor?"

Helen looked back at Cash as the doctor again said he didn't know. "Hey! Look at his eyes, they're moving." His eyes were closed, but moving rapidly, like he was dreaming.

"Huh. That's strange…" and the doctor bent over Cash.

Then a murmuring sound came from Cash and he slightly moved his lips.

"He's trying to talk!" Exclaimed Tony.

"I highly doubt it," said the doctor.

But he was. Cash murmured again and Helen put her head close to his. "He's saying, 'Save her,'" Helen said confused.

Then they all heard it. "Save her. You have to save her. She's going to get hurt."

They all looked at each other perplexed.

"Boris! Boris! Save her before it's too late!" Cash's desperate words hung in the room like a fog. Boris' face turned white and his eyes showed fear. "Save her, Boris!" Cash's head limped to the side and he was silent again.

At the last admonition, Boris backed away from the group, turned, and ran out of the room.

CHAPTER 5

MISSING MEMORIES

Dark gray clouds like an evil fog floated through Cash's vision. He wasn't sure if he was asleep or awake; if his eyes were open or closed. Someone's words floated near his ears. Low. A man's voice.

"He has a fever," the voice said.

Cash tried to close his eyes, but they were already closed, so he tried to open them. They slowly cracked open a sliver. His eyelids felt like lead and threatened to close again. Cash recognized the face of Dr. Keller hovering over him with his hair slicked and perfectly parted down the middle. Johan's eyes were too close to focus on and awkwardly close. Was there a hand on his forehead? There was. It moved to his cheek.

"The best thing for him is to keep sleeping," muttered Dr. Keller.

Cash's drooping eyelids won and he drifted back to sleep as he heard a woman replying to the doctor, but Cash was already back in the arms of slumber.

The next time Cash phased back into reality, his eyes weren't quite as heavy as before. It felt more like a natural waking up, though his entire body still felt exhausted. This time the face hovering over him was Ringmaster Elon's.

"Ah, my boy," he said in his raspy voice.

Cash squinted to try and get the ringmaster's face into focus. All he could see was the handlebar mustache twitching as Elon spoke.

"You're going to be feeling all better, right? Get right back on the trapeze aren't you? Yes, of course you will. You're my star!" The ringmaster encouraged.

Furrowing his eyebrows, Cash tried to recollect what Elon was talking about, memories floating around the edge of his remembrance. He closed his eyes to try and call the memories back. Did something happen? But before he knew it, sleep had once again taken over.

––––––––

Cash jumped! This time his eyes flew open wide as a loud creaking noise woke him from his dreamless sleep. He couldn't see anything, it was pitch black.

Night, he thought.

The noise sounded like a squeaky floorboard. No, the door had creaked. Tap shuffle, tap shuffle. His heart raced and pounded in his head. Someone was in his room! As he lay in the bed, waiting for something to happen, he listened. Breathing. Not his. Tony? Tony… Tony… who was Tony? The thought distracted him for a moment before he recalled that Tony was his roommate.

The breathing was so close now. There was a slight, low rumbling in the person's lungs as they breathed. It felt like they were staring at him. The pitch-dark of the room only showed a dark outline slightly darker than the rest of the room.

He might have heard a barely distinguishable whisper say, "Dream, dreamer, dream," whatever that meant.

Footsteps lightly padded back across the room, away from him, and the door opened with a creak and closed again. Several minutes passed. Cash began to calm down, but waited to see if the person would return. Eventually, he faded into sleep once again.

Noises drifted into Cash's mind as he moved from sleep to merely sleepy. This waking was different. There wasn't a muffle to the noises he heard. The birds chirping outside was a crisp, vibrant sound. He could hear the wind blowing the branches of a tree into each other. It sounded like spring. Could he sense light beyond his eyelids?

After a few moments of relishing the normal, yet life-giving and vigorous sounds around him, Cash eased his eyelids open. He lay in a bed that wasn't his own. The room was bare, definitely not the caboose. A figure leaned into his line of vision. Bella. He felt relief at how quickly the knowledge came to him. Her brow furrowed in concern and she reached out her hand, putting her cool flesh on Cash's forehead. Her face caved into a smile of relief and the stress drained away. Her hair was a mess. Had she been there the whole night?

"Cash? Cash? Can you hear me?" Bella cooed.

"Yes," creaked Cash. His voice felt like it hadn't been used in days. *What happened?*

"Do you know who I am?" the beautiful acrobat asked.

"Bella," Cash whispered.

A sound halfway between a laugh and a cry escaped Bella's mouth. Her hand went to cover her lips.

"Oh, I'm so glad you're OK," she said. Now quiet tears were sliding down her cheeks.

"Where… what happened?" Cash said, realizing he still didn't know why he wasn't in the caboose.

"Do you remember anything?" asked Bella.

Cash reclined back onto his pillow, closed his eyes, and tried to remember what came before this bed.

"I…I… remember going to bed in the caboose. Maybe bits of practice. But that could have been any day." he paused to try and identify the emotion at the edge of his consciousness. "Panic. I remember panic."

"You fell during practice, Cash. There was an accident and you fell. All the way from the top. You were knocked unconscious… we can't believe you're even alive." Bella cried, holding back a sob.

Panic found him again. Cash hadn't even tried to move his body. Maybe he was paralyzed. He leaned his head forward to look at his toes. They were wiggling just like he commanded them to. Relief flooded him. His gaze slowly moved up his body as he assessed any damage, and looked for any pain. His right arm was in a cast.

"My arm…" he said.

"Broke when you hit the net. It was broken in several places. Took a couple of days for the swelling to go down, but then Dr. Keller was able to set it," she explained.

"Days?… How long have I been out?" Cash croaked.

"Five days, Cash. We were all so worried," Bella let out the sob she had been holding back.

And he could see the worry still etched above her eyes.

Before Cash could respond or even comprehend that he'd lost five days of his life, the door creaked open. He saw the familiar, painted face of Bonkers. Then there was a loud "HONK" as he stumbled and tumbled into the room. Behind him came Helen and Tony, looking elated.

"You're up!" cried Helen, clearly forcing herself to hold back a giant hug.

"The 'boose hasn't been the same without you," said Tony in his easy manner, but the giant grin on his face betrayed his cool.

"Hey, guys!" Cash beamed.

"Glad to see you're feeling better!" said Bonkers.

"Yeah. Bella was just telling me what happened. Things are still a little foggy. I don't remember falling," Cash replied.

"It was so terrifying! I landed on the platform and turned around and you weren't on your trapeze and I looked down and…" Bella paused to contain her tears, "You hit the net so hard. I thought for sure you had… that something much worse had happened."

"Not too bad to get out of that with just a broken arm," chimed Tony.

"It's so good to see you awake, Cash. We've all been taking shifts and staying with you," Helen added.

A large silhouette appeared in the doorway behind his friend.

"Out, out. No more visitors today," a harried nurse pushed past them. "Time for pain medication. Then the doctor will be in. He needs to rest." She methodically placed a cup of pills on the bedside table and pulled Cash forward to adjust his pillows.

"See you, buddy" called Tony.

"HONK." Bonkers departed.

Bella rose, scooted past the nurse, and slipped out the door with a quick wave to Cash.

Helen paused for a moment, looking like she was going to ask the nurse something, but she changed her mind and gave Cash a warm smile.

"I'll be back to check on you soon."

The nurse turned and gave her a hard stare.

"Fine. I'll be back tomorrow."

The nurse nodded and Helen left, closing the door behind her.

Cash watched as his friends filed out of the room. He looked around the room in a moment of calm after they left. Suddenly, he realized that his bladder was quite full.

"Um, where is the bathroom?" Cash blushed as he asked the nurse.

"Down the hall," she tilted her head to indicate the direction.

The nurse moved to his bedside as Cash wiggled his legs to double-check that they still worked, and moved them toward and over the edge of the bed. She held his good elbow as he rose. Standing made him a bit dizzy, but it soon passed and he shuffled toward the bathroom. He paused at the door. Whispers, barely audible, floated timidly into the room. Cash stepped closer to the door, trying not to betray his location.

"I told him what happened, but not everything," Bella whispered.

"Did you tell him what I did?" Helen replied quietly.

"No, I didn't. I also didn't mention why he was unconscious," came Bella's quiet response.

"Why aren't you telling him? He should know what happened. What you did!" Tony added heatedly.

"No! It's better for him to not know — for as few people as possible to know. We have a chance to protect him.... and protect us," responded Helen.

"Fine. I don't like the idea of lying to Cash, but… you might be right," Tony conceded.

Another voice piped in. Cash realized it must be the doctor. Several people spoke at once and then he heard people walking away. He opened the door to find Dr. Keller. They were almost the same height. The doctor raised his eyebrows in surprise.

"Off to the bathroom," Cash muttered.

———

Helen paused to watch as the door to Cash's room opened. The doctor stepped back and she caught a glance of Cash as he headed the other way down the hall with a hand on the wall to support himself. Bella and Tony were already down the hall by the exit, so Helen watched Cash for a moment longer and took her time exiting the medical tent, chewing on her lip and lost in thought. The cook squinted at the morning sun and guessed it was time to get back to the cookhouse to clean up breakfast. She aimed to the right when a large hand grabbed her arm and jerked her along the side of the medical tent. Elon pulled, then pushed Helen roughly in front of him, his hulking physique obscuring her from the view of passers-by.

"Why is my star acrobat in a cast?" he growled.

"It takes time." Helen set her chin to look up at the ring-master, despite the sick feeling in her gut. "I haven't had more than a minute alone with him between Dr. Keller and the nurses and visitors. And I still have an entire circus to feed. I can't wait around all day."

"Finish it, Helen."

"I will. I'll take care of it," she assured him.

"You had better. Don't forget our agreement. You do the few, little things I ask of you and I let you stay here and go about life like a normal person. Every now and again I hear rumors of people at other circuses with your… talents. Working sun up to down down, so tired that someone has to feed them. I'm sure we could arrange a trade. Other ringmasters aren't nearly as kind to their *talented* staff as I am. My brother, for example." Elon stared at Helen for a moment then turned to go.

"Elon," The ringmaster paused and turned toward her. "Maybe you should be thanking us that the fall and head injury didn't kill him. A cast is better than dead."

Elon grimaced and stalked off without a word. Helen watched him go, took a deep breath, and relaxed her hands. Her fingernails left half-moon imprints on her palms.

———

Cash awoke to a tap on his door. Slowly, he opened his eyes. The door was open and Tony had one hand on the doorframe and the rest of him was leaning into the room. The knocking was to wake up Cash, not ask for permission to enter.

"Hey, Tony. Go away, I'm sleeping," Cash murmured with a slight, sleepy grin.

"Maybe, but doc says you're cleared to go home! And by home I mean our wonderful, lovely, decrepit caboose!

I'm here to escort you and make sure you don't, you know, fall over and break your other arm or something. Lorenzo would really kill you then," Tony said.

Cash chuckled and looked around the room.

"Here. I brought you some clothes so you wouldn't have to change back into your trapeze costume," offered Tony.

Cash gratefully got dressed in his jeans and dark blue, long-sleeve t-shirt as quickly as he could, which wasn't very quickly at all considering his broken arm and that his head ached when he moved.

Tony led him out of the medical tent, waving to the nurses as they went. Walking out into the bright day, the sunlight hit Cash like a bolt of lightning. He immediately squinted and felt dizzy. The world moved between his feet. He stopped and doubled over.

"Oh, sorry. Meant to tell you the doc said you might be a bit sensitive to light for a while," Tony added apologetically.

From his bent position, Cash turned his face up towards Tony. "Did he mention anything else?"

"Yeah. That you'd probably be hungry," Tony glanced at the cookhouse. "Flag's up. Looks like breakfast is ready. Let's go." Tony took the baseball cap he was wearing from his own head and shoved it towards Cash as he started walking.

Cash put on the cap, thankful for the shade, and followed after Tony.

Tony pulled back the tent flap and heavenly aromas of all of Cash's favorite breakfast foods clouded his senses. Bacon and sausage. Pancakes and… hash brown patties. He was hungry. Very hungry!

The first shifts had already gone through for breakfast, so the boys didn't have long to wait. Cash grabbed a tray from the closest stack and stood in line. Glancing ahead to decide which delicious options he wanted to stack up on, Cash caught Helen's eye as she served French toast. They looked at each other for a moment in a strange pause. Helen leaned toward Billy who was serving next to her, whispered something, grabbed an empty dish, and headed into the kitchen.

"That was strange," thought Cash as Tony nudged his shoulder to get him to move forward.

Everything on the buffet looked magical to Cash. He loaded his tray as full of plates and bowls as he could manage. When Tony had his breakfast as well, they wandered past the managers' table on its raised platform toward their usual spot. Elon and Lorenzo were finishing their meal. Lorenzo gesticulated grandly while telling some story about his own days as a trapeze artist. Elon looked on with his usual sour and indifferent expression. The acrobat trainer froze mid-story and stared at Cash. Elon turned, carefully wiping his flawless mustache. They both scrutinized Cash as he and Tony walked by. Their gaze made him sweat as he imagined them whispering about when he would perform again.

Cash turned down the next row of tables toward their usual spot and saw Bella sitting eating her oatmeal alone. A brief glimpse of concern flashed on her face before it changed into a smile and she waved them over. They weaved their way between the benches and set down their trays at Bella's table. Tony started talking right away, but Cash studied Bella, trying to figure out what had his normally optimistic friend upset.

Halfway through his stack of pancakes, Cash asked the question that was bothering him, "Hey, is Boris sick or something? I know he doesn't like hospitals, but I was waiting for him to come by yesterday and he never did."

Bella looked uncomfortable. For once, Tony had a serious look on his face as he stared at her.

"He's not here," Bella said timidly.

Cash was shocked. He glanced at Tony to see his reaction. Tony looked worried, but not surprised.

"What do you mean he's not here?" Cash whispered aggressively so other tables wouldn't hear. "You don't just leave the circus. Where did he go? Where *could* he go?"

"He told Lorenzo it was pneumonia and left a couple days ago," Bella replied, trying to be nonchalant.

"Is he coming back?" Cash couldn't believe this.

Bella started to reply, but Tony cut her off. "You know Boris, he does what he wants."

They paused awkwardly. Cash thought about what Tony said. Boris did do what he wanted, but never irresponsibly. Not without having a plan and letting everyone know. It wasn't like him to sneak off secretly. Whatever was going on, it seemed that Boris and Bella were in on it too. Cash felt sick knowing his friends were keeping so much from him.

"Barnaby thinks he's close to getting another lion for the show," Tony said in an awkward attempt to change the subject.

"Oooh! How exciting!" Said Bella.

"Hmmm…" contributed Cash, not really paying attention to the conversation that pursued.

After breakfast, Tony and Bella went off to prep for the show that evening and Cash made his way to the caboose. He stepped in and looked around. The curtains were drawn and the interior was illuminated by muted sunlight. Five days had passed since he last entered the 'boose. On his nightstand were several cards and a stuffed bear, left by friends. Cash smiled. His arm ached and his head hurt. He felt worn out. Not quite tired enough to sleep, he sat in a chair at the kitchen table and tried to remember the accident, unsuccessfully.

He couldn't remember the day at all. He remembered the night before, Tony joking about some of the townies as they got ready for bed. What a strange feeling to know he lived the day of the accident, but couldn't remember it. Like walking into a room and forgetting why you did it. He assumed it was a normal day that included waking up, eating breakfast with his friends, and going to practice. His memories failing him, he recalled what everyone told him.

It happened during rehearsal for the evening show. He and Bella were practicing their routine on the high traps. Then what? Bella said he had fallen. An accident. Did he let go? Did he get knocked unconscious when he hit the net? Did something break? Maybe Bella messed up and everyone was protecting her. And why did his head hurt so badly? If only he could remember!

CHAPTER 6

THE REPLAY

The old, familiar pang settled tightly in Cash's chest. He wished with everything in him that his parents were there now in the Caboose explaining life and what was going on to him. He wished they hadn't died and he hadn't come to this crazy circus. His eyes stung and burned as thoughts of running through the old, wooden front door and falling into their arms taunted him. It had been almost eight years now, but he still felt like someone punched him in the stomach when he thought about them. He missed them so much.

Fighting back tears, Cash ran both hands through his wavy blonde hair and pulled it back in exasperation. He glanced up at the mirror above the basin across from the table. The image in the mirror surprised him. He stood and moved closer to his reflection. Again he pushed the hair from his forehead and looked at himself. There was a scar on the left side of his forehead, about two inches long.

"When…. did that happen?" he said out loud. Had he forgotten about another accident? Cash worried that more of his memory had been damaged than he thought. Maybe he couldn't even trust what he did remember.

Frustrated and with his mind spinning, he decided to

go watch the other acrobats in rehearsal. Maybe something would help him remember, or at the very least, distract him.

He shoved his hands in his pockets and dropped his face as low into his collar as he could. The wind bit through his jacket anyway as he scurried down the nearly empty midway. Food carts, carnival games, and stages for the magician, sword swallower, and more awaited customers. He got to the tent quickly. As he walked through the back entrance, he immediately felt his anxiety and sadness melt away as the familiar atmosphere enveloped him. As much as he longed for his old life, this felt like home now. The hallway was dark, but he saw the golden light flowing in from the ring entrance a few feet away. Lorenzo's amplified voice bounced down the hallway and Cash smiled. He headed into the ring and paused in the entryway where he had watched his first show with Boris. The acrobats were out practicing their tumbling routine. To his left, Flora awaited her cue. Cash got lost in the lights, the rhythm, the noises. He chuckled at Barnaby when Flora tapped him on the shoulder with her trunk and he turned around to see who was there. He appreciated an elephant with a good sense of humor. Flora and Major performed their routine without a hitch. During the transition into the equestrian performance, Cash noticed Bonkers. The clown was standing uncharacteristically still over by the next entrance. When the other clowns came out, Cash looked to see if Bonkers was still watching from the side. He was. This time Cash noticed that Bonkers had a camera in front of him. He'd never seen one like it before. It had a large round wheel that was spinning. Cash headed over, mesmerized.

"Whatcha got there?" Cash asked.

The clown jumped a bit and only glanced at Cash quickly before returning his eyes to the contraption.

"Hey, Cash. Good to see you up and about. Quite a scare, huh?" Bonkers asked, slightly distracted.

"Yeah. But except for a headache and broken arm, I'm feeling pretty good," Cash replied.

"Good. Good, good." Bonkers muttered, focused on the camera still. "Oh. This is a Mikroteknico 470. The newest moving film camera."

"Wow. It's not a still camera then?" Cash asked.

"Nope. Well, technically it takes 24 photos every second, but play them back and it's moving pictures." Bonkers explained.

"Where did you get it?" Cash questioned.

"Lorenzo asked for it. Said the big shows are using them on their best acts. They film the act and watch it back slowly to see where they are off - you know, things that happen too quickly to notice when the show is going. Anyway, Elon said no, it's too expensive. But Sacha got him thinking that they could make some short films to play in theaters before a movie. People can then see a glimpse of what we do and come to the show."

"Like a moving poster," Cash said excitedly.

"Exactly. Sacha said he'd figure out how to cut the film strips together. So, I film the acts and give him the reels to cut and paste together," Bonkers replied.

Cash watched Bonkers for a moment as he moved the camera around, following the tumblers when he had a thought.

"Bonkers, when did you start filming the acts?" Cash asked casually.

"Well, let's see. We got the camera a week ago. The first time I used it was on Saturday..." Bonkers slowed his talking and looked away from the camera. His eyes met Cash's, who finished the thought.

"The day of my accident," Cash said quietly.

"Yes, Cash. But leave it be," Bonkers pleaded, as he realized what Cash was going to do next.

Cash looked around the ring quickly, frantically, then asked, "Where's Sacha!?"

Without another look at Bonkers, Cash turned and ran out of the ring. He darted through the dark hallway on a mission: find Sacha, find the film, find out what happened.

———

Bonkers juggled the heavy camera and lowered it to the ground as quickly but gently as he could. He ran out of the tent, knowing he wouldn't be able to catch Cash before he found Sacha. Instead of heading toward the red wagon, he veered into the cookhouse.

"Helen!" Bonkers yelled as he slowed his awkward run. He picked up his pace again, hiking up his feet to run over his big shoes, and ran into the kitchen.

Helen and Tony looked up from popping popcorn as Bonkers clambered through the flaps into the kitchen and they both stared at him.

"He knows," Bonkers huffed, trying to capture his escaping breath. "He's about to know. Cash knows about the film, he's going to watch it. He's going to know what you did. He's going to know everything!" Helen dropped the pot she was washing into the metal sink. They all shuddered at the bone-screeching racket.

"Where is he?" Helen asked determinedly.

———

Cash ran as fast as he could, his head swirling in pain. He had to get to the Red Wagon. He arrived, ran up the steps, and threw open the door. He glanced around. Nina was absent, and Sacha, standing next to a projector, looked up at him like a kid caught with his hand in a candy jar. Except in this case, it was a knapsack sitting on a chair.

"Cash," Sacha said smiling, pulling his hand out of the knapsack. "I'm so glad to see you up and about. I've been worried sick." His tone indicated otherwise.

"Sacha, where is the film from the accident? I have to see it," Cash demanded.

"Oh, sure. I heard you had a bit of amnesia surrounding the accident. Hoping it'll jog your memory, hey?" Sacha asked mockingly.

"Yeah. Something like that."

Sacha dramatically waved Cash toward a chair on the other side of the projector.

Cash sat and watched Sacha as he reached back into the knapsack, pulled out reels of film, and looked at strips of tape on them, reading the notes. Finding what he was looking for, he unhooked the reel carriage and threaded the film through. Sacha switched on the machine and the sound of the gears whirring broke the silence in the office. Cash heard a click and the lights went out in the room. A small, flickering square of light appeared on the blank wall in front of him. After a few seconds, images began to play.

At first, Bonkers' face took up the square. It looked like he was adjusting the camera. When he stepped back, Cash could see the ring with the tumblers meandering around and Lorenzo walking forcefully, hands waiving, mouth moving. The film had no sound. Lorenzo looked comical with no words coming from his jabbering lips. Cash recognized the flow of practice. The older man waved at the tumblers and they moved toward the bleachers so he could focus on the next segment of practice, the trapeze.

The camera panned from Lorenzo to reveal who he was gesturing to now. Cash saw himself, in his performance vest and leggings, nodding at Lorenzo's instructions. The look on his face projected on the wall was all focus and determination. He would have been nervous, but it didn't come through in the film.

It was like watching a robot. A silent representation of himself, acting out some drama he knew he should know but couldn't remember. The version of himself on the wall climbed the ladder up to the high traps and approached the edge of the platform. Jojo hooked the trapeze and brought it into Cash's realm of grasp.

Cash had never seen himself perform. He was amazed at his ability, grace, and athleticism. It occurred to him that he was really good on the trapeze. Then the film neared the end of the routine. Cash, like his friends watching that day, saw him let go of the trapeze and then, right after he let go, how one end of the trapeze snapped from its wire and began swinging around wildly, like a rampant fire hose. Equipment failure.

Suddenly, his stomach contracted. He would have yelled, "No!" if all of the air in his body hadn't disappeared from the horror of watching the violent, renegade trapeze strike the side of his forehead as he pirouetted back toward it, desperately grasping at the air. The body on the wall morphed from an athletic, agile young man, to a string doll flinging like spaghetti. Cash touched his forehead and the mystery scar. It was right where the trapeze struck him.

The angle of the camera suddenly dropped. Bonkers' back filled the frame for a moment as he ran towards the net. The camera kept rolling, focused on the net. Cash's limp body fell through the air. People say tragedy happens in slow motion. Even on film, it seemed slow as Cash's vulnerable body descended toward the net. In the room, Cash closed his eyes. He couldn't bear to watch himself land.

When he opened his eyes, Boris and Tony were on the net. Tony stood over him without a shirt on, and Boris was on his knees near his head while Helen struggled onto the net. She approached Boris and Tony and from the way the boys looked at her, she wasn't being quiet. Helen dropped to her knees next to him, threw what looked like a rag at Tony, and grabbed Cash's head. Boris and Tony gestured wildly and looked like they were yelling at Helen. Then they each seized one of her arms and dragged her away from Cash's body while she struggled to stay near it. Cash leaned forward and squinted, trying to make sense of the strange scene, and his friend's odd actions. What had happened on the net?

Cash heard a flipping sound and the room went black. He sat in the hovering darkness for a moment absorbing the images he'd seen. The room was silent. Sacha must have slipped down the hall while Cash was watching the film. Suddenly, the door flew open, and light from the front of the building poured in. Cash looked over his shoulder to see Tony, Helen, and Bonkers' faces illuminated in the yellow light, looking at him with concern.

CHAPTER 7

THE BIG REVEAL

Elon paced his decadent train carriage. The other cars were purple with paintings of animals, acts and circus escapades, but the exterior of his car was red to stand out from the rest of the cars. He had chosen a deep green for the inside of his dwelling.

"The color of money," he thought. "Money makes everything happen." He realized night had fallen during his strategy session and he reached a hairy hand to the light switch. Quiet buzzing filled the car and the warm bulbs lining the ceiling flicked on a couple at a time. His car was as close to the front of the train as he could stand from the sound from of the engine.

He stopped his pacing by the large oak desk that took up the entire front wall. Twelve neat stacks of bills created a geometric grid on the desk.

A good haul for such a small town, but Elon felt none of the elation, none of the static electricity that usually accompanied a successful show. The whispers in the town were rising to conversation, to solid fact. "The boy, the star acrobat, he fell. He'll never perform again."

Elon wasn't sure if the last part was true, that was up to Cash. But he'd seen enough performers suffer traumatic accidents to know that well after their bodies healed, the mental anguish kept them from the ring permanently. Fear was a dangerous captor. Only waiting would reveal if Cash would ever fly again. He needed Cash — needed him to become the famous star he envisioned. The star Lorenzo assured him the boy could be.

In the meantime, he was out of his main act. Elon turned from the desk full of money and returned to pacing, his large hands clasped behind his back. He would usually promote Boris' act but who knew when he'd be over pneumonia if that was even what ailed the big man. Two acts down. He would figure it out. He always did.

Pausing by the door, he ran a finger over his satin stage jacket hanging on a hook. Also green. Though he constantly worried about money, he had never had a show at less than half of the capacity of the tent which meant they could comfortably continue things as they were.

"The phenom" they called him when he started. "He can sell tickets to ants in a fistfight."

The rest of the show was solid, but Elon needed the extra money Cash's act was already starting to bring in. With a famous act, he could compete in the big cities. He dreamed of building a permanent tent. No more trains, no more setups and teardowns, and blindingly boring days on the rails with nothing to look at but blurry trees. Glints of permanent stardom taunted him. They could have a show every day. Multiple shows. It would be an extravaganza people would travel to. The money would flow in. And that happened with a real tent, a permanent show, and a star performer. He had to make sure Cash got back on the traps.

A sudden, sharp rap on the door made him jump. His face flushed and anger caused his body to tense. No one bothered him after the show. They knew better.

"The tent had better be on fire," he growled as he headed to the door. He swung it open to reveal Sacha with a strange, smug look on his face. "Sacha, what…?"

Sacha came up the steps and slunk past Elon without being invited in, like an intruder.

"Well, Uncle, I just overheard an interesting conversation between your boy Cash and his friends," the younger man gloated.

Elon rotated to remain facing Sacha as the young man made his way in, touching Elon's jacket, picking up his top hat, and eyeing the money on the desk.

The ringmaster raised his eyebrows with a blank expression, but his mind was whirring. He felt trapped but wasn't sure why.

"Seems your cook has a secret." He paused hoping Elon would confess. "A *healer*. At your circus. I can only imagine how helpful that would be with all the things that can go wrong at a circus."

The ringmaster's heart pounded, he could hear blood coursing in his ears, which he felt turning red with anger.

"I've heard stories at some of these remote towns of people with more-than-human skills. Thought it was folklore." Sacha picked up a gold coin from the table by the door and flicked it so it spun in the air. He caught it and said, "Guess I was wrong." He looked right at Elon. "Is this why your shows are so successful, Uncle? Whenever a performer gets hurt you heal them so they're right back in the show?! That's how you run at such a grueling pace rushing from town to town?!"

The nephew had gone from inquisitive to accusatory.

"Are you accusing me of cheating?! How dare you question me about my show and my workers! How I run my show is my business not yours!" Elon spat back.

"Maybe if my father had a healer, his show would be more successful than yours!" Sacha replied, both of their tempers rising.

"If your FATHER had healer he would threaten her and treat her like an animal. Make her perform like a monkey! Cutting people to have her heal them in front of a crowd. Your father is a MONSTER!"

Sacha's face turned white then splotches of red appeared as the two men stared at each other in thick silence. The only sound was the slight creaking of the train carriage in the wind.

The young man turned away and flew out the door, slamming it behind him.

Unclenching his fists, and allowing his body to relax a little bit, Elon stepped backward, looking for a chair. He dropped into it trying to understand what had happened. Cash knew about Helen's gift. Sacha knew about Helen. What other secrets had Sacha uncovered? As he sat, Elon thought about another train car, with another show many years in the past.

Twenty Years Ago

Elon paced his bare carriage. Plain, splintered wooden slats made up the four walls. His stomach turned in knots in anticipation. The show had wrapped an hour ago and the money from the ticket sales was on his makeshift desk. It was their biggest show so far. Every penny was accounted for. A loud knock made Elon jump. He wiped sweat from his forehead as he reached for the door. Before he could open it, his older brother barreled through the entry. Even though Elon was larger than the average man, his brother still towered over him. Louka ducked into the car and turned to get his broad shoulders into the room. The giant man straightened out and looked down on Elon. His top hat was in his hand as it wouldn't fit on his head in the train carriage.

"Hello, brother." Louka eyed the money while addressing his brother. "Looked like a big crowd tonight. Did we set a new record?"

"Y-yes. Beat the old attendance record by almost 50 people. They were shoved in the stands like sardines," stuttered Elon.

"Excellent. That's what I like to hear." Louka reached for the piles of money and collected every last one. Elon began to sweat. He thought of all the things he wanted to say to his brother. Tonight was the night. Elon cleared his throat to confront his brother.

"We agreed to split the proceeds 60/40. I've increased your sales by 200%. We were supposed to be partners," Elon appealed. Louka whirled around and with one large step was right in front of Elon glaring down at him.

"Without me you have nothing. You could never do what I do and run the entire show. You'd be poor. A beggar. Or worse, shoveling the elephant car. Do you want to shovel the elephant car?" He paused and examined Elon's eyes. "I didn't think so. You get what I give you." Louka pulled a couple of bills from the stack, held them out, and dropped them. Elon watched the bills float to the floor.

Louka backed away, straightened the money into a neat, thick stack, and walked out of the car, putting on his hat as he walked into the cool, crisp night.

It took years for Elon to get away from Louka. Their show became so successful that they broke the circus code and set up in a town where another show was already playing. Their competition was a small, fledgling dog and pony show. The old ringmaster, Emil, should have retired years before but didn't know what else to do with his life. He kept going out of routine. The acts were lackluster and unexciting.

Louka's show dazzled the townspeople. Eventually, the old man's shows were empty and he was forced to leave town. Elon watched Emil and his crew pack up their train cars. As the defeated circus was about to pull out, Elon made a life-altering decision. He ran and hopped onto the caboose, leaving all of his things behind him and, more importantly, leaving his brother behind. Elon made his way up a couple of cars and found a place to sleep for the night. The next morning he found Emil and the men struck a deal. Elon ran the circus, and after a few short years, had enough money to buy the circus from Emil who married the old seamstress and finally retired. Success came easily to Elon, but at night after the shows, he was perpetually haunted by thoughts of his brother; always feeling like Louka was one step behind him seeking his revenge. Over the years, Elon heard whispers about his brother's show. At one point the story was that Louka fired everyone but the acrobats.

Two Years Ago

Elon exited the ring and cut through the backyard, still elated from the adrenaline of the crowd. He quickly noticed an unfamiliar young man lingering along the fence and staring at him. The lanky teenager looked around 15 or 16.

"Excuse me," the teen said.

"If you need a job, Barnaby will be out in a minute. Talk to him," Elon replied and kept walking.

"Wait! I'm your nephew," the boy replied earnestly. Elon froze. Was Louka nearby? Even after 18 years, the thought of Louka made cold fear trickle down his spine. Elon turned towards the young man, scanning the area around them, expecting his brother to step out from behind a cart or tree.

"Why should I believe you?! Is your father here? Why are you here?!" Elon shouted.

The startled young man removed the knapsack from his back and withdrew a black top hat. He held it in both hands for a moment, then handed it to Elon who examined it. The familiar black, silk rim and red band. He flipped the hat over expecting what was inside. His brother's name was scripted on the white inner band.

"What am I supposed to do with this?" Elon spat.

"It's my father's hat. I showed you so you'd know I'm his son."

"Why isn't he wearing it?"

"He has a new hat. A white one. He got it when he changed his show," explained the young man.

"The acrobats..." Elon said quietly.

"You heard. It's a contemporary show now. Just acrobats," the young man added.

"If you are his son, why are you here instead of with him?"

The young man looked down into the open knapsack.

"He's horrible," he whispered, then looked up again. "When Father fired everyone, one of the old riggers took me aside and told me about the old days of the circus. The days when my father's brother - you - were part of the circus. He said you started your own show and it was successful, so I looked for an opportunity to get away and find you. You can't imagine the fear of living with him, never knowing when he's going explode. He's like a snake, but also a snake charmer. He always has a way of making you feel horrible and getting what he wants. I wanted to get out."

"What's your name?" Growled the ringmaster.

"Sacha," the young man replied.

Elon knew exactly how Sacha felt. Against his better judgment, he told the young man, he could stay. Sleep escaped Elon that night. If the boy was Louka's son, was he really running away? He knew his brother was harsh, but was he harsh enough to drive his own son away? How did Sacha find him? Surely it meant that Louka was on his heels. Or maybe he wasn't. Maybe Louka cared more about his show and money than finding his kid. He could always be a spy. Anyway, Elon was going to keep an eye on him.

———

Present Day

Again, Elon wrestled with questions throughout the night, questioning that decision from years ago to take in Sacha.

Had Sacha been playing him for years? Was he a spy for his father? A tool for his brother's revenge? This time though, he drifted into a short, uncomfortable sleep. And he dreamed.

———

Cash ran from the Red Wagon. Not thinking about where he was going, he ran as fast as he could. He felt skewed and off-kilter. He needed to get somewhere to think. He ran along the train cars and stopped at Major and Flora's car. It seemed like a good place where people wouldn't look for him. He opened the door a crack and pulled himself inside. He paused for a moment on his hands and knees, looking out at the circus through the open door, catching his breath. His head swirled from the conversation with his friends, from running, and from his injury. He leaned forward over the edge of the train car and threw up. Cash stood, closed the door, and leaned against it.

"It's just me," he said quietly to the rustling elephants. "It's just me." Cash closed his eyes hoping it would ease the pounding in his head. Flora took a step toward him and nuzzled her trunk against his cheek in a comforting gesture. Cash petted her back absent-mindedly.

Superpowers? His friends hadn't used that word, but isn't that what they had implied? When he was younger, his father had frowned upon comic books featuring super-human beings. "Why fill your head with things that aren't real?" But Cash read them anyway. Stories about strong men - stronger than Boris, invisible women and kids with speed like a cheetah. Helen healing him didn't make sense, but it explained how he had an old scar on a new injury, which also didn't make sense. Could two things that didn't make sense explain each other? It was too much for his head. He cleared his mind and played with the hay on the ground. He weaved the fiber through his fingers, and it calmed his nerves. Sitting in the dark, he listened to the occasional movement from the elephants and the distant noises of everyone preparing for the show that evening. Normal noises. Things that made sense to him. Sleep came slowly and gently.

A quiet rapping woke Cash sometime later.

"Cash are you in there? I'm opening the door," Tony said quietly, concerned.

Cash scooted over so he wasn't leaning on the door as it opened. His roommate stuck his head in and looked around until he found Cash.

"Come back to the 'boose, man. At least get a good night's sleep. If you don't want to see me, I'll sleep in here."

He must have slept through the show. To his stiff neck and back, his bed sounded like the best thing on earth. Cash swung his legs around and over the doorway. He jumped down and lost his balance, dizzy from just waking up and his semi-healed state. Tony caught him and put an arm around Cash for support. The boys walked to the caboose in silence.

CHAPTER 8

BETRAYED

In the morning Cash awoke from a comatose sleep. Consciousness came slowly, but Cash realized he felt much better. He wondered how long he had slept. The sun shone bright and the grounds sounded quiet, but he remembered it was a pull out day. They were moving on to the next town. Everything should be close to packed, it was just a matter of feeding everyone and letting the animals stretch one last time. His stomach grumbled. As quickly as he could, he got up, splashed water on his face, threw on a somewhat clean shirt, and headed to the cookhouse.

———

"Do you think he'll show up?" Helen asked, worried. The peacemaker of the group, Helen always looked for ways to mend rifts in the relationships of her friends. Bodies weren't the only thing she healed.

"I dunno," said Tony with a mouth full of eggs and bacon, "He was still passed out when I left. Didn't move or make a peep when I was up and getting ready. Thought he should rest."

Helen asked worriedly, "But do you think he's mad at us for not telling him what happened? For what we told him?"

"He didn't say a word to me last night. I couldn't tell if he was tired or mad," added Tony. Glances bounced around the group. Everyone was there except for Boris.

"Hopefully he's had some time to think about it," chimed in Bella.

"Here he is. I guess we'll find out," said Bonkers, looking toward the tent flaps where Cash had just entered.

———

Cash looked around the tent and noticed his friends at a table in the back, then headed for the food. He needed another minute before he faced them.

Like an automaton, Cash stiffly went through the line, barely paying attention to what was piling up on his tray. The hubbub of the tent created a nice background of noise. He grabbed a cup of orange juice and set it on his tray. Cash froze as he realized the entire tent had gone silent. He slowly looked over his shoulder and turned.

Everyone looked toward the entrance where Magda stood, hair whipping in the wind, the glowing, golden morning light silhouetting her. The old woman rarely left her tent for food or anything else. This morning she hobbled down the center aisle, one pained step at a time, leaning heavily on her gnarled, wooden cane. Heads turned to follow her path. Her cane thumped on the ground until she arrived at the first row of tables in front of the platform. Elon sat frozen with a forkful of food halfway to his mouth. He stared down at Magda who stared up at him.

"Beware, ringmaster." The old woman's raspy voice boomed with surprising might. The entire tent heard her. Several cups rattled as people jumped in their seats. "Be on guard! The dream you had last night," she continued. "was a warning. In the dream, you were a plant in a garden. You were the biggest and you watched over all of the other plants. But the one next to you was a dangerous weed." Elon's face turned gray and his mustache began to twitch. "Then the weed disappeared and you thought everything was fine. But when you didn't expect it, the weed came back and strangled you!"

Elon dropped his fork. It clattered on his plate. Everyone in the tent froze. Fear hung in the air like a heavy tapestry. In one quick movement, Elon reached under the table, and overturned it. Plates and chairs flew all over the platform. He was on his feet and approached the edge of the platform. Magda stood unflinching and staring at the ringmaster.

"We pull out in one hour!" He bellowed forcefully. "Anything or anyone who isn't ready will be left behind!" His face was red and he was shaking. Everyone stared. "This isn't a joke! MOVE, MOVE, MOVE!"

Instantly everyone in the tent shot to their feet. People scrambled over benches and ran to finish packing. Cash watched the chaos burst out of the tent. A tornado of motion flurried around Magda who stood frozen, still staring at Elon. Helen ran toward the kitchen and started dishing out orders to her boys. Cash grabbed the pancakes from the serving tray, wrapped them around pieces of bacon and sausage, and shoved them in his mouth in two bites. He threw his tray on the stack of dirties and took orders from Helen since she had the most to clean up.

Bella and Tony ran over to help while Bonkers left to check on the clowns. Cash helped the best he could with his one good arm. He and Tony bussed tables, threw dirty dishes into bins, and took the bins to the storage cars. They folded up the tables and shoved them into the car as well. As soon as the furniture was out, they recruited some of the boys and began to disassemble the tent. The tent was down in 40 minutes, which left 20 minutes to finish packing up the kitchen and get to their cars. At that moment, the clowns came running up in a line.

"Quick, throw the pots and pans in their bins, get them on the storage car!" Cash yelled to Bonkers. The clowns, some with their faces still painted from the night before, began an assembly line - throwing anything and everything into the storage bins and passing the bins towards the car.

"Where's Boris when you need him to move big equipment, huh?" said one of the clowns to Cash as four of them hefted a stove onto the car. Bella, standing nearby, overheard the remark, and Cash watched horror wipe across her face.

Cash felt sick with the realization that Boris might get left behind, wherever he was.

Bonkers threw an elbow at Cash to get his attention. Cash remembered the rush and shoved the box he was carrying into the car. Five minutes and a few more small things to get. The last whistle blew. The clowns closed up the storage car and ran to their car. Bonkers, Bella, Tony, Helen, and Cash grabbed the last few cables and things as the whistle sounded and the train started moving.

"To the caboose!" yelled Tony. The crew all angled toward the back of the train. Cash arrived first and threw open the door, then turned to help everyone up. Everyone tumbled inside and he stood on the back platform, watching as they pulled away from a mess. Elon prided himself on leaving a place as clean as they found it so they would be invited back. This time, papers rustled in the gusting wind and Barnaby's cat wandered through debris.

A few chairs and boxes were left behind, but it seemed like everyone was on board. The train rounded a bend and Cash looked toward Boris' car, wishing his friend was there. As he stared, the curtains of Boris' window parted. Cash stared and tried to figure out if it had been the rocking of the train or someone in Boris' car. He took one last curious look, but the train was on a straight path now, and Boris' window was out of view.

He turned to see that everyone had found a spot to sit. "So I'm guessing Magda has… she can… you know… one of those gifts?" Cash sputtered.

"Yeah. Her fortune-telling is a load of elephant poop. But when it comes to dreams…" Tony filled in.

"She not only interprets them, she can tell you *what* you dreamed," finished Bonkers.

"Spooky." Cash whispered. "But the warning she gave Elon. That was intense. Do you think it's real? Is something going to happen?" The others shifted uncomfortably.

"It's hard to tell," said Helen. "I've been at the circus for a long time. Magda can tell you all sorts of things about yourself just from your dreams. When it comes to predicting future events, it's kind of like the chicken and the egg. No one really knows which one came first. And with warning dreams like that, she might be right and the thing happens. But if it doesn't happen, was she wrong, or did the person heed the warning and it didn't happen because she warned them? Either way… we should all be on guard."

Bonkers had his legs tucked up to his chest and was rocking. Bella stared off at nothing. They all looked worried. They clearly believed in Magda's gift.

"So Helen can heal, Magda can interpret dreams. Are there… other gifts?" Cash looked at Bella, Bonkers, and Tony.

Bella responded first. "I'm normal."

"Hey, like we're not?" Asked Tony, slowly breaking into a smile.

"You know what I mean," she continued. "I don't have a gift. But my brother, Martín did. He could always predict and sense the weather. It started small, with thunderstorms or snow. As he got older he could tell what the weather would be in faraway places. Helpful for traveling so much. Elon used him a lot. 'East or West?' he'd say. But it wore on Martín. The gift and the pressure of being right. So I understand. I get what you all go through."

"Martín was such a sweet boy," added Helen thoughtfully.

A faraway look came over Bella's face and she was lost to reverie.

"I can feel what people are thinking," Bonkers jumped in.

"Oh gosh! You can read thoughts?" asked Cash.

"No! Well, not really. I feel their emotions. Either the general feeling in a room or an individual person. When I'm doing my act out in the crowd, I can feel people's excitement… or their fear if I come up to them. That's how I can always choose the right people to interact with," the clown explained.

Cash thought about it for a moment.

"Does Elon use your gift too?"

"Yeah. After a show I let him know which acts the crowd was interested in or not. What they want to see again. Sometimes I catch people who aren't there to have fun. Other circuses send spies. Things like that. But it's going all the time. Right now, Cash, you're intrigued and disbelieving and wanting to believe and confused and… a little bit sad."

Cash's eyebrows shot up in surprise.

"Yeah… I am all of those things. I had to think about it, but that's exactly what I'm feeling. Interesting. Do a lot of people at the circus have gifts? Is it everyone but Bella and me?"

Helen's face turned serious before she replied, "That's a tricky question, Cash. This whole business of gifts is delicate. Until your accident the only person who knew about my gift at the circus was Elon."

"Besides Elon, only a few of the clowns know about me. And now you all. So don't, you know, say anything," added Bonkers.

"It can be a dangerous thing, to be special," continued Helen. "Some people see the gifts as a means to gain power or money. Either with their own gift or by using people with the gifts. Many of us with gifts keep it secret. Regular people don't always understand. We get put in institutions or locked away somewhere or manipulated."

"It's crazy…" muttered Bonkers.

"I'm sorry we were so secretive after your accident, Cash. The moment you fell, I… " Helen looked away, sniffed, and slowly brushed tears from her eyes. "With the head injury and being so high up, I knew I wouldn't have much time. I had to get to you and didn't consider who was around. Afterward, I felt so exposed that Boris, Tony, Bonkers and who-knows-who-else saw my gift. I asked them not to say anything. I'm sorry. We should have told you right away." Helen said.

"We were protecting Helen, and all of us with gifts, really," Tony spoke for the first time in a while.

"I forgive you, Helen and Tony. Bonkers and Bella. It's a lot to take in. I can't even imagine what you all go through." Cash looked down at Helen. "And thank you for saving my life." Helen smiled warmly at Cash. "It wasn't just me." She nodded at Tony.

"Tony, you can heal too?" Cash gasped.

"No," A sly smile spread across Tony's face. "I can manipulate time. How people or things move *through* time, more specifically."

Cash's jaw dropped.

"Not for very long." Tony said.

After a moment of silence, Cash realized what had happened. "You slowed me down. That's why the fall didn't kill me."

"Just for a few seconds, but it was enough."

Cash nodded his head.

"That wasn't the only time," Tony added.

"What do you mean?" Cash tried to think of another scenario where he had needed Tony's gift.

"Remember the day Lorenzo discovered you?"

"Yeah…"

"You weren't going to make the train."

Cash gasped. "I remember a weird feeling in my stomach. It was quick. Almost like a rope was tied around my middle and it was tugging me forward."

"Yeah, that was it."

"Whoa." Cash looked at his friend with admiration.

"Well, I think Elon has a gift," Bonkers asserted, changing the subject. "He's hard to work for, though what boss isn't? He knows about our gifts but he doesn't exploit them too much. There's the occasional veiled threat, but it could be a lot worse. He could put us on display and have all of us in a sideshow, but he doesn't. I don't think it's because he's compassionate, because he's not. The only reason I can figure is that he has a gift himself and he could get exposed if we all were," he looked around and noted contemplative nods from Helen and Tony.

"So, what is his gift?" asked Tony, thinking hard.

A sly smile curved Bonkers' lips. "When Nina and I were going out, she told me that we've never lost money on a show. Even in small towns. It doesn't make sense. You've seen some of the tiny places we've played."

"Wait! You and Nina?! When did that happen?" Cash stared at the clown.

"Oh, a few years ago. She dumped me pretty quick so it didn't get around."

Bella leaned toward Cash and whispered with a grin, "Bonkers likes older women."

The clown shrugged in response. "Can't deny it."

"Back to Elon. So you think he has a gift with money?" Tony asked, eyebrow raised.

"That's my guess. We're obviously not rolling in dough, but if the show always breaks even, that takes away some of the risk if, say, your star act gets injured."

"Huh. I've never heard of that one. But it makes sense," said Tony, thinking through his years at the circus.

Suddenly, Bella, who hadn't said anything in a while,

let out a shriek. Everyone else's heads whipped towards her. The thin acrobat was leaning over her knees, hands covering her face. Helen moved next to her and put an arm around her shoulders.

"I'm worried about Boris. I don't know where he is! I'm afraid we left him behind!" she wailed.

"He doesn't have pneumonia, does he?" whispered Cash.

"No," Bella admitted.

"When was the last time you saw him?" Cash asked. Though the question was addressed to Bella, the caboose suddenly became tense. It didn't take Bonkers' gift to tell that there was something his friends weren't telling him. Again.

"What? What is it this time!? I can tell there's something I don't know here," Cash was exasperated.

Bonkers looked at Cash with a mix of pity and empathy. "The last time any of us saw him was in the medical tent when you were unconscious. We were all together with Dr. Keller when Boris left."

When Bonkers didn't explain further, Cash looked around desperately seeking answers. His friends were avoiding his gaze.

"Please! Tony, what happened? Why did he leave?" Cash pleaded.

Tony sighed. "You… you said something and he left."

"What? I was unconscious. How could I say something to make him leave?"

"Cash, honey. This might be hard or confusing for you to hear," said Helen quietly. "There's a good chance you have a gift."

"No. No, no, no. I'm normal. I don't have a gift," said Cash, confused that she would even think that. "I can't heal or or or or talk to animals or manipulate things or whatever else there is!"

Tony and Helen looked at each other, and Helen nodded to Tony to continue.

"When you were unconscious, it seemed like you had a vision or a dream or something. You were stirring in your sleep and then you began to speak without really waking up. Then you shouted at Boris to 'go save her' and he ran out of the room. We were shocked at what happened, but apparently it meant something to Boris and we haven't seen him since."

Cash's vision went gray. He could barely breathe, let alone think. He wanted to get away from his friends to figure out what was going on. If the train hadn't been moving, he would have left the car. He buried his head in his arms to block them out and try to remember. He hoped he'd have some memory of what he told Boris to drive him away, but the events from the day of the accident still hadn't come back to him, let alone what happened when he was unconscious. It was too far-fetched to make up. Were they trying to blame him for Boris leaving? Were they making all of the gifts up? He peeked through his fingers. No, his friends were concerned for him.

"Have you ever had really memorable dreams? Or dreams that came true?" Helen asked quietly.

And Cash remembered the dream he had before his parents died. He looked up, feeling shocked and sick to his stomach. His face turned white.

"Two days before my parents died," Cash whispered. "I had a dream that the three of us were birds, flying in the air. And suddenly they were gone. A hunter…" Cash couldn't finish. A lump had appeared in his throat, threatening tears. "I thought it was a coincidence." He couldn't believe it. He thought about some of the other vivid dreams he'd had. Some made sense, some were abstract. "NO! This can't be real! This is a curse! I'm making the people around me die and run away!"

"No. Of course not, Cash. I think it's more of… insight into what's happening or going to happen. Surely you've had good dreams too?" Helen comforted.

Cash didn't respond. Had he?

Then Cash did remember something from before the accident. "I saw Boris fighting with a man. A local I think. The day of the accident. I couldn't understand them, I don't know what language they were speaking."

The tone in the caboose changed suddenly. A spark of interest bloomed and floated through the room.

"That's right. He brushed off the conversation when I asked him about it. But I bet it *was* his brother-in-law!" Bella said.

"Maybe he just went to visit his sister?" Tony suggested hopefully.

"And he didn't make it back because we pulled out early," added Bonkers eagerly.

"But why wouldn't he tell us? Why would he just leave so upset?" asked Bella, clearly hurt.

"I don't know, Bella. I don't know," said Helen, giving her a squeeze. They rode in silence for some minutes. Until Tony changed the subject and Bonkers quickly had them laughing at a new gaff.

Cash went to sleep later that night full of emotions: confused that he might have a gift, scared that it drove Boris away, amazed that more people at the circus had gifts, slightly fearful about what he might dream that night and that it would drive more of his friends away. As he slept that night, the train pulled into the town of Avantré. Even the raging thunderstorm couldn't wake Cash from his thankfully dreamless sleep.

CHAPTER 9

BORIS RETURNS

"NOW, NOW, NOW!" Shouted Lorenzo. With a flick of his wrist, Cash lit a match and the large ring dangling in the center of the arena burst into flames. Cash backed up a few steps just as Jamie, one of the equestrians, jumped through the blazing ring on her horse. Jamie and horse were unscathed, yet Cash smelled singed hair. When he realized it was his own, he swatted frantically at his head to dampen the sparks burning his blonde locks.

"Well done, Jamie! Well done!" Lorenzo walked towards her while starting a slow clap. "Elon always has a nose for new acts, and he sure was right about you." Lorenzo moved towards Jamie with a hug. She stepped back and Lorenzo suavely turned the movement into petting the beautiful, brown horse at Jamie's side.

"Attention, everyone! Jamie's routine will be at the end of the Second Act. Coming out of Bonkers' chasing the ballerina's act, we'll need her horse prepped. Understood? Good!" He grabbed his megaphone. "That's a wrap! Get some dinner!"

Cash turned quickly, and discovered that the other

acrobats had crowded in behind him to congratulate Jamie. He shoved his way through them and set his path toward the exit. The patter of small feet hurrying to catch him hit his ears, but he didn't say anything when Bella caught up to him.

"Cash, I know it stings to get replaced, but it's only temporary," she said.

"You don't know it's temporary. All I know is that there are no guarantees. Getting replaced is the worst thing that can happen to an acrobat!" he paused and saw her skeptical glare. "Fine. Second worst."

With Boris gone and the revelation of his and his friends' gifts, Cash had barely thought about his act and getting back to rehearsals. This first rehearsal was harder than he anticipated. He didn't realize how much he had come to depend on his talent, on his act, and on the admiration of the crowd. What would he do and become now? There wasn't even a chance of swinging anytime soon with his arm in a cast. And he couldn't bring himself to think through any of his routines without knots of fear in his stomach and breaking into a sweat. "You'll get better and we'll start training again and we'll be back in our spot, you'll see. Lorenzo had to do *something* until you're swinging again." She grabbed his good arm and he stopped his exit march. "You're going to be OK, Cash. I know it."

Her words made Cash uneasy. Without Cash, Bella had been demoted to a simple routine with a couple of trapeze tricks at the beginning of the show. He knew she was trying to encourage him, but she was also depending on him getting back into the swing of things.

"I…" he trailed off. The thought of standing on the platform made his head dizzy and his stomach queasy. He snapped his mouth shut and brushed past Bella.

"I hope you're right," he forced without turning to look at her again.

Cash mindlessly followed the crowd heading to the cookhouse for dinner when he realized he wasn't hungry. He changed direction mid-stride and turned back towards the caboose.

A stone in his path received a swift, distracted kick. He understood he had to be replaced, but it was still embarrassing. His body ached and his arm was in a cast for a couple more weeks. Quite suddenly, his entire life was different; he wasn't a star and he might not even be an acrobat, his friends had super-human gifts, apparently he had a gift that had driven his best friend away and maybe killed his own parents. He wished for something normal and familiar, but it wasn't there. It was like falling through the air all over again.

Bella's encouragement echoed in his head, but it still made him nervous. He wanted to believe he'd be the star again. As an acrobat, he'd fallen before. Lorenzo made them practice falling safely, but never from that height. And who could have predicted a freak accident? If Helen and Tony hadn't used their gifts on him… he didn't want to think about that. He hopped up onto the caboose platform and paused to look at the landscape. The forest to his left and the track they came in on straight ahead. He spied houses off in the distance, and the circus set up to his right. A lonely bird chirped in the skeleton trees edging the train. Cash leaned over the side rail and looked up, thankful for any distraction. The air pricked his skin with hints of cool.

A flash of color caught his eye among the dark brown and pale yellow of the late fall landscape. Cash turned to see Bonkers in his garish red and white suit, carrying a tray of food. He looked like he didn't want to be seen, so Cash pulled himself as far back onto the platform as he could while still keeping an eye on the mischievous clown.

Bonkers turned and knocked on one of the cars. He waited, rocking on the heels of his big shoes. He raised his hand to knock again but hesitated. Finally, he set the tray on the top step, straightened up, looked around, and ducked through the nearest opening between cars.

Cash counted the cars and a surge of excitement shot through him. Bonkers had been at Boris' car! Maybe they hadn't left him behind after all. His first reaction was to run and bang down his friend's door, but he stopped himself.

Maybe he's sick, or hurt, or not even there, Cash thought. He took a calming breath and hopped down from his platform, then casually headed up the line of cars.

When he was a little ways off, the door opened and Boris' hand shot out to take the tray. In a snap, the plate disappeared and the door slammed closed again. He was there! This time Cash disregarded any doubts, ran the distance to his friend's door, knocked quietly, and whispered.

"Boris, I know you're in there. What's going on? Are you sick? Or hurt?" Cash listened for signs of movement. Patience for his friend ran out and Cash let loose on the door, making a racket. "Boris! I don't care if you want to see me or not, I need to talk to you and know what's going on if we're still friends!"

The door flew open mid-knock and Boris' giant arm shot out. He grabbed Cash by the front of his shirt, pulled him up off his feet, and into the car in a violent motion and closed the door again, just missing pinching Cash's feet in the swinging door.

"What in the world, Boris?! Have you gone crazy?" Boris clapped a hand over Cash's mouth and put a finger to his lips, giving an urgent plead with his eyes for silence. Cash stilled, eyes wide open. He took in his friend's face. It was the same but older somehow, or maybe just tired. His normally jovial eyes were stressed and urgent. Then Cash looked around with Boris' hand still on his mouth. He hadn't spent much time in Boris' car before. A built-in bookshelf on the opposite wall caught Cash's eye. It was full of trinkets and photographs. One frame showed a smiling Boris with an older couple and three pretty women.

———

Ten Years Ago

Boris sat at the foot of his bed, his knees tucked to his chest. He looked out at the almost full yellow moon highlighting the ravaged landscape, and he tried to ignore the gnawing in his stomach and in his chest. Civil war had torn through Russia for the past year. Between the war and unfavorable weather, most of the country was starving. The famine explained the pain in his stomach, but the pain in his chest was due to the conversation he was about to have with his mother and father.

For a few more minutes Boris sat in the silence, staring out the window, beginning to distance himself from this place and the people in it. When the whispers and rustling from the next room subsided and he was confident that his sisters were asleep, the large young man unfolded his legs and gently padded across the room and opened the door. The short hallway lined with photographs and framed newspaper articles led to the kitchen where he would find his parents.

Boris stood in the doorway to the small kitchen and committed everything to memory. The little white stove, the open wooden shelves with wooden plates and cups. Most of the room was filled with the hefty dining table where they shared meals. He caught a glimpse of his parents sitting quietly across from each other on the benches, staring silently into each other's eyes. In his mother's hair shone glimmers of silver he hadn't noticed before. His father turned to look at him with sorrow in his eyes like he knew what was coming. Boris walked to the chair at the end of the table and sat down. The chair gave a creak of resistance to his weight.

"I'm joining the army," Boris said in a hushed, but decisive manner.

"No, Boris! Why?" his mother asked, worried.

"There isn't enough food here for all of us. If I go, you'll be able to feed everyone."

"Son, we'll figure it out. We'll keep all of you fed." his father said unconvincingly.

"So many boys don't come back from the war. Please, Boris, we don't want to lose you. Stay. We will make it and this spring will be better. We'll get more from the garden. Your father will have work again." She reached out and grasped his wrist, emphasizing the stress in her eyes.

"Your mother is right. We have some money we've been saving in case things get worse. Don't join the army, son." His father rarely let emotion show, but Boris could hear the anxiety in his voice. Boris knew joining the civil war was extremely dangerous, but he also wanted his family to survive the war and the famine.

"I'll think about it," Boris said, squeezing his mother's hand before pushing back from the table. He got up and returned to his room. All he could think about was how his parents had sat there and lied to his face. They had no plan, no money or food in savings. They didn't even believe things were going to get better. He had to leave to save them.

The next evening Boris grabbed an old travel bag and began to load it with his few possessions. The floorboards near the door creaked. Boris paused his packing and looked over his shoulder. His sister Nadia, the youngest, stood grabbing the door frame. Her jaw-length black hair framed her skeletal face.

"Where are you going?" she asked directly.

"I'm joining the army." he replied.

"Why?"

"So you all have enough to eat. I'll be taken care of there and you will have more food to go around here," Boris said in a forceful whisper.

"But mother and father said there will be enough," she stated, clearly believing them.

"I know." Boris sighed.

"You don't believe them?" Nadia queried with doubt finally lacing her voice.

"That's just what they told us so we wouldn't be scared," piped in a third voice. Marian, the oldest and the realist. She stood several inches above her younger sister. Her long, dark hair was in a braid that draped over her shoulder. "I got up to get water last night. They were talking in the kitchen. I stood in the hall and listened. I shouldn't have spied, but Mother was crying and said she didn't know what to do. She was afraid we'll starve this year because all the money is gone."

Nadia's face turned white as her nightgown. "What are we going to do?" her voice raised in pitch with her rising panic.

"Shhhh!" Boris prompted. "I already told you. I'm leaving so you all can eat."

"When?" whispered Marian.

"In a few hours. Once I'm sure mother and father are sleeping. Now go back to bed so they don't get suspicious." Boris hugged his sisters, softly pushed them out of the room, and sat back on his bed to steel his mind against the emotions of leaving. With his ear against the wall, he listened to his parents shuffle to their bedroom. A few minutes later, he jumped when his door opened. Marian darted in and gracefully shut the door in silence. She sat next to him on the bed and they both stared into the moon, saying silent prayers.

"I'm sorry I won't be here for Maya," he whispered, avoiding his sister's gaze as he thought of his niece.

"Me too. With her father gone, she looks up to you. You're the strong one in the family, Boris," Marian said.

"That's not true. You're the one whose husband went off to war and are raising a child by yourself," Boris encouraged his older sister.

Marian didn't reply, but looked across the cold, apocalyptic field outside the window.

"Are you going to tell them?" Marian asked, still facing the moon.

"Tell who what?" Boris played dumb.

"The army people. That you have a gift with languages?" Marian, with her head on her tucked-up knees turned her doe eyes to her brother.

"No."

"But maybe they'll make you an officer, and keep you out of the fight," she pleaded with him.

"Or they would subscript me to the army for life once they found out what I can do. That wouldn't end well. Who knows how often they would let me see the family. I'd be a government secret." Then he added, "I'll take my chances and be careful."

Marian stared at her brother for another moment and then looked back to the moon with a sigh. An hour later Boris was walking across the barren landscape in the starlight. All the while he could feel his sister's eyes on him, watching her only brother go off to war.

***

Present Day

"My family," Boris whispered, freeing Cash's mouth.

Cash turned his head away from the photographs to look at his friend, but Boris wasn't looking at the photographs on the shelf. Instead, his eyes were set on the bed. Cash followed his friend's gaze and looked over at the bed with the dark, red canopy and black comforter. The black of the comforter began to shift as someone underneath it began to stir. Cash whipped his head back to look at Boris. Finally letting go of Cash's shirt and setting him back on the ground, Boris quietly walked toward the bed. Cash followed hesitantly behind him. Boris leaned over and pulled the covers down a little bit to reveal a mess of dark brown hair. The sleeping figure rolled toward them. Cash gasped so hard he almost choked.

The silky hair belonged to a girl. He had no idea if she

was pretty or not because her face was distorted. Her left eye was swollen shut and the bruise around her right eye ran into the bruise around her nose which was broken in at least one place. Her lower lip was split down the middle and her jawline was red like the fighters Cash saw sparring for money around the shadier parts of towns they visited.

Cash stared at her and shook his head, unbelieving.

"Who… what… what happened? Was she in an accident?" he whispered up at Boris.

"No accident," he replied flatly. "Her father. My sister's husband. My sister made me take her. Now I'll protect her." Cash gaped up at his friend. Boris' voice was flat, but his eyes burned with something Cash had never seen there before. Fury.

"What about your sister? Is she OK?"

"She got away. I came north, she went south. Her husband cannot search two directions at once. We will meet again in the west," Boris replied flatly.

"What are you going to do with her until then?"

"You'll help me. Be her friend."

With that simple instruction, Cash decided to be friends with the girl with the beat-up face.

"What's her name?" Cash asked.

"Maya."

Cash and Boris stood silently looking at Maya. Then Boris walked to the table at the other end of the car and gestured to Cash to take a seat with him.

"Cash, this must be our secret. I'll keep hiding until I know she is OK. OK? Until she can take care of herself. Elon can't find out yet. She's… not like other people."

"You can't keep hiding in here," Cash urgently whispered.

"If I noticed, others will too."

"I… I don't know what else to do," Boris whispered hopelessly.

"You need help taking care of her." Cash thought for a moment, running through an idea in his head. "I can do it! I'm barely doing anything right now since my accident." There was a solemn and silent moment as Cash and Boris both realized they hadn't seen each other since before Cash should have died. Boris extended his paw-like hand to Cash's shoulder and pulled him in for a hug.

"I'm happy you didn't die, friend."

"Yeah me too," Cash choked back a gulp of emotion. Thankful to be alive, thankful to have his friend back. The tension of the morning melted at the normalcy of talking to Boris like no time had passed.

"And I'm sorry I wasn't there after. But… you see," Boris glanced at Maya. "I couldn't wait any longer." After a moment, he added, "How did you know to warn me?"

"I don't remember anything. Helen and Bella and everyone think I have one of those 'gifts'," Cash explained.

Boris leaned forward and studied Cash with a serious face. He reached up and roughly pushed Cash's hair back to examine the fading scar on his forehead.

"Helen told you?"

Cash nodded.

"I've never seen a gift like hers," he released Cash's hair. "Usually gifts aren't so physical."

"So what happened, exactly?" Cash asked.

"What, your accident? No one told you yet?"

"Not that. I don't want to hear it again. After. Did I really talk to you while I was unconscious?"

The big man nodded.

"It was strange. You weren't moving. Then it was like watching someone having a dream. You stirred and muttered. Then you went stiff and and talked to me, 'Save her, Boris, save her.' I got in a fight with Marian's husband earlier that day. Marian sent me a letter a month ago and it was different. I began to suspect what was going on. When he showed up at the circus, he threatened me and told me to stay away from them. So when you said that, I knew something really bad was going to happen and I had to go. I got there just in time. You see what he did to Maya. Marian looked just as bad. I sent Marian to the train station and put Maya outside while I made sure her father wasn't able to follow us."

"Oh saints, Boris. Did you kill him?" Cash dared to ask.

All emotion left Boris' face. "He was still breathing when I left him."

The train rocked gently as they rounded a bend. Maya stirred in the bed and settled again. Cash had almost forgotten she was there.

Boris and Cash sat silently for a moment.

"It took so long to get back, with Maya and her injuries. She's been in and out of consciousness."

"Boris, she needs a doctor."

"No!" he hissed. "No one can know yet. Cash, her gift is a dangerous one," and he grabbed Cash's arm in his iron grip. "And I don't want too many people asking questions about where I've been. I just need a little more time."

"She could be really hurt. At least let Helen look at her?" Cash offered.

"OK. Bring her tomorrow. Tell no one else," the big man said.

CHAPTER 10

HELEN'S GIFT

Helen trudged through the early morning darkness. She cursed the new moon as she stepped on a rock and almost upended the carton she was carrying to the kitchen. Her frustration evaporated as she pushed her shoulder through the flap and into the kitchen. Most people thought the circus happened in the ring, but Helen relished the refined chaos of her kitchen. She took in the sight of her boys already getting started for the day. Tony, perched atop one of the storage racks, was tossing frying pans down to Billy.

"Who put this bin on the top shelf anyway?" Tony called down as he dropped another pan. Much to Helen's relief, Billy caught it in his hands and not with his head.

"Good morning, boys!" she called.

"Good morning, Helen!" the boisterous replies echoed off the pots and pans and steely surfaces.

"Mornin', mum," came a mumble from the oat bin. One of the smaller boys had most of his upper half stretched into the container with his feet off the ground. Helen walked over and pulled the mystery child by the back of the sweater until the chest and head of Ralph appeared. "Couln'a reach the scoop-uh," he explained with a shake of the head that sent oat bits flying.

"Ok, well, next time have one of the bigger boys help you." Helen rumpled Ralph's already messy hair.

She weaved her way past stools, crates, and small persons to throw the produce box on the counter with a harrumph. Behind her, pans clattered as Tony jumped down from the top shelf and toppled over Billy with his hands full of pans. In a smooth move, Tony grabbed Billy's hand to help him to his feet as he slid past him to arrive at Helen's side.

"Things are a mess, on account of how fast we pulled out of the last town," Tony reported.

"I know. I'm just glad we got everything on the train. We don't get any excuses. Breakfast has to be out on time no matter what. If we throw off breakfast, everyone's days are thrown off and you know how the ringmaster gets," she replied.

"Aye, boss." Looking into the box, Tony slid it across the table. "Billy! Catch this!" The surprised boy tossed the pans he had just recovered across the steel prep table and caught the box as it teetered and threatened to spill on the floor.

After the clamor died, Tony instructed, "Wash the potatoes and start grating them for the hash."

"Giving orders are we?" Helen teased in a motherly tone.

"That's the first food I've seen in this kitchen. Even if it weren't on the menu, it is now. It might be all the first shift gets to eat."

Helen turned to Tony and realized that at some recent point, he had surpassed her in height. His eager, sharp brown eyes peeked out from his dark hair that had the slightest curl at the end.

"Then I guess we had better find the rest of the food pretty quickly," Helen directed. They parted ways and began looking in every bin, crate, and hiding space for the rest of their ingredients and tools.

"I can't find the grater!" yelled Billy.

"We need pans, spoons, mixing bowls, whisks, knives, and the serving trays!" Yelled Helen.

"And food!" Hollered Tony.

"And the grater!" Piped Billy.

Suddenly everything in the kitchen moved at once as every boy dug through bins, tore open boxes, climbed shelves, and tossed items onto the prep area as they found them.

Several tense minutes later bacon was sizzling.

"I got the grater!" Ralph called, half buried in a wooden crate. He straightened and lobbed it across the kitchen. "Catch, Billy!"

"Hey! Don't throw that! I'll grate my fingers," replied Billy as the grater hit the floor with a clatter.

"Wash it and get going, boys!" Helen wiped sweat from her forehead as her experienced eyes quickly took inventory of the recovered tools and food. "All we need are eggs!" She announced with excitement.

"I saw someone load the egg crate into the animal storage carriage," offered Billy.

"Good! Ok. That's odd…" she muttered.

"They put them back with the animals!" Ralph realized excitedly.

Helen paused to reflect and then shrugged her shoulders.

"Tony! We need our eggs. Go talk to Barnaby," she gave Tony a very direct look to prevent any backtalk.

The young man's shoulders bristled, but he gave no objection. "Yes, ma'am," he said as he walked out of the tent.

Twenty minutes later in the cookhouse, Helen put out the last pan of their limited breakfast menu as the first member of the setup crew came in for breakfast.

"You boys serve it up, I'll be back in five," Helen said with relief.

She walked back into the kitchen and sat down wearily on a stool. Before she'd even caught a breath or felt the blood circulating in her legs again, Cash burst into the back of the tent. He caught eyes with Helen, then scanned the rest of the kitchen before returning his earnest gaze on Helen. In a few graceful strides, he was across the kitchen and grabbing Helen by the arm.

"I need your help!" Cash gasped.

"What? No! My kitchen is in chaos!"

He froze and his grip didn't ease up at all. "I need your *special* help."

"Oh... Ok. Show me," Helen replied in a low, steady voice. They exited through the back flaps just as Tony popped his head in the kitchen and caught a glimpse of Helen's retreating form and Cash's wavy, blonde hair.

They walked quickly in silence, Helen sensing that whatever was going on wasn't something Cash wanted to discuss in the vicinity of others.

Finally, she whispered, "Where are we going?"

"Boris' car." Cash didn't look at her as he said it.

Helen sent him a quizzical look but didn't ask any of the questions that jumped into her head. They crossed the midway from the cookhouse to Boris' car as the sun hinted at its arrival over the hills. Cash approached the car, knocked twice, and let himself in, leaving the door open for Helen to follow.

Large meaty arms grabbed her in an embrace when she entered.

"Thank you for coming," Boris said quietly to her as Cash closed the door with a soft click.

Helen, recovering from her initial surprise, stared at Boris in the dim light, her mouth open. She glanced around the unfamiliar car and saw outlines of furniture and knick-knacks.

"I... where did you?" Helen tried to grasp what was happening. Boris was back and someone needed healing and it didn't seem to be him. "Who?..." Helen turned a full circle examining the room, looking for someone else bleeding or sick.

"In the bed," whispered Cash. Boris led the way and the three of them crossed the room to the bed. As Helen approached she saw a small form under the blankets. Closer to the head of the bed, an involuntary gasp escaped Helen's throat at the sight of Maya and her face.

"She won't wake up," Boris murmured.

"What do you mean she won't wake up?" Helen queried.

"I tried to wake her this morning to give her a drink and she won't wake up. But she is breathing," he replied.

Helen leaned over the still body. "Barely," she whispered. Turning toward Boris she asked, "What happened to her face?"

"Her father," came the strained reply.

"Is it like that anywhere else on her body?"

"Everywhere I could see," Boris replied grimly.

"Ok. This could take a while. I need a chair."

Cash brought over a chair and Helen settled into it. Gently she pulled back the quilt and found Maya's limp arm. She straightened it and pulled it closer to herself, then grabbed Maya's forearm with both of her hands.

A minute passed in silence. Boris paced and Cash pulled another chair over to the bed, tapping his heel. Helen stared intently at Maya's face and thought one of the welts was looking smaller. As she stared, spots began forming around the edge of her vision from the energy being pulled from her.

———

13 Years Ago

Helen eased into the wooden chair, arms, and legs sore from harvesting all day. She swirled the cool jar of cider in her hand and took in the landscape from her favorite spot on the whole property. She and Henri built this home with their own hands. The wraparound porch was her idea. Rocking chairs were his. They spent many evenings quietly rocking, savoring the satisfying moments when the day's work was done.

Today was unusually warm for September. They'd started early to try and escape the heat, but the day wore on and the team worked harder and longer to try and get the apples in before they cooked on the branches.

"Just a few more days of this," Helen thought, "and we'll be done for the season."

The sound of someone barreling through the trees jolted Helen from her reverie. She heard her name being yelled from the orchard, but the late afternoon shadows hid the person calling. Suddenly her brother-in-law, Elon Mastiff, came careening into the dusky sunlight from between two apple trees, running toward the house at full speed. He was carrying someone. Henri.

"No, no, no, no, no. No! No! No!" Helen jumped up, throwing her jar to the ground. Cider splashed along her leg, but she never noticed. She was already around the railing and down the steps, running to the advancing men.

"Put him down!" she yelled as she approached. Elon tried to set his brother down gently, but his arms and legs gave out and both brothers hit the ground limply and hard. Helen ran the short distance and crashed to her knees next to her husband.

"What happened?" Helen asked, her eyes wide and heart pounding as she took in the motionless body. Elon pulled himself off of Henri.

"He collapsed," he gasped.

Henri's shirt was covered in blood. Helen began to unbutton his shirt expecting to see a gash. Her hands worked quickly and pulled the fabric aside, to find his skin perfectly intact. She prodded and pulled and desperately tried to find the source of the bleeding.

"Why's there so much blood?!" She cried frantically.

Elon turned toward Helen, looking dazed. She saw a gash above his ear gushing blood.

"It's you!" she said to him.

He touched the side of his head and looked down at his brother.

"When he fell to the ground I got down to get him. I hit a branch on the way up. I didn't think it was that bad..."

"What's wrong with him? Why isn't he breathing?" Helen asked, focusing back on Henri. She had both hands on her husband's bare chest. "Breathe, Henri, breathe!! Come on! Breathe!" She touched his face, his nose, his mouth.

"Let me see," said Elon, coming in from the other side of Henri's body, encroaching on Helen.

"No! Get away!" She looked at him with crazed despair, her hands never leaving Henri's skin. "I can save him! I have to save him! I just need more time!"

He backed away quickly. After another minute of Helen crying and screaming at her husband's body, her hands settled over his lungs, immovable as concrete. Eventually, Elon slipped one hand onto Henri's chest, then neck. He softly put a hand around Helen's wrist.

"He's gone, Helen. I think he was gone before I got him here. I'm so sorry." His voice cracked at the last word.

Helen threw her head back and let out a raw and untethered scream. Elon reached for her shoulder and pulled her toward him. She crumpled into him across her dead husband's body crying and screaming so loudly that Elon gritted his teeth and vainly attempted to hold back his tears.

"I could have saved him," Helen moaned in an eerily empty voice. They stayed there until both of them ran out of tears and the sun plucked its last rays from Helen and Henri's apple orchard.

———

Several days later Helen stood at the doors to the town church where she had married Henri, hugging friends and family as they exited the funeral. The line dwindled and Elon came and stood silently next to her.

"I can't believe he didn't show," Helen said quietly without looking at him.

"Sadly, I didn't really expect him to," he gritted bitterly.

"But still. His own brother. Your brother. You'd think…" her sentence trailed off and she stared into space.

"We both know Louka only cares about himself." Elon gave her a moment, then turned his head toward her. "There's something I wanted to ask you about. When I went to my room the other day after…" he cleared his throat uncomfortably. "The gash on my head was gone."

Helen whipped her head toward him. Her body seemed calm, but her eyes were dangerous.

"Did Henri know about your gift?" he asked so only Helen could hear.

"Yes," she barely whispered.

"Does anyone else know?"

"No. Not a soul." She continued to stare icily at him.

"Helen, come with me." He took hold of her upper arm. "There are other people at my circus like you. You have nothing here now. These small-town people won't understand if they find out."

Helen pulled away feeling vulnerable and uncovered. Her greatest fear was happening. Someone else knew about her power. Henri knew but she trusted him with everything, anything. But Elon… she wasn't sure about Elon. Though it might be better to stay close to him now that he knew.

She looked at him with a stony face.

"I'll come."

Present Day

"Helen. Helen!"

She heard the voice like a dim light through a fog. Her

eyes were closed and she wasn't sure she could open them. Her head felt like lead.

Cash pulled her arm and Helen slowly slid back, pulling her head up and sitting straighter. She opened her eyes a crack and saw a blur that she recognized as Cash.

"What happened?" she creaked.

"You were... working on Maya and fell over," Cash replied.

"Too much. I put too much into it. She was hurt worse than I thought." Helen gingerly pushed herself all the way back in her chair and let her arms hang limply at her side.

On the other side of the bed, Boris leaned over Maya to examine her. He looked over at Helen and smiled.

"She's looking like herself," he grinned.

"I'm sorry I couldn't get her all the way back to normal," Helen said.

"No, no. Thank you, Helen. I think you saved her." Tears gathered in the big man's eyes but didn't fall.

The bedding rustled as Maya stirred. Her eyes opened a sliver and Boris was back over her in a flash. "Maya," he whispered.

The young girl smiled and closed her eyes again. Boris reached out and touched her hair. She nodded slightly and drifted into a light sleep.

"She's going to be alright," Helen said with a tired smile.

A screech broke the untroubled moment as Cash rose from his chair. He silently grabbed the chair by the back and returned it to its place.

"I have to get ready for practice," he announced in a low voice.

Boris glanced between Maya and Helen in a torn way.

"And I must speak with Lorenzo before others tell him

I have returned. Can you…?" the big man asked without asking.

Helen didn't let him finish his question. "I'll stay with her. I'm sure people are getting fed without me there."

"Thank you," whispered Boris.

"I'll come fetch you if she gets worse," she looked at Boris intensely. "But I don't think she will."

He nodded and headed for the door Cash was holding open for him.

"And Boris," she added. "I won't tell anyone."

He nodded and exited his car.

Cash and Boris walked together in silence. Looking around everywhere but at his friend, Cash finally asked, "What are you going to tell people?" He felt nervous. Once any clown or acrobat caught a scent of drama, rumors would be flying around the circus faster than a tumbling monkey.

Boris exhaled a loud sigh.

"Something close to the truth, I guess. That I saved her out of a bad situation and she should be left alone."

"Why are you so set on keeping people away from her? Is her gift really dangerous?" Cash asked.

Boris took Cash by the arm and pulled him as close as he could while they kept walking. He responded urgently. "Cash, she can manipulate people by touching them. She can make anyone do whatever she wants." he trailed off as Tony came jogging up to them.

"Cash! Hey!" Yelled Tony.

"We will talk more later," Boris muttered as he released Cash from his grip. Cash tried to adjust to the quick change in tone. He desperately wanted to ask Boris more about his niece.

"Hey there, Boris," Tony smiled at Cash and assessed Boris. "Good to see you."

"You too. I have to go speak with Lorenzo." Without a smile, Boris headed toward the big top.

"Have you seen Helen?" Tony turned to Cash. "She's missing lunch prep. I'm sure she had something important to do, but those boys are unbearable without her around."

"Yeah, she…" Something nagged at Cash. "…she'll be along soon." *Unbearable…* He looked off across the midway lost in thought.

"Unbearable!" He yelled, turning back to Tony.

"What? Yeah… are you OK?"

"No! No, no, no." Cash grabbed his head as glimpses of bears and a cabin in the woods flashed through his mind.

"Cash?..." Tony stared at his friend's erratic behavior.

It all came rushing back. "Tony! I had a dream last night about bears! I think it means someone is going to die!"

CHAPTER 11

THE DREAM

Horrible thoughts ran through Cash's mind. Gory night-mare-scapes of all of the ways his friends could die. He stood in the big top and was supposed to be watching practice, but he was staring off into space with a sick feeling in his stomach. With every trick Bella performed, he jumped, and every time Boris lit something on fire, Cash feared the worst.

"Cash!" Lorenzo jolted him from his stupor. "Get on the trampoline. I can't stand you doing nothing anymore!"

Cash walked over to the trampoline and began to bounce absentmindedly. He occasionally added in a summersault to keep Lorenzo happy, but his mind tortured him with the stupid dream. If his friends were right and his dreams meant something, what did this one mean? His track record with dreams meant someone was going to die or get hurt. His uncle, his parents, Maya. He needed to find out what it meant before something happened to one of his friends.

"Everyone gather 'round," shouted Lorenzo, flapping his arms in an exaggerated gathering motion. Cash bounced off the trampoline and joined the acrobats, tumblers, and clowns making a half circle around Lorenzo. "That's all for practice this morning! You have three hours until you're back here for the show. Tonight, I don't want to see any sloppy back handsprings." He turned a hawk eye to the tumblers who performed right before Boris. "The rest of you, pay attention and be ready for your cues. Let's keep it seamless." Lorenzo dragged out the last word and laced his fingers together in illustration. He looked all the way around the half-circle at everyone. "Go!" Everyone dispersed, but Bonkers caught Cash's eye from across the circle and gave him a direct glare. Cash waited as the clown walked over to him.

"Walk with me," Bonkers didn't look at him or even pause to wait for him. They headed toward the side exit, away from everyone else leaving to get a snack or sneak in a nap. "Why do I feel like you have a sick feeling in your stomach, Cash? And don't tell me it's indigestion." They had reached the curtain into the back hallway. Bonkers popped his head through the curtain to make sure no one was on the other side before staring down his large red nose at Cash. Recalling Bonkers' "ability", Cash felt trapped. He had never knowingly been the recipient of it before.

"Stop panicking. You're making the feeling in your stomach worse." The clown raised his overly large eyebrows.

Cash realized he wasn't going to get out of this without saying something. Maybe Bonkers could help keep an eye on everyone for him?

"I had a dream last night," Cash admitted, crossing his arms across his body, looking around. "The kind I've had before…"

Bonkers nodded slowly.

Cash continued, "I'm afraid someone is going to get hurt or die. That's what usually happens when I dream."

"Yeah. You have a bad track record. Have you talked to Magda yet?"

"No. Why would I talk to her?"

Bonkers reached into his pocket and triggered the water from the fake flower on his costume, splashing Cash in the face.

"Ack! What was that for?" Cash asked, swiping his face with his sleeve.

"Hello! Magda interprets dreams. Maybe you should go over there and find out what is going on before your dream kills someone. Someone like ME!"

Cash realized Bonkers was right. As much as he tried to avoid Magda, he needed her help.

"Yeah, I guess you're right! Thanks…I'm still kind of new to all of this stuff."

"Why are you still here? Get going! Before... before..." Bonkers made fake choking noises, contorted his face, and grabbed his throat. "Before I die..."

"Fine! I'll see you later." Cash went through the curtain, down the hall, and out of the tent.

With a deep breath, he headed towards Magda's tent. When he was younger, there were all sorts of rumors about what she kept in the back of her tent. Tony told her she had frogs in jars and that she ate them and that was why she never joined everyone for meals. He knew it wasn't true, or at least hoped it wasn't true. He'd seen people run screaming from her tent after a bad reading. She thought it was funny, but Elon didn't since those people generally did not return to the circus. He made it halfway to her tent when Helen careened around the caramel apple booth and crashed into him.

Helen exclaimed, "Cash! I was looking for you! Come with me." She grabbed his hand and turned.

"I can't, I have to..." but he didn't finish his sentence.

"She's awake," is all Helen said. Cash followed.

Helen opened the door to Boris' car and Cash followed her in.

Boris sat on the edge of a chair as close to the bed as he could get. He hovered over his niece with a glowing smile on his face.

"Cash!" he yelled. He hopped up and knocked over his chair. The form under the blankets recoiled at the noise. "It worked! She's up! You saved her! Both of you!" He looked at Helen and then at Cash.

He leaned over the bed and whispered to the girl. Putting a hand behind her, he helped her sit up.

"Helen, Cash, I'd like you to meet Maya, my niece," he added unnecessarily.

Cash full on stared at the girl sitting in the bed. She looked about his age, maybe a year younger. Her dark hair cascaded around her shoulders and framed her face. Her perfect, spotless face. Taking a couple of steps closer, Cash examined her visage, looking for the bruises, welts, and cuts that had disfigured it the day before. Maya followed his gaze. Cash looked her in the eye and was taken aback by the energy and knowing in her translucent, almost transparent, light blue eyes. Captivated, Cash reached out to shake her hand. Maya slipped a tan hand into his and suddenly Cash felt warm static running up his arm. Looking into her pale blue eyes, Cash felt completely exposed, like every hidden thought and feeling was being broadcast to the world through this girl.

"Don't touch her!" Boris ripped their hands apart. Cash gasped and took a step back. Maya continued to look at him, but now her eyes were relaxed and inviting instead of intense and piercing.

"It's nice..." she began, but her voice caught and she cleared her throat. "It's nice to meet you, Cash." Her voice was pure and penetrating like a perfect melody.

Cash couldn't respond. His mind whirled trying to understand what had happened when they touched. He looked from Maya to Boris who was shooting a warning look at Maya. Helen looked around at everyone, not quite sure what just happened.

Cash remembered his mission to find Magda, thankful to have a reason to leave.

"I have to go. I need to find Magda before the townies start coming in." He awkwardly looked around the room and quickly exited, avoiding everyone's gaze as he left.

Boris looked at Maya happily sitting in the bed. He collapsed in the chair by the bed and put his head in his hands.

"Please try to keep your gift hidden, Maya." The big man raised his head to look at her, his eyes filled with concern. His look was so different from the hatred and disgust that used to fill her father's eyes when he told her the same thing. "It's for your benefit," he whispered to her.

"For all of us," she added knowingly.

"Yes. For all of us with gifts," Boris confirmed.

———

Lorenzo strode up the steps of the red wagon and flung open the door with flair. Nina didn't even look up from the long line of townies purchasing their entertainment for the evening. Annoyed by the lack of attention he walked down the back hallway to the business office where he would find Elon. His cane tapped along the hallway. The sprightly, old acrobat rapped on the ringmaster's door.

"Come in," growled the ringmaster.

Lorenzo opened the door. Elon looked up from his desk and raised an eyebrow at the old man. "You wanted to see me, ringmaster?"

"Lorenzo, you know I always have my ear to the ground."

"Of course, Elon."

"I hear that Cash is checked out. Unengaged."

"His arm is still in a cast. I put him on the trampoline today. He's progressing," replied Lorenzo.

"That's *not* what I'm worried about. It's the mind games. You should know that. If you wait to get him back on the traps, it means he has more time to mull over the accident. Over and over. Fear will set in permanently," Elon rose, moved around his desk, and stood mere inches from Lorenzo. "Get him back on the traps, even if he's hanging one-handed," Elon demanded.

"Of course, ringmaster."

"Make him fall. Again. And again until he isn't scared anymore." Elon stepped closer to Lorenzo and looked down at him. "He has to fly again. Everything is hinging on him."

"I have other acts. Our sales have still been good..."

"It's not enough!" Elon lost control, grabbed a glass from his desk, and threw it against the wall. Glass exploded and clattered to the ground. Water dripped down the wooden wall.

"Is it your brother?…" Lorenzo took a guess.

"Yes," was the dangerous, whispered reply. "The rumors are true. He's scrapped everything and turned his circus into one of these modern affairs with nothing but acrobats and silk ropes and pantomimists with painted faces doing stunts. It's ridiculous! But people are attending. The talk is about his star, a girl from the East. They say she's more graceful than a dove." Elon paced the length of the office and back again. "We need a star acrobat to stay in the game. We need Cash back on the trapeze. Or else he won't be the only one out of work." Elon threatened as he glanced at Lorenzo. He turned and brusquely sat down at his desk.

Lorenzo knew their meeting was over. Glass crunched under his shoes as he exited. If Elon wanted Cash back on the traps, they were going to start now. He made a beeline for the big top, weaving through families and couples wandering the grounds before the show. Normally he would stop and talk up the show, but he had to hurry to get Cash in the ring before the doors opened.

Just as he was about to go inside, he noticed Cash heading in the direction of Magda's tent.

"Cash!" he yelled. Cash kept walking, he was too far away to hear. Lorenzo looked around and waved his cane at the young boy keeping guests out of the big top. "Run and fetch Cash. Bring him here immediately." The little boy who couldn't have been more than seven, scampered off in the direction Lorenzo had gestured. He watched the silent interaction as the young boy tugged on Cash's jacket and Cash's startled response. The pair walked over to where Lorenzo waited.

"Follow me," Lorenzo instructed, turning his back on Cash and walking into the tent. He marched up to the ladder leading up to the trapeze. "Up!"

Cash looked at Lorenzo in horror, but quickly realized the man wasn't joking. The climb was awkward since he could only grab the ladder with one hand. When Cash pulled himself up onto the platform, Jojo scrambled up behind him and hooked the trapeze, surprised to see anyone there so close to show time. Cash put his toes to the edge and looked down. His lunch came back up his throat, but he swallowed it down again.

"Grab the bar with your good hand," shouted Lorenzo from the bottom of the ladder.

Cash's head spun. This couldn't be happening. It was too soon. He couldn't even look down at the net without feeling sick.

"Step off!" came the next instruction. Cash had the trapeze in one hand and edged his toes to the side of the platform. His heart felt like it was beating far too fast. He took deep breaths to try and regulate it. All he could see was the film of his limp body falling through the air.

"Now! Now! Now!" yelled Lorenzo.

He let one foot dangle over and his vision started going black and his ears shut out the yells from below.

Then he heard a whisper right beside him, "Sorry, kid," and he felt Jojo's large hand shove him over.

Suddenly, he was swinging on the trapeze. He swung out, his body flinging lopsided with just one hand on the bar. His lanky body cruised through the air, and his stomach seemed to completely leave his body.

"Fall!" barked Lorenzo again.

Cash's heartbeat throbbed in his head. He barely knew what he was doing as he let go. He closed his eyes as tight as they would go and tucked. The fall wasn't nearly as far as "the fall", but it seemed to last forever. When he did hit the net, his stomach slammed back into his body. He rolled over onto his knees. This time his lunch did come back up and he vomited over the side of the net. He weakly let himself down from the net, wiping vomit from his mouth. Lorenzo stared at him unblinking.

"Again!"

Cash coughed and spit. Stumbling to the ladder and climbing up again, Jojo gave him a sympathetic look as he hooked the bar.

"Seems like he has a bee in his bonnet. I really don't want to push you again, but I will if you need it," Jojo offered. Only able to focus on the task in front of him, Cash nodded, grabbed the bar with his good hand, and stood shakily on the edge.

"Hep!"

With eyes closed, he stepped off and swung, gripping the bar as hard as he could. At the next command, he let go and fell. Another wave of nausea hit him as he fell. This time he managed to keep from throwing up, but the gagging made his eyes water. He felt seasick.

Lorenzo repeated the exercises four more times. Each time Jojo tried to encourage him at the platform. Each time Cash fought off nausea, weak legs, and fear that made his vision go dark around the edges.

Finally, the boy that had fetched him came in and said something to Lorenzo that Cash couldn't hear.

"Last one!" shouted Lorenzo.

Cash swung and fell one more time and staggered off

the far side of the net, trying to get away from Lorenzo as fast as he could.

He headed for the nearest tunnel. His head was swirling and his path swerved like a drunk person. The tunnel was an obstacle course of animals, clowns and acrobats buzzing before the show. Not realizing tears were streaming down his face, he shoved through and into the back corridor. He fell to his knees just as a familiar voice yelled "Concessions coming through!" around the corner.

Tony rounded the corner and saw Cash on his knees, heaving and gagging.

"Cash!" Tony unstrapped his tray of popcorn and set it on the ground, quickly bending over his friend. "Boris, I need Boris," he said to no one. He ran down the corridor to the dressing stalls.

"Boris!" Tony called as he ran down banging on each dressing door. Screams and shouts emitted from the dressing rooms until the last one. The big man flung open the door.

"What?" his voice was muffled by the boar's head costume.

"Cash is sick, Boris. Can you carry him to Helen?"

"Where is he?"

Tony and Boris, still in costume, ran down the hall to where Cash was now lying on the ground. Boris scooped him up, flung him over his shoulder, and headed toward the kitchen.

Holding open the back flap into the kitchen, Tony let Boris and Cash go in before him. Boris flopped Cash onto one of the stools around the prep table and held up his slack body.

Helen turned around at the commotion.

"What happened?" She asked, hurrying over to him.

"Not sure. I found him puking in the hallway," Tony offered.

"Billy! Crackers!" Helen yelled. Billy clattered in a bin while Helen went to the sink and came back with a cold washcloth. She put it on Cash's forehead and Billy set the crackers in front of him.

Cash reached for a cracker and nibbled on it.

"Sorry for the drama. I'll be fine," Cash said after finishing a cracker.

"What happened, Cash?" asked Helen, sitting next to him.

"I was heading toward Magda's, but Lorenzo found me and made me practice."

"Practice? On the trapeze?" asked Tony incredulously.

"Yeah. Climbing up, swinging, and falling," Cash explained wobbly.

Helen gasped. "It's too soon!"

"Yeah. Guess my body thought so too. I kept seeing the film of my accident playing in my head. Over and over each time he made me get up there. My heart was racing and head throbbing and the nausea..." Cash squinted up at Boris. "Don't you have a show?"

"Oh yes!" The big man cried.

"My popcorn!" Tony and Boris exited the tent in a hurry.

Cash put his head on the table. Helen got up and went over to a large pot on the stove. She came back with a bowl of stew.

"I can't..." whispered Cash.

"Give it a minute," she replied.

Homey scents enticed him from the bowl. Carrots, celery, cumin and a touch of cinnamon. After a few minutes, his appetite did return and he set into the bowl. He ate every drop and pushed the bowl away. Gradually, he felt his strength return. Some of the weakness lingered in his bones, but overall he felt better than he had in weeks. He looked from the bowl up to Helen and back again.

"Did you?... Can you do your thing with food?" he whispered.

Helen smiled a large, warming smile and chuckled.

"No, my gift is only when I touch people. I'm just a really good cook." She winked at him. "I wish I could take away all the effects of what happened today, but my gift doesn't help that sort of, er, injury."

"What do you mean?" Cash asked.

"I think what you experienced today stemmed from panic because of your accident. It's very traumatic, almost dying. Today you experienced the physical effects of fear."

"Have you ever been in an accident like me?"

"No... but someone very close to me died and I couldn't save him." Her voice became quiet and her eyes went soft. "That was really, really difficult to get over."

"How did you? Get over it, I mean," he asked.

"Time helps, but until then you have to find your grit and carry on," she explained. "I found my reason to go on. Now you have to find a reason to get back on the trapeze that's stronger than fear."

"What could that be?"

"I'm not sure, but I hope you find it soon." Then Helen dropped her voice. "While you're here. I can work on your arm." She glanced down at his cast. "I'm not sure if we'll be able to convince Dr. Keller to remove the cast early, but I can help the healing along."

Helen put a hand on his arm, just above the cast, and kept talking so it looked like they were having a normal conversation. Cash couldn't focus on her words though.

He was distracted by a sensation of heat growing in his arm. It began spreading like putty filling a crack. The heat eventually expanded all the way up and down his arm. Helen's eyes began to droop as she spoke. Suddenly the heat vanished and Helen removed her hand. Cash wiggled his fingers. He smiled as he realized that his wrist didn't hurt.

"Thanks for the stew," he said with a big smile.

"You're welcome, Cash, honey," she said knowingly as she picked up his bowl and Cash exited the kitchen.

———

Feeling revived, Cash resumed his mission to find Magda, who wouldn't be working now that the show had started. He walked quickly, kicking at rocks and watching the evening sun drop slowly toward the horizon. The silhouette of Magda's daunting purple tent loomed in front of him. He paused, reminding himself she wasn't a witch, just another person with a gift that could help him. Cash approached the entrance and froze when a leaf crunched under his shoe. The tent didn't stir. As lightly as he could he tip-toed the remaining three feet to the entrance. There he paused to gather the bits of courage that hadn't fled yet. His heart pounded and he tried to ignore all of the circus' favorite rumors running through his head.

She has 49 varieties of frogs in her bedroom for experiments and potions… *Magda doesn't sleep. She walks around camp muttering at all hours of the night.*

Especially after the breakfast incident with the ringmaster, the chatter became more vivid.

She can read minds and hear your thoughts.

None of that mattered right now. Cash didn't care if she could read his mind. He needed answers.

Ignoring the voices of fear whispering in his mind, he took one more deep breath and faced the purple tent. He was so close that the soft fabric brushed his nose a couple of times. Cash listened, trying to tell if she was in there. He attempted to prepare himself for whatever she said about his dream, no matter how bad it was. Cash finally raised his left hand and stuck his fingers through the flap. Slowly, he pulled the tent flap back, letting in the last gleams of the day's sunlight. A beam of light illuminated dust floating through the air and a sliver of the table where Magda read fortunes. The cards and the crystal ball and even the black tablecloth were gone. A bone-dry bamboo table sat alone in the middle of the room. Beyond the table Cash saw shelves with books and trinket boxes, abstract black and white photos that looked like images of ghosts. Next to the shelves was another flap that led into Magda's bedroom.

Cash stayed in the entrance to the tent and said, "Magda". His voice cracked as he inhaled dust.

"Come in," her old voice moaned from the back. Cash entered the room darkness wrapped around him as the tent flap closed behind him. He stood uncomfortably and a frog croaked quietly on the other side of the shelves. Subtle noises made him wonder what other things were scurrying around. Doubts filled his mind. Maybe it would be better for the dream to remain a mystery. He turned to leave when a crack of light showed from the back room.

The flap opened and Magda emerged. She carried a small candle that illuminated her craggy face.

"Sit," she whispered, emphasizing the T. Cash obediently moved to the table and fumbled with the chair, heart and chest racing.

What am I doing here?! he thought. *She could use me for her next experiment and no one would know until morning.* He took several deep breaths.

Magda pulled her own chair out from the table and sat slowly, all the joints in her body protesting with loud creaks and pops. Cash grimaced.

"They called you the star of the air!" she began. "But now I hear that you are on the ground. You are the boy who is too scared to fly again." Cash's stomach fell and he missed a breath. I*s that really what people were saying about him?*

"What do you want?" she asked directly.

"I… I…" *Pull it together, Cash!* He was caught off guard. Another deep breath. He closed his eyes. Maybe not being able to see her would help with his fleeting courage. "I hear you can tell people what their dreams mean."

"Yes."

"How do you? er… How can I?" another deep breath and he continued. "Can you tell me what my dream means?"

"Yes," another simple answer from the decrepit fake psychic.

"Should I… How should I…"

"Tell me your dream!" She shouted at him impatiently.

Startled, Cash yelled back, "I walked into a house! … Sorry, I walked into a house." Cash recalled the dream in as much detail as he could.

———

I opened a door and entered a cabin. There was light and dark wood everywhere: the floor, tables, chairs, and stairs. I looked around the house and I was in a big living room with large, overstuffed chairs. To the left was a kitchen. In front of me was a stairway that went up to a balcony with rooms off of it. I climbed the stairs to see what was up there and one of the doors opened. A large bear came out of the room at the end of the hall. I was terrified and backed up against the wall at the top of the stairs.

It, er, he. It felt like a he, walked toward me. Terror froze me to the wall, but I slowly realized that I somehow knew the bear, and that he wasn't going to hurt me. He came closer and when he was about halfway down the hall... it sounds weird, but he smiled at me. He kept approaching and went faster, almost to a run. But he tripped on the rug that lined the hallway. It seemed to happen in slow motion. His paw got stuck on a wrinkle in the rug and his feet got all tangled up and the momentum from his run hurled his body along. He hit the banister, broke through, and fell to the floor. Hard. I ran down the stairs, but when I reached the bear, he wasn't moving. I knew he was dead.

I went to explore the rest of the cabin: the kitchen, the other bedrooms, and there was a study. When I got back to the door, a clock chimed. I turned around and there was another bear that had been following me around. He walked right up to me and got in my face, almost like he was going to say something.

During the retelling, Magda's eyes had slowly drifted shut and her chin drooped against her chest. Cash paused at the end of the dream and stared at her.

Quietly, he said, "Magda, were you listening?" Her head jerked up and her eyes opened as wide as they possibly could. Her eyes sparkled with ancient wisdom.

"You fool! You didn't even know what was right in front of you! The house represents generations and your family line. Did you live in the country?"

Cash nodded.

"The dream is about your family. What has happened and what is to come. The bear that fell represents your father. He died in an accident, yes?" Cash nodded again, eyes growing wider. "An accident that was nobody's fault. Suddenly he was gone."

"Yes. Then does that make the other bear my mother?"

"Hush, boy! Didn't your mother die in the accident too? It could not be her. The other bear, you called him a he. What else do you remember about him? "

Cash paused to think. "It was almost like he had a beard and he seemed older than the first bear."

"Then that bear is NOT your mother. But it is someone else related to your father. Someone who is still alive. Someone you came into contact with after your parents' death," she surmised.

"It couldn't be. There is no one else. I'm the only one left."

"Clearly, not everyone is dead. Since the bear came into the *living* room, it represents a man that is still alive. Since you have not had contact with him yet, then that part of the dream lies in the future. Did your father have an older brother?"

"No, he was an only child," answered Cash.

"Then being the older bear and in the same house or family line, that only leaves one possibility. This older bear is your father's father," she said.

Cash stared at her, struggling to connect the dots.

Magda laid it out for him. "Your grandfather is still alive."

Cash gasped. Could that be true? Could he still have family? "But... but..."

Magda continued, "The clock chiming means it is time. Perhaps he has been following you, looking for you, but he is closer than you think or know. "

"But… but… I don't know anything about him. He and my dad had some falling out. My parents never talked about him. I'll never be able to find him. I don't even know his name."

"Maybe fate has given you a clue." Magda closed her eyes. Cash could see her eyeballs moving rapidly beneath their lids. "What else do you remember about the dream? Anything that stood out."

"Well…" Cash thought through the dream again. "I guess it's kind of weird, but all of the walls in the cabin were orange."

Magda's eyes opened wide and drilled into Cash.

"Yes! Do you have in your possession an item that belonged to your father or grandfather? Something that is orange? Perhaps what you seek is encased in orange."

Cash bolted up, hit the table, and knocked his chair over. The candle on the table shook and fell over.

"Boy!" Magda cried. But he was already out of the tent, the flap waving behind him as she put out the flame. *He had to get to the 'boose.* He ran as fast as he could, not caring that he was missing the show. He jumped onto the platform, flung open the door without bothering to close it, and fumbled to light the lamp by his bed. He scrambled to the trunk under his bed. The key, the key. Cash reached for the tin box in his nightstand and dug out the old key to the trunk. With shaking fingers, he undid the lock on the trunk. Cash clawed through blankets, pouches, bits of money he'd been able to save until he got to the bottom.

Cash pulled the small rectangular book from the trunk

and held it up to the light. It had been years since he had looked at the book. He had packed it away with his memories, trying to move on with his new life. Could everything he'd ever hoped for - a family - be hidden in this book?

Slowly he creaked open the orange cover. In pencil, he recognized where he had written his own name in the book as a small boy. "Cash Connolly". Above that his father's handwriting spelled out "William J. Connolly". But, Cash saw with amazement, above his father's name in scripted handwriting and dark ink read another name, "James Howard Connolly". The book had belonged to his grandfather. Cash had a name.

CHAPTER 12

CASH'S PLAN

Cash paced the caboose vigorously. He allowed himself to remember all of the memories of his mother and father that he had locked away like the book inside his trunk. Visions of holidays and trips into the city; digging in his mother's garden and walking around the university with his father. Hugs and snuggles and bedtime prayers. Cash absently sat on the bed as the pain of his lost family tore through him. He always focused on the present: his friends, his job, and getting to the next town. Years ago he learned to shove away thoughts of what could have been if his parents hadn't died. Now the thoughts overwhelmed him. Stability, someone to look out for him, to pay for his clothes and books, to love him.

Occasionally on his days off from the circus, Cash would walk around the town where they were stopped. One spring when he was twelve years old he stopped in front of a grammar school. The boys were in blue shorts and the girls in matching blue jumpers. The kids were in the fenced schoolyard and Cash watched the unfamiliar scene. Boys played soccer and girls along the edge of the soccer pitch leaned together and giggled. Normal. That was what normal kids experience. He remembered school, but barely. It seemed like a different world now. His education at the circus was with the old seamstress. She gathered all of the young kids together in the ring before shows and taught them to read, do math, sew a costume, tend to a burn, feed the animals ,and do anything else that would be beneficial to life in the circus. He could have been one of those kids in the yard, leading an ordinary life, but he wasn't. He knew he missed out on a lot growing up at the circus, but what hurt the most was not having his parents anymore. They loved him well and left a large gap in his heart.

His friends were great and he would do anything for them, but it wasn't quite the same. Cash wanted family, real family. He had to find his grandfather if there was even a chance that he was still alive. Maybe there was still an opportunity for him to know the unconditional love of family again. With that thought, hope sparked in him for the first time in a long time.

———

The next morning Cash woke to Tony leaving the 'boose. Through his morning daze, he remembered what Magda had revealed and he sat straight up in bed. Hope filled him again. A rush of the potential of finding his family. Then just as quickly the previous day's "rehearsal" came flooding back and his stomach tightened and stayed that way.

"Oh no...." Cash moaned out loud. How could his life be so wonderful and horrible at the same time? His stomach was still in knots and he was disgusted by the thought of trying to eat anything for breakfast. He got dressed and made his way to Boris' train car.

Cash approached the door and knocked quietly, then harder. Boris whipped open the door and had a big smile on his face.

"You don't look like death's door!" In typical Boris fashion, he grabbed Cash by the shoulder and pulled him into the car.

"Coffee? Tea? Biscuit?" the big man offered.

"No... no thanks. Still don't have much of an appetite," replied Cash.

"I heard about what happened with Lorenzo."

"I... I can't go back, Boris," Cash looked at his friend desperately, tears beginning to build up on his bottom eyelids.

Boris examined him and nodded knowingly.

"I'll tell Lorenzo you're sick. But you can't hide forever, Cash." Boris' face was concerned.

"I know. I just need to get myself together, and get ready for it."

"OK. Well, you can keep Maya company while I go to practice." The big man left the car confidently.

Cash slowly turned to look at the bed. He had forgotten about Maya until Boris mentioned her. She was sitting up in bed looking at him with big blue eyes the same color as Boris'. Sharp cheekbones hollowed out the sides of her face but were balanced by round lips.

"Good morning," Cash sounded as awkward as he felt. "So you're feeling better." He rocked on his toes and didn't know what to do with his hands.

"Mmmhmmm," she affirmed.

"You definitely look better than when I first met you. Though you were unconscious... you don't remember that."

"I remember more than you'd think," she said mysteriously.

Cash looked at her confused, not sure what she meant, when Maya threw off the covers and jumped out of the bed.

She wore loose pants and a long-sleeved top in brown and darker brown. Cash eyed her as she approached, forceful, yet somehow light on her feet at the same time.

"Do you know you're famous?" she walked right up to him and stopped. He was almost exactly a head taller than her, and her head was tilted up examining his face. Her dark and almost black hair cascaded down her back.

"I... I... I don't know," the words wouldn't come out right. For such a small girl Maya intimidated him.

"I heard about you before Uncle Boris rescued me. The girls in my class were whispering and giggling."

Cash stared at her, lost in her semi-transparent eyes and also lost for words. Maya cocked her head.

"That means they *liked* you." When Cash didn't respond she continued, "They wanted to be your *girlfriend*." She took one step back, with her feet pointing at 10 and 2 like Bella. One side of her mouth tipped upward in a quirky half-smile. "Do you have a girlfriend?" She waited for a response. When Cash shook his head, she took several steps back and walked around Cash to the table where she folded herself down and put an elbow on the table.

"What happened at rehearsal yesterday?" she continued the one-sided interrogation and flicked crumbs from the table.

Cash regained his composure and sat at the table so he didn't have to look at her. Maybe if he didn't look into her eyes he'd be able to think.

"Lorenzo, he's in charge of the acrobats, made me rehearse on the trapeze," Cash finally admitted.

"Why's that so horrible? You're an acrobat, aren't you?"

He held up his cast.

"I almost died in an accident and it's been challenging getting back on the traps. My stomach contracts into a brick and my vision goes dark. I can barely breathe. Yesterday Lorenzo made me swing and fall, swing and fall, swing and fall. I saw a film of my accident and every single time Lorenzo commanded me to let go, the tent disappeared and I watched myself falling over and over again."

"You're afraid," she stated simply.

"Yes," Cash looked down at the table as the word caught in his mouth. "I don't want to die."

Maya reached out and touched his arm. Cash sat up like he'd been shocked. It was that static feeling again. It ran up his arm, then felt like it was going into his brain.

Suddenly the door flew open and banged against the wall. Cash and Maya jumped at the sound and the bright light. Maya let go of his arm. The morning light was eclipsed by a large shadow, but it wasn't Boris.

Elon entered the car and looked left toward the bed, then right and his intense eyes settled on Cash. A slow smile spread under his perfectly manicured mustache as a faint scent of pine and sweat drifted into the train car.

"Boris said you weren't feeling well, my boy. So I rushed over to check on my star acrobat. Lorenzo told me you got back on the traps yesterday. I was very glad to hear it." Elon grabbed the chair next to Cash at the square table and turned it straight toward Cash. The big man lowered himself down into the chair and leaned forward with his arms on his knees, closing in on Cash.

"You know, every time you don't perform, my dear Cash, I lose a lot of money in ticket sales."

"Yes, sir." Cash glanced at the table and back at Elon.

"If you want to stay on the acrobat team and not on Barnaby's clean-up crew, I need you to perform." Elon eyed him sharply.

"Yes, sir." Cash steadied his eyes on the ringmaster noticing his abundantly hairy eyebrows, mustache, and stubble.

"But I know sometimes we all need a little motivation." Elon's tone became frighteningly friendly as he leaned back in the chair and reached into the pocket of his green velvet jacket. When he slapped his hand on the table, there was a metallic ring. Two gold coins shone on the table when he removed his hand.

"Consider this a deposit. There's more when you fully rehearse, and when you get back in the show. Are we in agreement?" He raised one of his dark eyebrows. Silence. His mustache twitched.

"Yes, sir." Cash looked Elon in the eye, full of resolve.

"Good! That's what I like to hear!" He pushed his hands against the table, about to stand up when he noticed Maya across from him.

"And who are you?!" He asked, his eyebrows raising in shock.

"Maya. I'm Boris' niece."

"And how did you get here, Maya?" His voice was too sweet.

"I lived in the last town and hid in Uncle Boris' car until you left town. I wanted to get away from my parents."

"And how old are you?"

"Sixteen." She conversed with the ringmaster like an adult.

"A teenage runaway. Not as original as you think. Well, you have to work to stay here, like everyone else. You'll assist Barnaby. He's had trouble keeping help since this one left." He gestured at Cash.

"I'd like to be in the tent, sir," she countered.

"Ohhh. Boris' niece wants to tell me how to run my show?"

"I ran away to be at the circus, so I'd like to be in the tent to see everything. I hear that your show is the best, sir." Cash gaped when she batted her eyelashes at him.

"Hmph. Fine. Lorenzo could use an assistant. He's been running around like mad lately. Report to him tomorrow morning!" He stood dominatingly over Cash and Maya and his eyes turned to slits. "Stay out of trouble. Both of you."

Without saying anything else, he turned and left the car like the wind off of a tornado.

Maya turned to Cash with her eyes dancing.

"Let's go to the cookhouse. I'm starving!"

———

Cash held back the tent flap for Maya and she went in and stopped, her sky-blue eyes taking in the scene in wonder. She looked at the buffet that ran the short side of the tent, up to the platform for the managers and ringmaster where Barnaby was finishing a late breakfast.

"The clowns are in their costumes, even outside of the performance!" In her excitement, she grabbed Cash's arm and the static feeling began again. "Sorry!" she jumped and let go. "Uncle Boris said I'm not supposed to touch you. I keep forgetting." Looking up at Cash she added, "Thank you for keeping me company. I'll answer your questions once I get some food. Where do I start?"

Cash led Maya toward the buffet and handed her a tray.

"You can get whatever you want and as much as you can eat," he instructed.

Her eyes grew large as she looked down the buffet at the warm apple popovers, thin pancakes, trays of sausage, scrambled eggs, and fresh fruit.

"Oh it smells delightful," Maya gushed.

Tony stood behind the line with a serving spoon ready.

"Is this who I think it is?" he asked Cash, nodding at Maya with a grin.

"Yep. Tony, this is Maya, Boris' niece."

"Nice to meet you," Tony said examining her. "I've heard a lot about you from Helen."

"And I've heard a lot about Helen's cooking," Maya barely looked at Tony as she replied, focusing on the food.

"Ha! A girl with a healthy appetite. I like it." Tony smirked and grinned at Cash before loading Maya's plate with eggs, potatoes and bacon.

"Yessss," whispered Maya looking at the heaping food on her tray. Glancing up and locking eyes with Tony she added, "Thank you." Tony looked startled and Cash thought he saw pink spreading across Tony's cheeks.

"Where do we sit?" Maya asked, addressing Cash.

Cash looked toward his regular spot, disappointed to find that his friends had already left. He headed in that direction anyway.

"Usually I sit with Bonkers, Boris and Bella. Helen and Tony join when they're done serving," he explained as they sat down at the empty table.

Maya shoveled a large forkful of eggs and potatoes into her mouth in a surprisingly ladylike way.

"So what do you want to ask me?" she said with her mouth still half full.

Cash sat back, surprised by her abruptness. He looked past her trying to identify the best way to ask what he wanted to know.

"What's it like having a family?" he finally asked.

Maya paused with her fork midway to her mouth. She closed her mouth and put her fork down.

"Well, you saw me when I got here. Some parents are nightmares."

"Was it always like that?"

"No. No, it wasn't." Maya poked at the eggs on her plate. "It was only the last few years that were frightening. My dad lost his job and… descended into a pit he couldn't get out of. On top of that, my gift got stronger and it frightened him. Before that we were happy." Sadness crept into her eyes as she continued, "My parents loved each other and laughed a lot. They threw me the most elaborate birthday parties. My mother always read fairy tales to me before bed. But the kind where the girl is the hero, not the lame princess who always needs some boy to protect her. And my dad made breakfast. I would come home from school to my mother doing wash or preparing dinner. It was normal. It was wonderful. Then it became hell and every night I prayed for an angel to come rescue me. Maybe Uncle Boris is my guardian angel." She quickly looked at her food and took another bite. "What about you? Where's your family?"

Cash filled her in on what happened to his parents.

"How long ago was that?" asked Maya

"Seven, almost eight, years now," replied Cash.

"So you've lived almost half your life here?" She asked, surprised.

"Yeah. But I wish I had a family and a normal childhood," Cash confessed.

"But you're a star! How many kids would die to be an acrobat in the circus?" They both winced. "Sorry. Not that someone has to die to be in the circus."

"Yeah, I guess. Though right now I'm not even an acrobat. I'm nothing."

"Are you still scared of the trapeze?" Maya asked.

"Yeah. If my parents could die in a freak accident, it's always been in the back of my mind that it could happen to me. Then it did."

"But you beat it! Defied it! And there's something else now…" She looked at him seriously and Cash looked up to meet her gaze as she leaned in. "When I first met you, you were possessed with fear. But now there's something pushing away at the fear. What changed?"

All at once, Cash's heart fluttered, reminded of the hope, but he hadn't even told Tony or Boris. Even so it came flooding out, "I found out that my grandfather is alive," he whispered so others couldn't hear, but his excitement was clear. "All I knew about him was that he moved across the ocean to teach at a university right before I was born and my dad took it really personally. He never talked about him, so I always assumed he had died, but I had a dream and Magda told me that it means he's alive and he's nearby. I went back to my caboose and pulled out an old book that my dad gave me, but it had originally belonged to his dad and his name is still inside, so now I know his name!" Cash exclaimed with excitement.

"Wow! Ok! So for the last seven years, you thought you had no family and now you think your grandfather is alive? That's crazy! Have you contacted him? Where is he?" Maya pelted him with questions.

Cash's excitement deflated. "I have no idea where he is. He could be anywhere. All I know is his name. I don't even know how to start."

"Oh. Well, the circus travels a lot. Maybe you can ask around the towns for him," Maya suggested.

"Yeah. But I can't ask that many people. I barely have time to leave when we're in a town."

"Then who does go into town?"

Cash looked off over her shoulder to think when he saw Tony behind the buffet, pretending not to look at them.

"Helen's boys do. They're always running into town to get supplies."

"Do you think they'd ask around for you?"

"Yeah, actually. I know Tony would!" Cash began to get excited,

"Alright! We have a plan!" Maya exclaimed.

Cash smiled the biggest smile he'd smiled in a while until a thought crossed his mind.

"But when I find out where he is, I can't just walk out of here with nothing. I don't have *any*thing. Just a few pairs of clothes and books. What if I have to travel? The circus will be gone. Or what if I find him and he's poor and can't take care of me? I'll need money."

Maya rolled her eyes and stared at him. "Are you kidding me?"

"What?"

Maya leaned in and whispered forcefully.

"The ringmaster of the whole circus walked in and handed you gold coins this morning and told you there'd be more."

"That's right!" He said excitedly, then everything connected. "Ughhh.... that's right."

"So all you have to do is get back on the trapeze and he'll give you more money. Simple." Maya cheerfully finished his thought.

Cash leaned forward and knocked his head on the table and moaned. "Of course, I have to get back on the traps to get out of here and find my grandfather."

———

The next day, Cash walked into the medical tent for his follow-up with Dr. Keller. Cash sat on the metal table, paper crunching underneath him and the cold from the table seeping through his trousers.

"Hello, Cash", the doctor drawled. "Thank you for going to get an x-ray. It's not often we're in a city with an x-ray machine, but I'm afraid it will have been a waste of time. Broken bones take time to heal. I don't know why Elon insisted you go get it done." Cash shrugged, but the doctor was already reaching for a manilla envelope on the counter.

"Let's see what the images show us." The doctor flipped the switch on a large white box on the wall and it lit up. He opened the flap of the envelope and pulled out a dark, transparent sheet.

"So you can see here..." Dr. Keller began as he held the image up to the light box when he paused. He pulled the image closer and looked at the sticker in the top right corner.

"Huh. This seems to be yours. And it's from today," he muttered more to himself. He set the image on the counter and reached into the manilla envelope and extracted a second image. He held the second one to the light and started, "Like I was saying…" he attached the image to the lightbox and stood back with arms crossed and one hand supporting his chin. "Well, that doesn't make any sense."

"What doesn't, sir?"

"I can see where the bone was broken," he leaned into the image, tracing his finger along the radius bone. "Here. And here." The doctor examined the image a little longer. "It's not broken anymore."

"My arm is healed?" Cash asked hesitantly.

"It doesn't make any sense, but, yes. It appears so. Must be your young bones," the doctor turned to him. "And I'm sure Helen had something to do with it."

All color escaped Cash's face. "You know about Helen?"

"I'm sure she made you eat and drink plenty of calcium. Good for bones, you know?"

"I… yes. Definitely. Yes! Lots of calcium. So much calcium," Cash stuttered.

"Well. Let's get this cast off!"

An hour later Cash left the tent examining his arm. The flesh was white and still a bit clammy, but he felt good. His arm felt strong. He was ready to practice. Physically, at least.

———

Maya exited the big top with a flourish and shook her head to get her long, dark tresses out of her face. She shielded her eyes from the bright sun and squinted to take in the sights and smells of the circus. Townies were already milling about. She could feel the excitement in the air.

With Cash's arm out of the cast, Lorenzo was preparing for his big return. He had already sent her out into the city to spread the word that Cash would be coming back. However, they didn't know that it wouldn't be tonight. They definitely didn't know that she had just left him recovering from a panic attack.

Maya walked slowly through the crowds towards the red wagon and she ran into the bottom stair and, startled, looked up at the building. There was a huge line of townies waiting to buy tickets. She walked up the stairs and let herself in. Nina scurried from the towering safe in the corner to the ticket counter with a folder in her hand. She looked backward at the safe.

"Maya! Can you close the safe door, please?" Maya padded over to the safe and glanced inside. The top shelf held even stacks of gold coins. The shelves below held rubber-banded stacks of bills and manilla files full of documents. She pushed the heavy door until it clicked. She twirled the handle until it stopped. Turning back towards Nina at the ticket counter, Maya realized that Nina was the only one there taking tickets.

"Do you need help?" Maya asked as she approached where Nina was seated.

"Oh, yes! I've been short since Sacha left, Penny was supposed to be here 10 minutes ago and I have to run these documents over to the tent." She stood and grabbed the folder from the counter. "I just filled the drawer with change and I'll only be a few minutes." Nina moved to the door and added, "I owe you one, Maya!"

Maya sat down at the counter to help the next customer and smiled.

A girl about her own age stared up at her with eager eyes and handed her money.

"Is Cash performing tonight? I saw him in his very first performance. He's wonderful," she gushed.

"And you loooove him," her friend teased her. The girls with the money blushed.

"He's not performing tonight, but he'll be around watching. Any day now he'll be back in the air. You'll have to come back again to see him perform." Maya handed the girl her change and the teens giggled and ran off.

Nina returned twenty minutes later to a much shorter line.

"Thank you Maya, if Lorenzo gets upset tell him I asked you to help." Nina and Maya switched spots.

"Lorenzo actually sent me to get some posters. Do you know where they are?"

"Oh, they're in the hall closet." Nina pointed over her shoulder without turning away from her customer.

Maya craned her neck down the hall and headed toward the sliding door on the left. She pulled back the door and faced a wall of white bags. They felt like they had tubes in them. She pulled one out and opened the top. There were rolls of paper inside. She pulled one out and admired the two-color print with a large illustration of Elon in front of the tent. Then she had an idea. As requested, she took the posters to the kitchen for Helen's boys to post while they were around town. Except for one bag with 250 posters which she took to her and Uncle Boris' car.

———

11 Years Ago

Boris leaned on his axe to give himself a break and a chance to wave at his older sister Marian and her daughter Maya as they walked up to the house, full grocery bags hanging from Marian's arms. Five-year-old Maya sucked a lollipop and skipped happily to the front door. He set another piece of wood on the old stump and swung his axe. The two halves tumbled to the ground. As he was placing the next piece of wood in its spot, he heard yelling from the house. With the log hovering over the stump, he paused to listen. His mother rarely raised her voice, yet it echoed from the small wooden house. The door flew open and Marian ran out crying and quickly rounded the corner of the house toward the woods in the back. He hesitated for a few moments, unsure if he should go after Marian or find out what happened. Striding toward the house, he saw his mother at the kitchen table with her head hanging heavily in her hands.

As he stepped into the house, he saw that the grocery bags had been dumped out on the table and flung to the ground.

"What happened?" he asked, confused. The table was covered in candy and toys.

His mother dropped her hands from her face and sank back in the kitchen chair.

"Ask your sister. I sent her with the grocery money for the week and she comes back with this. She spent it all, Boris! We can't eat this!"

Fear gripped his already rumbling stomach. He turned to see Maya in the corner, still sucking on a lollipop and twirling with a new doll.

"I'll find out what happened."

He swiftly exited the house to find Marian, rage building in him as he went. How could she do this to the family?

Sobs reached his ears before he reached Marian. She sat on the ground against the house with her knees pulled into her chest. As he approached she looked up at him. Her tears indicated sorrow, but her eyes were sharp with fear.

"I don't know how this happened!" Marian pleaded. "I didn't mean to come home with all that. I promise!"

Boris stared at his older sister for a moment then sat on the ground next to her. "What happened?"

"Maya and I were in the store. She asked for a sucker and I said, 'no' and explained that we had to buy vegetables and grains. We held hands and wandered around the store so I could look at all of the prices to see what we could afford this week. A few minutes later Maya asked for that doll and I put it in my basket. Then she asked for more candy and more treats and I just put them in the basket. It didn't seem right, but I just… did it."

Marian struggled for the right words and Boris assessed his sister. She wasn't one for exaggeration or making up stories. Of everyone in the family, the war affected her the most. His once-spirited sister had become serious and protective. Boris trusted his sister, but couldn't make sense of her story.

———

Present Day

Tony saw Maya approaching the kitchen with a trolley full of bags and jogged over to her. "Here, let me help." He took some of the bags from her. "Where you goin' with these?"

"To the kitchen," she said in a happy voice.

"I don't remember ordering..." Tony felt one of the bags, "Tubes?"

"Nope. It's a bunch of posters. Lorenzo wanted to see if you and the boys could put them up around town when you're out."

"Didn't the advance team already paper the town?"

"He wants, 'More, more more!' He seemed pretty stressed about it."

"Of course. I'll put them up myself," Tony smiled at her and reached out to grab the rest of the posters. Their hands touched and neither of them moved. The butterflies Tony felt when he saw Maya multiplied. Their eyes locked and her eyes pulled him in, like an icy blue river. Time slowed and the sounds around him dimmed. Static danced up his arm.

Just then Cash came around the side of the tent, surprised to see Tony and Maya holding hands.

"Um, bad time?" Cash asked, not sure what to do.

Tony jumped back.

"Not at all. I'm delivering some posters. Lorenzo wants more around town," Maya said quickly.

Tony finally pulled his eyes from Maya. "Wait! Where's your cast?" he asked, eyes wide as he looked at Cash's right arm.

"I got an x-ray and Dr. Keller just removed it."

Tony gave him a knowing smile. "That's awesome, man!"

"Did you talk to Tony about your side project?" Maya raised her eyebrows at Cash and tilted her head toward Tony, who looked interested.

"Oh yeah!" Cash filled Tony in on Magda's interpretation of his dream. "I've started asking the townies who come to the circus, but I need someone asking on the outside. I was hoping you and the boys could ask around for me."

"Yeah, we're already going to be hanging the posters. We can ask as we do that. A lot of the town folk don't trust us though. Might be kind of tough to get answers out of them," Tony said doubtfully.

Cash gave a quick glance at Maya, and she slapped his side pocket with the back of her hand so the coins inside jingled.

"I have money!" Cash reached into his pocket and pulled out one of the coins Elon gave him. "In case that will help someone talk."

Tony's eyes lit up. He reached out and took the coin, quickly depositing it in his pocket. "Perfect!"

Cash filled him in on the few things he knew about his grandfather.

As Cash walked back to the caboose he allowed himself to feel the feeling that had been begging for attention the last few days: hope.

CHAPTER 13

A WARNING

Tony ran down the main street of Avantré. He ducked under an awning and folded himself into the shadows of a doorway of a closed furniture shop, desperate to get out of the wind-driven rain. Raindrops splattered the shop entryway as he shook his head.

"Of course, it had to rain today," he said to himself. "Look who it is," he leaned forward a little bit to spy Boris and Bella across the street, dashing under an awning, also trying to stay somewhat dry. Tony watched them talking, looking around, most likely trying to figure out where to go. They were dating, but Tony never really thought of them like that since there were always so many people around. Boris leaned down and kissed Bella on the lips. His left arm wrapped around her and she relaxed in his embrace. They made the perfect couple. Something inside of Tony twinged. Maybe he did want that. He'd never had a serious relationship before. The only girls his age at the circus were tumblers, who were all ditzy and silly. There weren't any other girls until now.

When Boris and Bella made a run for it, they headed south. Tony headed north, not wanting to disrupt their time away from the circus. He went into every shop and restaurant up and down the main drag, asking the managers to put the circus posters in the windows. When the unavoidable questions about Cash's return came, he stayed positive, assuring the fans of everything except Cash's actual return date, which no one knew yet. Tony left a men's clothing shop, pausing to look at the suited mannequin in the window. His fingers toyed with the gold coin in his pocket. His reflection in the window showed his small jacket and worn sweater. He knew he looked tattered. Finally, he pulled his eyes away from the tailored masterpiece. He opened the poster tube he was carrying and looked inside. One left. He pulled his hat lower to try and keep the rain out of his eyes as he headed to the café next door.

A bell tinkled as he stepped through the dark wooden door. Similar dark paneling ran around the edges of the room where a handful of diners were scattered. The scent of freshly baked muffins wafted from the kitchen and tempted his senses, and the coin in his pocket. Again, he resisted the urge to spend Cash's money. He walked up to the host stand, which was at the edge of the dining room, but separated by a glass wall. Tony asked the host if they would hang the poster in their front window. The young girl took it to find her manager, leaving Tony alone at the stand. He leaned a shoulder against the partition when familiar voices drifted towards him. Without turning to look at them, he knew Bella and Boris were in the dining room.

"This has been wonderful, I'm glad we were able to get away," Bella's dainty voice floated toward Tony.

"Me too. You've been working so much..." Boris' husky voice trailed off. "I know you care about Cash, but you're driving yourself to exhaustion practicing your current routine and your old routine and helping Cash and training with him."

There was a gap in the conversation filled by slight shuffling and the creak of a chair.

"I know. It's not just about Cash. It is partly…he reminds me so much of my brother, I can't help but want him to succeed," Bella said quietly. Another heavy pause.

"Bella…what is it?" A tenderness Tony had never heard in the big man's voice caught his attention.

"Lorenzo said that if Cash doesn't perform again, I won't perform again either."

Tony choked on his spit and ducked down while he coughed through it. He knew Lorenzo was tough on his stars, but had never heard of him threatening the partner's career. While he was still on the ground the hostess returned. Composing himself, he stood up to see what the verdict was regarding the poster.

"Yes, we will be happy to hang your poster," the girl, about his age, batted her eyelashes at him. Her red, chin-length hair was pulled halfway back and her green eyes sparkled at Tony.

"Thank you," Tony winked at her and turned to leave.

As he got to the door, he remembered his second mission. He turned back around and the girl's face lit up in expectation. Tony leaned on the hostess stand conspiratorially.

"Have you ever heard of a James Connor around here? He's a professor or something."

The girl looked slightly disappointed, but thought about it, probably longer than necessary.

"No. No, I can't say that I have. Is he someone you know?" she asked, hopeful again.

"One of our acrobats. It's his grandfather."

With both of his missions accomplished for the day, Tony exited the café quickly, debating whether or not to tell Cash about Bella's plight.

———

Cash filled his lungs with clear, crisp mountain air. As he inhaled, he forcefully flapped his wings, taking him higher and higher. He flew far above a mountain peak. He looked around taking in the bright green valleys spotted with gray boulders, looking like toy ants from his height. Suddenly he hit a draft. He stopped flapping and soared. The wind rushed over and under his static wings, supporting him. He dipped one wing and began a subtle descent in a spiral around the mountain peak.

Suddenly, a flock of blackbirds erupted from the ridge of the mountain. They got their bearings and headed straight for him. He tried to alter his path, but the current that was an advantage to him a moment ago was now a trap. He managed to turn around, but the blackbirds were already upon him. One nipped at his wing while another clamped its beak around his leg. Then the largest of the blackbirds crashed into him and the bird locked in on his leg, knocking both of them from the jet stream and they began to fall to the earth, totally out of control.

———

Cash's eyes popped open, he gasped for air and pushed himself up onto an elbow, taking in his view of the caboose. It was just the caboose. He was OK. He wasn't falling to his death. The clock on the wall ticked steadfastly. His heart rate slowed back to normal. Tony was asleep in his bed.

Everything was OK. Or was it? Cash quietly creeped out of bed and peeked out of the curtain. The sun was just beginning to cast light on the barren trees. Silently padding around the caboose, Cash layered on clothes to protect against the chilly morning and then let himself out of the door and into the breathtaking cold morning air.

"Oooh!" Cash moaned into his dark blue mittens as he bounced from foot to foot to circulate his blood. He jumped from their back platform and headed towards Magda's purple tent. The grass and dead leaves crunched under his feet, but he kept moving. The need to get warm pushed away the nerves he still felt about approaching Magda. He hadn't interacted with her since she interpreted the dream about his grandfather. This time Cash didn't hesitate at the flap. He let himself in, knowing that her living quarters were in that back, and not really caring about anything except getting out of the bitter wind.

As his body adjusted to being out of the cold, he looked around the tent. It looked much the same as the last time he visited, but what stood out the most was the silence. His heart beat in his chest from the brisk walk over, but aside from that he only heard the muted sounds of the autumn wind outside.

"It must be too early," Cash thought. Embarrassed about his sudden and thoughtless journey to Magda's, Cash turned to leave when he heard a creak from the back of the tent.

"Hel... hello? Magda?" Cash called.

"Who is it?" croaked the woman's voice like sandpaper from the back.

"It's Cash." He said louder and slightly more confidently.

"Come on back." she creaked.

Cash edged around the table where they sat last time and approached the tent flap next to her display shelves. He eyed a crystal ball and fermented frog in a jar on the shelves as he passed by. Putting one hand through the gap, he let himself through.

The morning sun provided a bright haze in the room through a transparent piece of plastic on the roof. Magda sat in a rocking chair in the corner of the room, her gray wiry hair spread in a crown about her.

"I'm sorry to disturb you so early..." Cash began.

"No...I barely sleep when it's this cold," she sighed as she spoke. Her eyes were closed and remained so as she addressed Cash. "Excuse me for not getting up. My joints aren't what they used to be... might as well be frozen with what this weather does to them." She rolled her head to the side and finally lifted heavy lids to look at Cash.

She hinted at the bed with her chin and Cash looked over, sitting down on the foot of the bed to face her. His hand ran across a blanket on the bed that was as soft as a kitten.

"Would you like a blanket, Magda?" he asked. A slight jerk of her head in the upward direction confirmed the answer. She closed her eyes again.

Cash rose with the blanket, and gently laid it across the arms of the rocking chair and her lap. One side of her mouth twitched upwards in appreciation.

He settled back down on the foot of the bed and began. "I had another dream last night."

"Ah. And you want me to interpret it," she said in his direction.

"Yes! I mean, 'yes'. Please, it felt so real."

"No," was all she said.

"No?" Cash whispered more to himself. "Please, Magda, I'm just beginning to understand this gift... *all* of these gifts. If someone is in danger, I need to know. I have to protect them and warn them!"

"*I* won't interpret it. *You* will. I will teach you." She opened her eyes. This time they were alive and full of electricity.

Cash started and wondered if gifts looked like something. If they did, that look in her eyes was it.

"Ok...I'll try, but you have the gift." Cash said.

"You have the gift, boy. Yes, I know interpretation. Yes, I can tell people what they dreamed and when and the implications. But I began like you. I began by dreaming and noticing patterns and asking questions. I interpreted my own dreams before I ever interpreted anyone else's."

Cash paused.

"I didn't know gifts could grow," he said, marveling.

"Oh, of course," Magda laughed at his innocence, only to have it turn into a fit of body-jolting coughs.

"Many people are satisfied with the gift that is given to them and never bother to push it or explore what it could be," she continued. "There are no limitations, boy. If you can dream it, you can get there with persistence and belief." She closed her eyes again and breathed deep, raspy breaths. "Pun intended," she added with a soft smile on her face. "Dreams often carry common elements. You can discern much just by asking basic questions. First question: were there three parts to your dream?" her eyes were open again. Alert and piercing through Cash.

"No. It all happened in one piece." Cash answered.

"Ok. Three parts represent the past, present, and future. One scene is usually the present or near future unless there is something in the dream that would indicate otherwise. So this dream is about something happening or about to happen." Cash nodded slowly, absorbing what she said. Magda continued. "Did you recognize anyone in the dream?"

"No. It was me and then a group of birds came in," Cash thought hard about the details.

"But they didn't look like anyone?"

Cash replayed the dream in his head. "No. It was almost like the birds' faces were blurred or I couldn't see them. Definitely didn't recognize them."

"Ok. So it's someone you don't know. As an example, let's say you dreamed about your roommate. Tony?" Cash nodded. "If you dreamed about Tony and it looked like Tony, then the dream is most likely about Tony. If it's Tony in the dream, but you know it doesn't look or act like Tony, then it's a representation. The dream isn't about him, but perhaps the things he believes in or characteristics he possesses. But in this case, you couldn't identify the other people or animals in the dream, so it's probably not anyone you know."

Cash nodded again, thinking through other dreams he'd had. In the dream about his parents dying, they were animals, but the birds were strikingly similar to his parents in their mannerisms and his father-bird even had glasses.

"So people can be represented by animals?" he asked.

"Yes. Not to all dreamers, but that seems to be the way the dreams speak to you. Everyone has a different dream language."

"What is next in the dream interpretation?" Cash asked.

"Now, tell me the dream," she commanded.

Cash relayed the dream in as much detail as he could.

"That's good. You have a very clear revisiting. Tell me again."

He told her again, leaving out a few of the details.

"Again!" she said forcefully.

"I was a bird. I was flying high above the mountain, looking down on the valley and rocks. I was soaring and then a bunch of birds attacked me," Cash said as simply as he could.

"Good, good," she commented quietly. "Did you listen to yourself?"

Cash was confused. "Yes?"

"No!" she exploded. "If you were listening you would have heard the interpretation. Many times you'll hear the interpretation as you say the dream out loud. Again."

"I was flying high, above the mountain and valleys. Then I got attacked and fell, out of control."

She stared at him, waiting.

Cash heard what he said, but didn't want to believe it. "I'm going to be attacked?"

"Yes," she said quietly.

"But, by who?" he got scared.

"Strangers. Don't you see? In the dream, you're flying high. Either physically, as in the trapeze, or emotionally flying high. And then suddenly there will be an attack by strangers or people you don't know, as we already established. Someone you didn't see coming. They will try to knock you off your path."

Cash held his hands in his face and dragged them down his cheeks.

"Ok. Ok. Ok. Ok." He stood up. "Ok. That makes sense. I don't like it, but I see what you did. It was all there and wasn't hard. I said it out loud. I just have to listen. Ok... So I'm not going to fall off the trapeze again?"

"You did last time," she said, looking at him seriously. "But this is a warning dream. Be careful."

Cash nodded in disbelief. He headed to the exit. Magda grabbed his wrist.

"Cash, it's important that you remember what we spoke about today. The keys to interpreting dreams. You must write it down. You need to remember," urgency flooded her voice.

"Ok," he said distractedly, running through scenarios of how he might get attacked.

She gripped his wrist harder.

"You must!" The fog cleared for a moment and Cash's eyes focused on Magda's.

"Ok. I will. I'll write it down."

Cash exited the tent, quietly committing everything they discussed to memory until he could write it down.

———

Helen and Tony stood close together behind the cookhouse. Tony bounced up and down while Helen rubbed her upper arms to stay warm.

"You're sure he's at practice?" Helen chattered.

"Yeah. He left fifteen minutes ago. We should get going. Everything needs to be done in an hour and a half," replied Tony.

"I'll finish up in the kitchen and meet you at the 'boose," Helen said quickly.

"Great. I'll head over there now and start moving my stuff."

Helen turned to head into the kitchen but paused and grabbed Tony's arm. "Do you think he suspects anything?"

He looked at her seriously. "No. Not a thing."

———————

Cash jumped off of the trampoline and landed with a huff. He had never been so ready for practice to be over. Stalking over to the bench where he left his water and towel, he avoided making eye contact with the acrobats and tumblers. He grabbed his towel, wiped his forehead, and threw it onto the ground in frustration. After a swig of water, he sat down hard on the bench. Light footsteps padded in his direction and stopped in front of him. He tilted his head just enough to look at her with one eye.

"Tough practice?" Bella's thin frame overshadowed him.

"Yes." Cash sat up with a sigh. "I'm so close! I can feel it! But I just can't get my body to let go!" Cash slammed his water bottle on the bench and water flew out splashing him.

"That's a good sign!" Bella said cheerfully as she wiped water drops from the bench and sat next to him.

Cash looked at her skeptically, so she continued.

"You were so terrified for so long. I really didn't think you were going to get back up. But now you're determined! Your mind is back in it and your body will follow."

"You're sure?" he asked hesitantly.

"Mostly," she grinned. "You're not the first acrobat to get in an accident, you know."

"Yeah. I always knew it was risky and there was a chance something would happen. But, it really freaked me out. If Helen hadn't gotten to me…" Cash shook his head. "I didn't think it would be this hard to get back up."

"You're by far the bravest artist I've worked with. The moves you pulled are crazy. The bravery is still there." She looked him in the eyes like she was pushing the words into him. "It might get trampled down for a while, but it's not gone. I still see it in you." They looked at each other for a few moments.

"Come on! Let's get out of here!" she said and slapped him on the knee.

Cash looked up to an empty tent. "Wow, this place cleared out."

"Well, it's a night off. They probably have plans. Let's go find everyone. They're probably eating dinner."

Cash and Bella exited the tent.

"I hate the cold," Bella muttered as a frosty burst of wind hit them. She looked over at Cash, "Where's your coat!?"

"Ugh. Oh. I guess I forgot it. I'll just be a sec." Cash ran back into the tent and Bella stepped into the back hall to wait for him. He soon jogged back in and shook his head. "I must not have brought it," he said out loud to himself and the empty tent.

"We can swing by the 'boose. Can't have the star acrobat catching a cold," she teased.

They quickly covered the distance to the dark caboose and took the two stairs up to the back platform. Cash opened the door and all of the lights suddenly flicked on.

"Surprise!!!" At least a dozen people were crammed into the tiny caboose around a long, thin table running down the middle of the car. Cash looked around shocked.

"Happy Birthday, Cash!" they all shouted.

The caboose was transformed. Dark red velvet draped from the ceiling and a string of lights shimmered down the center of the ceiling, above the table. The long table boasted baskets of crusty bread, pots of delicious smelling soup, boats of potatoes and bowls of salad, and most importantly, a giant layered cake in the middle with white frosting and blue puffs along the edges.

"I.. I can't believe... I barely remembered." Cash laughed in pure delight and looked at his friends crammed around the table. Bella scooted around everyone and took her place next to Boris and Maya. Helen beamed at him and Tony looked proud. Even Nina left her post at the red wagon to join them. Bonkers sat with some of the other clowns and several of Helen's boys eyed the delicious meal.

"Hey, my jacket!" Cash pointed at Bonkers, who was wearing Cash's jacket. Bonkers honked his nose in response, and everyone laughed.

"Let's eat!" yelled Helen. Cash sat at the head of the table. It was moments before plates and bowls were being passed in a haphazard and jovial manner.

"More potatoes on mine!" hollered Tony, standing up and knocking over his chair to grab his plate from Boris. Helen popped open bottles of sparkling ginger soda and passed them down each side of the table. One of the boys' eyes opened wide.

"We never get soda," he whispered loudly to Bonkers.

"We're celebrating Cash! It's a special day!" Bonkers replied loudly, ruffling the boy's hair.

Boris reached for his glass of soda and raised it in a toast.

"To the birthday boy or should I say 'man'? To a new year, to new feats, to bravery in the face of fear. And to wild, fun, crazy times with your circus family! To Cash!"

"Hear, hear!" chorused the voices around the table as glasses clinked and splashed. Cash took a gulp of his soda and sat back watching his friends chatter and laugh. For the first time in a long time, he felt happy.

Cash dug into his dinner.

"Helen. This is so good. I mean I know you're a good cook, but this is amazing." He dipped a roll in the soup and shoved it in his mouth.

"Thank you, Cash. I saved a few nice ingredients. I wanted it to be special," she replied with a smile and Cash grinned at her with his mouth full of food.

Dinner passed in happy company. Tony, Helen, and Boris told tales of the early days when Cash first joined the circus. Though some of them were embarrassing, Cash didn't care. He was having too much fun.

"Now that you're a man, you get the initiation." Bonkers stood up and reached into his costume. He extracted a flask. "Take a gulp of that. It'll put some hair on your chest." He passed the flask down. Cash hesitantly took the cap off and smelled it. The scent burned the inside of his nose. He put it to his lips and pulled in a drink. His mouth was on fire. He sprayed the drink all over the table and everyone erupted in laughter.

"Awwgh. What is that?! It tastes like gasoline." Cash wiped his mouth on his sleeve. "It burns when I breathe," he rasped.

"Aw, fine. Guess you're not that much of a man yet." Bonkers grabbed the flask back. Cash shook his head and reached for his soda to wash away the taste of schnapps.

"Oh, Maya," said Nina, through a lull in the conversation. "I meant to find you yesterday. You got a letter," she said, turning to reach into the pocket of her jacket hanging on her chair. She rustled it out and passed it around the table towards Maya. Conversation in the caboose died down as everyone watched the letter make its way to Maya. Letters and packages were a rare occurrence for all of them. Maya took the envelope in her hands and stared at it, tracing the handwriting with her index finger.

"It's from my mother," she said excitedly.

"Must be nice to have one of those," muttered one of the clowns.

His words stopped everything in the room. No one moved. Cash's heart skipped a beat and the pang of loss and of absence hit him. Most of those in the circus were orphaned, abandoned, rejected, or forgotten by their families. For Cash, he had gotten used to not thinking about his parents. He told himself his friends were his family and left it at that. Tony seemed like his brother, Helen his mum, even Magda his weird, scary grandma. But they weren't really his family. He wasn't sure they'd love him unconditionally or stay connected if he left the circus. They all had different ways of coping with it, but mostly no one talked about this weird, faux family.

Maya's face turned to horror as she realized why everyone was quiet. She pulled the letter onto her lap.

"I'm so sorry. How rude of me," she whispered. A chair squeaked as someone shifted uncomfortably.

"It's OK, Maya," Helen said kindly, hoping to smooth over the moment.

"Quiet!" Cash said harshly. He turned his head so his ear was towards the door behind him. Then everyone heard the pounding footsteps. Someone stomped onto the platform and suddenly the door crashed open. Barnaby's form filled the door. His hair was a mess and he was panting. He took in the room with wide eyes.

"What're you all doing in here?! It's a rube!! A group of townies jumped the fence. They're threatening my boys. We need help! Let's go!" Barnaby cried.

The caboose erupted into chaos. Chairs skittered,

clowns tripped on them as they climbed over each other toward the door and everyone bumped into each other. Helen's two littlest boys tried to slip past her out the door, but she caught each of them by the shirt.

"Nope. You're not going. Stay here and don't let anyone you don't know in," she directed.

Everyone else pushed and tumbled out of the caboose. Barnaby was down on the ground pointing them toward the bigtop. The clowns were running in a line, all going as quickly as they could with their large shoes. Cash, Tony and Maya all reached Barnaby at the same time.

"Out behind the backyard" He yelled and pointed. Cash, Tony, Maya, Boris, Bella, Bonkers and Helen took off in a run.

"What's happening?" Maya gasped as they ran.

"It's a fight," managed Cash.

CHAPTER 14

IT'S A RUBE!

Cash, Maya, and Tony rounded the tent and stopped hard before they ran into the backs of Barnaby's small team. Facing them were at least twenty burly townie men. Most of them looked like they were in their twenties and thirties and, if Cash was right, some of them were drunk. In between the gang of townies and the assembling group of circus workers, two people were facing each other. What must have been the townie ringleader and Peter, who had replaced Cash as Barnaby's assistant. The ringleader was six inches from Peter's face and shouting.

"You come into our town and bewitch our girlfriends and wives and children!" The townie was yelling in the kid's face. "We come and spend our money and they're amazed, but WE know what you really are. You're FREAKS!"

"Uh oh," muttered Cash. "Freak haters."

"What does that mean?" whispered Maya.

"It means they're irrational. These are usually the worst fights," Cash told her.

They watched as the townie shoved Peter on the shoulder. Standing his ground, Peter shoved the large man back with two hands. The townie reared back and launched a punch at Peter who countered the man's momentum and pushed himself into the townie as the punch missed his face. They both collided and grabbed onto the other in a wrestling match.

"Go! Go! Go!" yelled Bonkers. By this time Boris, Bella, Helen, and the rest of their dinner party had arrived. The clowns ran toward the townies, who in return ran toward all of them. They clashed with honks, and cracking punches.

"Here we go!" said Cash as he and Tony took off. Maya started running behind them but stopped short of the fray next to Bella. Cash and Tony ran toward two twins about their size. Cash saw a punch coming and time seemed to slow down around him so he was able to quickly duck. Time sped back up and Cash quickly landed a punch on the man's ribs. As the fight went on, time seemed to keep ebbing, flowing, and changing speed, always at beneficial times. "Behind you!" cried Maya. Cash and Tony turned to see a third townie about to smash a wooden plank over their heads. Cash quickly landed a kick to the man's abdomen and Tony aimed a punch at his face. The man flew backward, board flying. He stayed down. They turned to address the twins they had been fighting, who had ugly, matching sneers on their faces. Out of the corner of his eye, Cash saw Helen running towards Chuckles the clown, who was on the ground, rolling in pain. Suddenly Boris barreled between Cash and Tony, grabbed one twin in each hand by the hair, knocked their heads together and the two men slumped limply where they stood. Boris let go and they collapsed in a heap.

"Ha! There you go!" he yelled.

From behind the twins came a wiry man with yellow teeth, wearing a dirty black vest for a shirt. He began speaking in a language Cash didn't understand. Boris went rigid with fury. The man nodded his head towards Bella and spat more words at Boris. The big man's fists clenched at his sides.

"No one says that about my Bella!" He roared and flung himself toward the disgusting townie. Before the man could react, Boris had him by the vest and pants and had hoisted him over his head, ready to launch him like a javelin. Boris threw the man towards another group of townies and five of them crumpled.

Above the cacophony, a familiar voice cried out. Cash moved to help Bonkers, who was fighting two townies, one of which had a metal pipe. The one with the pipe swung at Bonkers' midsection and Cash heard ribs crack. Bonkers dropped to the ground in pain but managed to leg-sweep the other townie. Cash dove at the man with the pipe, knocking him to the ground. They scrambled and the townie tried to reach for his weapon. Cash crawled over the man quickly and pushed the pipe away. Under him, the man squirmed to turn on his back and Cash got ready to punch him.

"No, please. I didn't even want to come." The man said. Confused, Cash paused. "Let me go," he begged. Cash slowly got off and the man half ran, half scrambled back toward the other townies like a mouse.

Suddenly a gunshot cracked through the night air. Cash dropped to his knees and covered his head. The fighting stopped as many of them looked around to see who had a gun and if anyone was hurt. Lorenzo stood at the edge of the fight with a revolver pointed in the air and a menacing look on his face. Gone was the flighty, demanding artist. Those who had been fighting disentangled themselves. Lorenzo moved through the crowd, lowering his arm, so the gun was still pointing up, but now closer to his shoulder, ready to extend and fire at any time. He had a mad gleam in his eye as he walked through and stared hard at everyone on both sides of the fight.

"You are *children*!" he shouted. "Throwing tantrums and dealing with your differences with your fists. Barbaric! All of you!" He made his way around the circle and walked up to the townie ringleader. Peter had given him a swollen eye and a bloody nose. Lorenzo lowered his gun, aimed at the man's chest and cocked it.

"Are you ever going to fight at this circus again?" he remarked quietly and threateningly.

"N...n.. no." The man stuttered.

"Good. If you do, I start shooting. I'll start with legs and move up from there. Have you ever seen what a .45 can do to a human knee?" He cocked his head to the side.

The man shook his head rapidly and turned to the other townies. He gave a nod and they all ran off, back to where they had cut through the fence.

Cash watched them run and then turned to look at Lorenzo in disbelief. He knew Lorenzo could be mean, but Cash never thought he'd actually hurt anyone. Lorenzo decocked the gun and saw everyone staring at him. "I wasn't actually going to *shoot* anyone. That was my last bullet." Cash let out a laugh of relief.

The clatter from moments before died down. Cash looked around at the retreating forms of the townsmen and at his friends, some unscathed and some hurting. Boris had blood dripping down the side of his face. Helen knelt over Bonkers, her hands pressed to his ribs. Cash's heart skipped a beat and he exhaled slowly as the adrenaline that had been pumping through his system dissipated. He felt shaky and sat on the ground. Maya soundlessly sat next to him and pulled her legs in tight. Tony collapsed into a heap on his other side and looked him over.

"Barely a scratch on you. How'd you manage that?" Tony asked Cash. The skin around his right eye was bright red and would most likely be purple and black by morning.

Cash responded, shaking his head, "I... I'm not sure." He turned to look at Tony. "Did we really just do that? Run into a fight?"

A creep of a smile turned into a large grin on Tony's face.

"Yeah, we did!" He smacked Cash on the back.

Cash let the feeling sink in and then laughed out loud. "We did!"

"You're not a scaredy cat anymore, are you?" Maya added slyly.

"Nope! Wait... who said I was scared?" He turned to look at her, but she only shrugged and raised a coy eyebrow before laughing.

The excitement only lasted a moment before it turned to regret and left a bad taste in his mouth. Cash watched more of their people limp back toward the big top and their train cars. One rigger cradled his arm, while an equestrian stood up holding his head, teetered, and threw up on the grass. Helen and Bonkers stood. Bonkers moved less gingerly, but Helen looked exhausted. Cash stood as they approached and he put an arm around Helen to support her. Bonkers, Tony, and Maya followed them back to the 'boose.

"I think that's it for your party, friend," Tony said as he slapped Cash on the shoulder.

"I'll come by in the morning and clean up," Helen gave a weak smile.

Maya added a quiet goodnight and Bonkers waved as they walked off and Tony and Cash went inside.

———

The next morning Cash rolled out of bed, groaning at the ache in his back and tightness in his legs. Eyes barely open, he ran a hand through his hair and immediately tripped on the table still running down the center of the 'boose.

"Owww!" Cash yelped.

"Shut up..." muttered Tony.

Cash hissed and grabbed his stubbed toe, hopping around. He laid back on the table and put his foot in the air, still grabbing it.

Tony sat up, hair disheveled. Cash looked over at his bunkmate and forgot about the pain in his foot.

"Tony, your eye!"

Tony got himself up out of bed and leaned over to look at the little mirror hanging on the wall.

"Sick!" he exclaimed.

His tender, red eye had turned into a proper shiner.

"I bet Maya will think you're rugged," Cash teased.

"You think?" Tony gently touched the dark bruise.

"Uh... I don't really know. Let's get to breakfast. You can find out."

———

Cash and Tony dropped their breakfast trays on the table at the same time and sat down across from each other. Bonkers raised his eyebrows at the piles of hash browns, sausage, and steaming pancakes on the boys' plates.

"Have you not eaten in a week?" he asked, leaning over and grabbing a sausage link from Cash's plate.

"Mphuff!" Cash tried to object through a mouth already full of food.

"We're growing boys," added Tony digging into his scrambled eggs.

Boris arrived and dropped his tray on the table with a thud. Bonkers, Cash and Tony all stopped chewing to stare at Boris' tray which made theirs look scant.

"Fighting makes me hungry!" Boris said too loudly. He sat down hard on the bench, making it wobble under Tony.

The tent flap whipped open and the morning sun pierced the dim lighting of the cookhouse. The Ringmaster's silhouette dominated the opening. He marched down the center aisle like a bull getting ready to attack. Cash's heart beat faster at the furious look on the ringmaster's face. His cheeks were flushed and Cash swore he saw steam coming out of his nostrils. The Ringmaster saw Cash and turned his course towards him. Cash subconsciously scooted back toward Bonkers as Elon swooped down toward him until they were face to face.

"You think you can get into a fight and I won't know about it?" he hissed at Cash through gritted teeth.

"No, sir," Cash whispered, his full voice getting lost in his throat.

Elon slammed the table with a fist, toppling Cash's orange juice and sending bits of eggs and hash browns flying into his lap.

"You're right! You can't!!" The ringmaster exploded. His hair escaped its molding cream and Cash could see every tooth in the Ringmaster's mouth as he yelled in Cash's face.

"You'd risk your life, your limbs, or break your arm again for a BRAWL with those stupid townie bottom-feeders?!" The Ringmaster stood to his full height and took a few steps back, speaking to Cash but addressing the whole tent, which by now was deathly quiet. No one even swallowed. He put up his arms in a show that he had nothing left.

"You're out of chances, Cash. You used them allllll up. If you'll risk yourself on a fight, then you can risk it up in the air." He put his arms down and stared straight into Cash's eyes. "If you don't fly in the show tomorrow night, you will NEVER be an acrobat in this circus again. I'm done waiting for you!"

Another moment of intense silence passed and Elon zipped up his posture and turned so quickly that his green tails whipped behind him as he headed for the door.

Cash's mouth dropped open in shock and he turned slowly to check his friends' reactions. Boris stared at him with a forkful of food stranded in the air. Everyone awaited his response.

"I'm not that hungry after all," Cash murmured as he shoved his tray away.

His gaze drifted back toward Elon who had been stopped by Peter on his stampede toward the exit. The Ringmaster was bent over listening to the teen, then took a sheet of white paper from the boy's shaking paw. Elon righted himself, head still looking down. Cash couldn't see his face.

"Whoooooah. Did you feel that?" Bonkers put a hand on Cash's back. "Ringmaster isn't mad at you anymore, that's for sure. Now he's really sad. I wonder what's in that note. Like one of those helium balloons you poke and it deflates and spirals to the ground." Bonkers shoved a piece of Cash's bacon in his mouth. "Yep. That's what just happened."

Now curious and somewhat concerned, Cash followed Elon's movements with his gaze as the ringmaster slowly spun on his heel and walked toward the platform where he usually took his meals. Elon lifted one foot to get on the platform like the most tired man in the world. The chatter that had built after Elon's tirade toward Cash now died down as others noticed that something was happening. Elon paused on the platform with his back to his workers. Head bowed, he stared at the note. The entire tent heard him inhale sharply. He turned toward them, face blank.

"Magda is dead," he bellowed. Cash's breath stuttered in his throat. He felt his face flush and he looked around at his friends, who looked as shocked as he was. The room tingled with whispers.

"She died during the night," Elon added, quieter this time. He stared at the path in front of him in an unfocused way, like he was lost in thought. Then he looked up and announced, "Circus funeral tonight at sundown. We'll start the show an hour late. Everyone will be at the funeral. No exceptions." With that, he walked off the platform and out of the tent, every eye in the place following him.

———

Cash dragged his feet up the steps to the 'boose. He leaned his head on the door for a moment before he opened it and drooped down onto his bed. Tony came crashing in a few minutes later.

"I can't believe she's gone." Cash looked up at Tony as he spoke.

"Yeah. It's been a while since anyone has died at the circus. People have left and then died. But... probably before you came, yeah?" Tony inquired.

"Yeah. I've never been to a funeral here."

Tony paused to look at Cash, a clean shirt in his hands.

"Sorry, man." He struggled out of his long-sleeved shirt and put on the t-shirt he had grabbed. Observing Cash's glum face he asked, "Were you close with Magda?"

"Not close. I spent all but the last couple of months at the circus terrified of her. You know all the stories people told about her. But she was helping me with my gift. Helping me understand it," Cash said regretfully.

"Your gifts did work together pretty well."

"I met with her yesterday and she taught me some things to do to interpret my own dreams."

"Did you write it down?" Tony's voice was muffled as he scrounged around his bed for his other work shoe.

"What she taught me?" Cash asked.

"Yeah. You know, since you won't be able to ask her again. While it's fresh on your mind," Tony encouraged him.

"Yeah. That's what she said too."

Tony held up the missing shoe. He sat down hard and changed his footwear. "I'm off to make popcorn."

Cash sat down at their table with a notebook and pencil as Tony dashed out the door.

CHAPTER 15

THE FUNERAL

Tony bounded down the stairs of the 'boose and caught a glimpse of someone leaving Boris' car. They were balancing a big box and standing on one foot, trying to find the next step down with the other. They clearly couldn't see past the box.

"Maya! Hold on!" Tony yelled.

Maya paused and retracted her dangling foot, standing firmly on the top step. Tony jogged over and took a step up to gently lift the box from her arms.

Her smile reached her pale blue eyes as she said, "Thank you."

"Where are you going with this?" Tony stepped to the ground to make way for Maya to come down the stairs.

"Bella's car," Maya replied, looking at Tony out of the corner of her eye and blushing.

"Is this her stuff?" Tony tried to peer into the box of what looked like clothes.

"No, it's mine. I'm moving in with Bella. Now that people know I'm here, it's kind of weird to share a car with my uncle. And Bella and her roommates have an extra bed."

"Yeah. That makes sense. Then you all can gossip." Tony added a girly giggle and Maya cracked a smile.

"I hardly know anyone yet. Not sure I have much to gossip about."

Before Tony could respond, Maya changed the subject. "Did you know Magda well?" she asked.

"She's been here as long as I have. I guess I knew her as well as anyone, which wasn't very well at all. Except for Cash. He seems pretty upset that she's gone."

"Hmmm," Maya added mostly to herself. They walked quietly the rest of the way, their feet eventually falling into step with each other.

"Here we are," Maya looked up at her new home. The purple and gold door flew open."Welcome, roommate!" Bella held open the door with a big grin on her face. "Come in, come in!" She waved them up into the car. Maya stepped in and Tony followed with the box. He'd never been in Bella's car before. There were bunk beds at each end and a dresser for each woman lining the wall opposite the door.

"This bed's been empty a while since Amalia left. I've been rearranging and making space around the car for you." She grabbed several leotards off of the floor and threw them on her pristinely made bed. Bella gestured at the neatly made bunk and Tony set down the box, then looked at the two ladies.

"Do you have any more boxes in Boris' car?" He directed his question to Maya.

"That's it. I didn't exactly bring much with me." She gave him a sweet, half smile that stopped his breath in his throat. She reached out and took his hand. Static jumped between them. His head filled with clouds and nothing in the room mattered except her pale blue eyes and the way she was smiling at him.

"Thank you, Tony. I really appreciate how helpful you are." Maya squeezed his hand and Tony felt like he would do anything for her. She let go of his hand and the room came rushing back into focus.

"You're welcome, Maya. I better be going."

Tony turned to leave the car and Bella quickly piped up, "Hold on, I'll walk with you. I need to talk to Helen." Bella grabbed a sweater from a hook near the door and pulled it over her head.

Turning to Maya, Bella said, "Make yourself at home. The pink dresser is for you and the empty shelf."

"Let's go, Tony." She put her hand on his shoulder casually, but then she dug in her fingers.

Surprised, Tony looked at her and quickly opened the door, then padded down the stairs. Bella followed and looped her arm through his as they walked toward the cookhouse.

"You know I think of you as a brother, right?" she asked, leading him at a fast pace away from her car.

"Yeah... what?" Tony replied.

"Be careful." A sharp edge in her voice caught his attention.

"Of what? Maya? It's just a little harmless flirting."

"No, it's not. You don't understand," Bella implored.

"I do! She's Boris' niece. Don't worry, I'll be the perfect gentleman," Tony rebutted.

"I'm not giving you the girl talk, Tony!"

"Then what?" Tony stopped walking. Bella went on a pace and then turned toward him. They were in an open space between the train and the main circus. No one was around.

"Why do you think Boris tried so hard to hide her?" She lifted her eyebrows at him, waiting for him to connect the dots. "Why do you think her own father hated her? Was *scared* of her?"

Tony opened his mouth but had nothing to say. He shook his head and shrugged one shoulder.

"Her gift is dangerous, Tony." Bella dropped her voice and stepped in closer. "When she touches people, she can manipulate them. The longer she holds on, the more control she has."

Tony's eyes grew large as he thought back through their interactions and the sparks he felt when they touched and even just now with the desire to do anything for her. Emotions fought inside of him: embarrassment, vulnerability, a creep of fear.

"Oh boy…ok. That's big." His head felt light. He staggered back.

"I see you're processing this, but take it one step further. Manipulation is very tempting, even when it seems like a good cause or at least a harmless one. I see the way you look at her. She's very pretty."

Tony nodded as he began to grasp what Bella was inferring.

"I'm not saying she's a bad person. I think she's a good person, but she's young and has an extremely powerful gift. What you think is going on might not be what's *actually* going on with her," she warned.

Maybe it wasn't attraction on his part. Maybe Maya *wanted* him to like her, and he only had feelings for her because she had touched him?

"Yeah. Yeah, OK. What do I do?" asked Tony.

"She needs friends right now. Her whole life has been

upended. But, maybe don't let her touch you for a while."

Tony nodded. "That's a good idea." They walked the rest of the way to the cookhouse in silence. He felt wary and disappointed, even sad that the spark between them might not be real. But maybe it was real.

———

That afternoon Cash stood alone in the caboose, slowly buttoning his black shirt. He stepped in front of the mirror and smoothed the front of it, then tugged at the sleeves. It had been more than a year since he had worn the shirt and it was snug. To fix the short sleeves, he methodically rolled each cuff over three times, then ran a hand through his wavy blond hair. It was long enough to cover the scar, but he held back his hair and traced along the scar with his finger, feeling the reminder that he shouldn't be alive right now. Gratitude filled him, then guilt as he remembered he was wearing black to attend a funeral. With time to kill before the event, Cash left the caboose and wandered the circus grounds. He saw some of the riggers building a large pile of wood about two hundred yards behind the train. Cash drifted in the other direction, passing the other cars, and listening to muted chatter from within. He headed towards the midway and all of the booths for games and snacks.

Eventually, his feet led him to Magda's tent. He realized for the first time that it was odd she lived in the same tent she worked in. Where she stayed when they traveled he had no idea. Looking around and seeing everyone busy with preparation for the show that night, he slipped inside her dark tent. Running a hand across the table in the front room, he recalled their first conversation about dreams and learning about his grandfather. Moving to the shelves dividing the tent in half, he took time to look at what was displayed. Some things made him laugh. The crystal ball looked cheap up close, a photo that could have been Magda many decades earlier, a skull from a small rodent.

He moved along the shelves until he reached the entrance to the back room. His heart began to beat. He slid his hand through the split in the fabric. So little time had passed since he had been here. Barely a day. He entered the back room and stood, breathing quietly in the absolute stillness. The same blue glow from the "skylight" cast soft shadows around the room. Her bed had been made, the black blanket pulled up and tucked in. Magda lay on a black stretcher set on top of the bed, with billows of dark velvet surrounding it. Flowers surrounded her in shades of pale pink and violet, popping against the black fabric and a prim black dress. Whoever had dressed her put a silver brooch on her that shone in the dim light.

"Goodbye, friend," he whispered, not daring to step any deeper into the room. Cash stood in silence as he took in the room. Someone had tidied since yesterday. Her books were in neat stacks on a shelf. And then Cash noticed the corner of what looked like a book sticking out from under the nightstand. With a glance at her body, he quickly walked over and squatted to grab the book. The royal blue cover had no markings. He opened it to discover a journal. There were bits and snatches of phrases. He flipped through. Some pages were packed full with tiny handwriting while other pages had large phrases or sketches. Cash wondered if it was a story, but it didn't make sense. Some of the pages had dates. Then Cash realized what he was holding. It wasn't a normal journal,

Magda had written down her dreams. Yes. Many of the pages had notes in a different color ink where she made interpretations.

"Come on! Let's get the body!" Cash jumped at the sound of Barnaby's voice so close. He was on the other side of the tent wall. Not wanting to have to explain his presence in Magda's room, he shoved the book in his shirt and quickly made his way out the front of the tent. He got far enough away to remove suspicion by the time Barnaby and his men came around to the front of the tent.

Cash headed straight for the 'boose, heart pounding, unsure if he had just done something wrong. He ran in and closed and locked the door behind him. Sitting at the table, he bowed over the book and began to read her notes. Some of the dreams were simple, and some were complex. Many were about Magda, but just as many were about others at the circus. The ringmaster, Helen, Boris. As he read through the dreams and interpretations, he began to see patterns in symbols and colors. He recalled their lesson yesterday and the farther he read, the more he began to know some of the meaning before he read her interpretation.

Suddenly, the handle to the car jiggled and Cash jumped up, the chair screeching.

"Hey, man. Why's the door locked? I gotta change." Tony banged on the door.

Cash rushed over and opened it.

"Sorry. I... I..." he backed up as Tony barreled in and both of their eyes landed on the table. "I stole a book from Magda's." The words practically fell out of Cash's mouth.

Tony looked at Cash, then back at the table, then back at Cash.

"Huh. That's weird. I gotta get out of these kitchen clothes."

Cash opened the door at the back of the caboose and paused to watch the procession of people walking toward the wood pile Cash had seen earlier. The sun had dipped past the trees to his left, creating spidery shadows across the ground and the funeral attendees. Tony quietly stepped out and closed the door behind them.

"Let's go," he whispered.

They walked silently toward the gathered crowd all in black. Boris, Bella, and Maya quietly caught up to them from behind and fell in step. Two rows of people formed a half circle a good fifty yards from the wood. The group slid into place behind everyone. Cash looked down the row in front of him and saw Helen wiping her eyes with a tissue. She stood next to a group of people he didn't recognize, at least not at first. He rarely saw the clowns out of costume. Bonkers wore a trim-fitting black suit and his short-cropped brown hair was slicked back. As Cash looked, Bonkers turned and returned the gaze. Cash was startled at the look of his friend without makeup. Somehow the lack of exaggerated emotion only heightened the deep, real sadness on his friend's face. Bonkers nodded a slow acknowledgment, then turned to whisper to the clown next to him.

Over the next few minutes, more people trickled over and the sun skittered closer to the horizon. A knot grew in Cash's stomach at the waiting and at the impending goodbye. He stared at the ground, lost in thought when the ringmaster's voice jolted him to attention.

"Tonight we mourn a great loss to our clan." Elon stood with a large presence to address the crowd. Despite the cold, he wore just a black dress shirt, black tie, and slacks. He paused in his speech and took his top hat off, holding it at his side reverently.

"Many of you knew Magda, many of you were scared of Magda," the ringmaster looked at the youngest acrobats and tumblers as he said that. "What many of you do not know is how vital Magda was to the success of our circus. I considered her a counselor and confidant. Her input, time after time, led us to where we are now." He gazed off past the crowd, breathing in steadily to try and keep his composure. Cash noticed red rimming his eyes. "I'm going to miss her," finished the ringmaster quietly.

He motioned with his hand and the crowd began to part. Barnaby and one of his men came down the newly formed aisle carrying the stretcher Cash had seen in Magda's tent. They walked slowly and people blew kisses, placed flowers on her, or touched her skirt where it hung over the stretcher. The men stopped with the body in front of the ringmaster. Elon reached out to Nina, who handed him a pink rose. The ringmaster gently tucked it between Magda's hands that were folded neatly on her chest.

The men continued on and walked past the ringmaster. They approached the pile of wood. With a bit of a strain, they hoisted the stretcher bearing Magda's body onto the pile of wood. The men walked off to the side to rejoin the crowd.

Elon slowly walked toward Magda's resting place. He bowed his head for a minute, then with the flick of his arm, the pile of wood was on fire. He turned around, facing the crowd. Cash gasped. Elon walked back toward the crowd, against the orange flames flickering and jumping behind him. His face was emotionless. He looked straight down the aisle and walked through the crowd, looking at no one.

Cash watched the flames skip and bow around Magda's body until he couldn't see it anymore. He felt sick.

"Why? Why? Why did he do that? She's burning!" He choked out a whisper to Boris. The big man looked down at him, worry showing in his eyes. "We should have buried her." Cash was beginning to panic. His head was spinning and his voice grew louder. "We can still bury her! I'll get a shovel." He grabbed Boris' forearm, getting more frantic. "You get water! We have to put out the fire. Then… then we'll bury her!" Cash looked at Boris frantically as attendees turned and looked at them.

Boris acknowledged the disturbance and shook his arm free. He firmly led Cash behind the crowd. By this time Cash was having a hard time breathing.

"This is what we do, Cash," Boris said calmly.

"No! You're supposed to bury people, not burn them!" Cash looked around, at the crowd watching the flame, at the fire, at the ringmaster's retreating form in the distance. He doubled over. "It's not right, it's not right."

"Where would we bury her?" Boris asked gently, putting a hand on Cash's back. "This isn't her land. This isn't the ringmaster's land. We don't belong anywhere."

"But how will people visit her?" Cash straightened, his face a swath of tears and snot.

"Who?" Boris wiped a tear from his own eye. "She didn't have any family. Saints only know if we'll ever come back here." They stared at each other for a moment. Boris looked off at the fire and sighed. "It's symbolic. We as the circus, we drift and never have a place to stay or a piece of land with our name on it. Most of us don't have homes or family except the circus. And when it's over this is what we do. So we remain travelers, blowing where the wind takes us, never settling anywhere."

Cash's head was spinning. "That would have been me!" Then he closed his eyes and repeated in a whisper, "That would have been me."

"It's hard to understand if you haven't seen it before, but this is the best way and it's better than what most of us came from," Boris said tersely. Then he remembered Cash's dream and the existence of his grandfather and replied in a gentler tone. "But maybe this isn't it for you, my friend."

That night after the show, Cash lay in bed, staring into the darkness, wide awake. Tony's light snoring kept a steady rhythm as he recounted the day. The news, the book, the funeral, the reminder about his grandfather. Cash knew one thing: he wasn't going to end up like Magda. No matter what happened, he was going to find his grandfather and get out of the circus.

———

Bonkers paced in the shadow of the ring doors gnawing on his thumbnail and occasionally looking up at the trapeze. Turning abruptly, he ran into Helen, peeling herself through the curtain. They skipped the apologies and disentangled themselves.

"How's he doing?" Helen looked up at the trapeze.

"Nothing yet," Bonkers mumbled, the corners of his painted smile turning down. He spit out a fragment of nail.

"Stop biting," Helen whispered and swatted at his arm, missing. Both of them gazed above their heads.

"Better than other...oh gosh!" Bonkers gasped.

Cash swung out towards Bella, their timing perfect. But Cash didn't let go.

"Thought that was it," Bonkers sighed, then finished his thought. "Better than other habits."

"It's OK. They just started, right?" Helen asked.

Bonkers sighed and looked across the ring at Lorenzo. In his typical black and white striped shirt, Lorenzo leaned forward in his chair, his back straight as a pole. He was atypically silent. Elon stood behind him, towering over him like a silent statue. It was a rare occurrence to have the ringmaster at practice, but everyone knew why he was making an appearance. Boris' niece stood a few paces away from them, eyes glued on Cash and Bella.

"One, two, three!" Bella's typically delicate voice cut through the tension in the tent. Again Cash didn't let go for his flip.

"Come on, Cash." Bonkers turned to see who spoke and found Tony next to him.

"It's not looking good. He's swingin' but hasn't let go yet." Bonkers filled him in.

Helen sucked in air through her teeth as Cash missed another perfect opportunity. Bonkers looked over and saw Maya walking towards them. She stopped next to Tony, who looked down and gave her a nervous smile. They both turned their faces to the air. Maya looped her arm through Tony's. The young man's eyebrows arched briefly and he turned his gaze back up to the trapeze, then as though remembering something, gently extracted his arm from hers.

Cash and Bella were both on Cash's platform. Bonkers wasn't sure what they were waiting for. Cash wiped his forehead and leaned on the protective railing. Lorenzo was climbing up Cash's ladder.

"I've only seen him go up the ladder once," Helen commented.

"And everything was OK, right?" asked Tony.

"Not exactly. It was the end of that acrobat's career," she replied solemnly.

"Yikes," Bonkers responded, rubbing his thumb and forefinger together, longing for a cigarette. He settled for chewing on his nail again. Looking around while Lorenzo and Cash talked, he spied Boris near the bottom of Bella's ladder. Bonkers noted the grim expression on his friend's face.

Lorenzo's hands flailed while he spoke. Suddenly Cash stiffened noticeably and Bella stepped toward Lorenzo and gestured toward Cash aggressively. Lorenzo finished his rant and poked Cash in the chest before turning with flair, dropping his cane over his forearm, and lowering himself down the ladder. Bella hurried down after him and jogged across the ring to her platform. Cash remained on his platform while Lorenzo returned to his chair. Helen gripped Bonkers' arm as the tension in the tent rose.

Cash and Bella approached the edges of their platforms as their trapezes were drawn towards them. Lorenzo settled into his chair and raised his bullhorn to his mouth.

"Ready!" Cash and Bella grabbed their bars.

"Set!" The two acrobats tuned out everything except for each other.

"Hep!" bellowed Lorenzo.

Everyone in the group stopped breathing momentarily as Cash and Bella glided into the air. They reached the center and transitioned into the swing back to their platforms, building momentum.

"Do it, do it, do it!" Helen gritted her teeth.

Cash swung his legs out in front of him, above the upper half of his body. He let go. Flipping his torso toward Bella he reached out his hands and connected with hers.

Bonkers grabbed his head in disbelief. Helen screamed and jumped up and down. Tony and Maya turned towards each other, cheering. They embraced in the excitement and quickly released in embarrassment.

Elon left Lorenzo's side and wordlessly headed toward the exit and the group.

"He did it! He did it!" Helen shook Bonkers violently.

"I know!" Bonkers yelled back.

"It's going to be ok." Helen wiped tears from her eyes.

Elon approached them with a scowl.

"It was one summersault!" the ringmaster exploded. "He has a long way to go!"

The group was silent as he furiously exited the tent.

"Eee!" Maya squealed. "He's going to be a star!"

"Again." Tony added.

CHAPTER 16

TONY'S TRIP INTO TOWN

Hey! Mind the road!" Tony ran to catch up to Billy who had his arms full and was teetering on a curb, about to tumble into the street. "If you get run over, all that lovely produce is ruined, and Helen will kill me."

"Sorry, Tony," Billy complied, peering around the load he was carrying. Tony reached him, rearranged the boxes in his arms, and grabbed a produce bag from the younger boy's hand.

Tony opened the bag and looked in.

"Ugh. All this shopping and vegetables, vegetables, vegetables! I'd kill for a doughnut or a pastry," Tony mumbled.

"Mmmm..." responded Billy, behind his boxes.

"Or a big piece of chocolate cake! I'm sick of the fried junk at the show. I want something baked, that comes out of the oven smelling like heaven." Tony grabbed a carrot from the produce bag, bit off the top and spit it into the gutter. "Guess this'll do."

"I miss my mum's fruitcake," Billy added cheerfully.

"Fruitcake? Fruitcake! Of all the desserts in the world, you miss fruitcake?"

"It was good," Billy mumbled, embarrassed.

"You're a fruitcake..." Tony stopped and turned. He inhaled deeply.

"She put fresh cherries in it along with the dried stuff. It was like a nice surprise... Tony?"

Tony backtracked a few steps and inhaled again.

"Come on, Billy, this way." Tony moved through the trickle of people, pausing every few seconds to smell the air and adjust course.

"What is it?" Billy asked, trying unsuccessfully to navigate without bumping passersby.

"Heaven." Uttered Tony. "This way, quicker!" The boys made their way through the crowd which was getting heavier as they went. Tony shoved and pardoned his way through beige trench coats and black wool jackets. Suddenly the crowd parted and Tony found the source of the smell he was following.

A boring-looking man sat on a bench wearing a tan hat and tan coat. The man glanced up curiously at the two rough boys who had just stopped in front of him. They were staring. He questioned them with his eyes.

"Oh, my saints. It *is* heaven." Billy said awed, as he adjusted his grip on the boxes.

The man on the bench had on his lap a cinnamon roll the size of a dinner plate. The white icing dripped down the sides.

Tony put a hand in his pocket and a flash of fear crossed the anonymous man's face. He still had Cash's coin.

"Where did you get that?" Tony asked, eyes locked onto the cinnamon roll.

The slight man gave a little cough. "Ehm. At the train station. There's a vendor in the lobby who sells them."

Tony's face lit up. "Thank you! Let's go, Billy!" He turned and jogged a few paces before stopping. "Which train station might that be?"

The man pointed in the direction they had just come. Two blocks down, turn right. Another couple of blocks.

"Yes, yes, yes! This is going to be so good," Tony said excitedly.

Tony threw open the door like he owned the train station. Large windows illuminated the space. Four ticket stalls lined the wall to his left and six rows of dark wooden benches filled the rest of the space. With a quick scan of the room, he saw a small green cart with gold lettering in the far corner, opposite the ticket counters. "Lina's Cinnamon Buns". Tony walked straight over to the cart and the small, old woman standing behind it.

"You boys look like you've been working hard. Fancy a treat?" Her voice was friendly, warm, and stronger than Tony anticipated based on her slight stature. Suddenly, Tony stumbled forward as Billy crashed into him from behind.

"Billy! Set the boxes down, we'll sit and eat." After several thumps, he answered the woman's question.

"Yes, ma'am," Tony addressed the vendor. "We saw someone with one of your cinnamon buns. The big ones." He gestured with his hands. "We'd like one of them."

"With extra icing," Billy suddenly appeared with a big grin and huge eyes.

"With extra icing," Tony repeated.

Lina grabbed several sheets of waxed parchment paper and opened her warming box. She set the bun down on the top of the cart and opened a metal container with a ladle sticking out. She poured fresh, warm icing on the steaming roll. Two heaping scoops.

"Four bits, sweetie."

"Cash won't mind," Tony muttered to himself as he reached into his pocket and took out the gold coin. Billy choked and fell into a coughing fit when he saw it. Tony gave it to Lina, who returned several silver coins to him. With two hands, Tony gently lifted the huge cinnamon bun and held it up to his nose. Billy got so close that he came away with icing on his nose.

"It's perfect," Tony whispered with his eyes closed.

The boys sat and Tony found the end of the roll, and, pulling off a piece, began to unwind it. Billy took a piece after him.

"Cheers!" Tony lifted his length of bun. Billy already had his mouth full.

Tony popped the warm dough in his mouth and savored the first bite. He opened his eyes and looked at Billy.

"Are you... crying?" Tony asked incredulously.

Billy's eyes opened wide.

"No! Yes! Don't tell anyone, you can't tell anyone, Tony!"

Normally he'd take a chance to exercise his place as oldest boy, but today was different. Tony let out a light-hearted laugh.

"Don't worry, Billy. It'll be our secret." He looked down at the younger boy. "You won't tell anyone about my coin, right?"

Billy shook his head fervently, his mouth once again full of bun.

The boys sat, happily indulging and watching the people in the train station. The waiting room slowly filled up. Cash glanced up at the schedule. The next train was leaving in 5 minutes. He vaguely recognized the town's name. It was to the north, but he couldn't remember how far. All the towns and cities blurred together after so many years on the rails.

Billy swung his feet and quietly hummed as he examined the icing running down his piece of cinnamon bun. Tony watched one of the tellers leave his counter and come out into the waiting room. He began talking to passengers waiting on the bench nearest him. Moving on to the next group, he had a quick conversation before moving on again. The man questioned everyone on that first row before stopping in front of the door to the platform. He took a deep breath like he was going to address the crowd.

Then the teller yelled across the lobby, "Attention, please! Is there a James Connor here? James Connor!"

Tony grabbed Billy's leg and turned to look at him, his eyes large and alert.

"What did he say!?" He whispered desperately. Billy gave him a blank look. Tony turned his gaze back to the ticket teller.

"There is a ticket issue with passenger James Connor! Please come see me!" the teller continued.

Tony saw someone begin to make his way toward the teller. In a moment Tony was on his feet to get a better view. He saw an older man with white hair and a white beard speaking with the teller.

"Oh my gosh, oh my gosh, oh my gosh." Without taking his eyes off of the man, Tony dumped the rest of the cinnamon bun in Billy's lap and began to make his way across the lobby.

Just then the conductor in his blue uniform and grey hat stepped into the waiting room and called, "All aboard!"

The room jumped to life as people stood and moved about to collect their belongings and funnel out the doors onto the train platform. An old woman walked in front of Tony, dragging her extra-long knitting project behind her. Once she passed he made little progress toward the man with the white beard before a boy about his own age carelessly turned and swung a large instrument case into Tony's shins.

"Aghhhh..." he gritted through his teeth. He hopped over a suitcase, jumped on a bench, climbed over, and shoved himself closer to the man who responded to James Conner. Thankfully, he was still talking to the cashier. A family with a gaggle of children crossed in front of Tony just as the man with the white beard nodded to the cashier and turned to go out onto the platform.

Delayed again trying not to trip over the toddler, Tony yelled out, "James Conner!" The man turned looking for who had called to him. He had the same nose and eyes as Cash. Now at the door, the conductor took Cash's grandfather's ticket and allowed him onto the platform.

"No!" Tony shoved and "sorry"ed his way through the crowd and tried to slip past the conductor.

"Ticket?" the collector demanded.

"I... uh... my grandfather has it, he's already inside," Tony tried to gesture.

"No ticket, no train," the collector who was two inches shorter than Tony looked at Tony's patched sweater disdainfully. "Go back and sit down." Tony peered over the ticket collector's shoulder and saw Cash's grandfather step onto the train at the platform.

Tony slowly maneuvered his way back to where Billy

was sitting with crusted icing on his face. He sat slowly and looked over at the empty cinnamon bun paper on Billy's lap.

"I ate the rest," Billy shrugged.

Tony stared at him for a moment and put his head in his hands. The platform doors closed succinctly. The waiting room was silent except for the low rumble of the train that was about to depart. Tony raised his head and watched the teller who had been speaking with Cash's grandfather lift the swinging door built into the counter and return to his window.

"I'll be back," he said to Billy without looking at him. Tony crossed the room quickly now that it was empty and approached the cashier at his window.

"Where ya goin'?" The man asked.

Caught off guard, Tony stammered, "I, uh, no. The man you were talking to, James Conner, can you tell me anything about him? Where *he* was going?"

The teller's eyes narrowed and his ginger-tinged mustache twitched.

"I can't share customer information with strangers," the man reached for a piece of paper to look busy and brush off Tony.

Tony stepped to the right so he was in front of the man again and he noticed the nameplate on the counter.

"Please, Mr. Simon. My friend's parents died, but he learned a while back that his grandfather is alive. His name is James Conner. I think that was him. Anything you can tell me would be helpful. He *really* wants to find him." Mr. Simon looked up with tired eyes. Tony reached into his pocket for the change from Cash's gold coin and slid it across the counter.

Mr. Simon's eyebrow raised and he put a hand over the coins and slid them off the counter, but he still eyed Tony with a measure of distrust. Then he reached for a tri-folded paper and set it in front of Tony.

"You would have figured this out eventually, so I'm not sharing customer information with you," Mr. Simon shifted uncomfortably. "In case anyone asks."

He flattened the map so it was facing Tony and grabbed a pen. "This is where we are," and he marked a circle around a dot on the map. "That train was going north... like this..." he drew a dark line along one of the train paths. "There are only three more stops on the line. Here, here, and here." Mr. Simon drew stars next to each of the three stops. "Which means your friend's, ehem, grandfather, is most likely in this vicinity." With that, Mr. Simon drew a circle around the three stops and the nearby villages.

Tony's eyes grew wide and he took the map.

"Thank you!" he gave Mr. Simon a big grin. Turning quickly, he waved the map in the air and yelled across the waiting room to Billy, "Come on! Let's go! I have to go find Cash!"

———

Maya stood next to Lorenzo's chair in the ring, watching the aerialists, equestrians, and tumblers trickle out of their final practice before the show that evening. Cash walked next to Boris and Bella who were both laughing. He smiled at them with a mixture of happiness, relief, and nerves before pausing, turning, and waving at her. Maya returned the wave, then turned her back on him to await her final orders from Lorenzo. The show director was correcting one of Bonkers' clowns very loudly. The clown was in his final pose and Lorenzo was shoving his cane at the clown's limbs and joints to perfect his posture.

"Hand above your head! Knee in the air and bent. Straight back like you have a plate on your head. Because tonight you WILL have a plate spinning on your head!" He stabbed his cane into the ground. "GO!" The clown scampered off to exit as quickly as possible. Maya almost laughed at his oversized shoes and bobbing wig. Lorenzo turned to her.

"And YOU, miss! I need you to go to the kitchen to find Helen. She MUST serve more protein on show days. None of these fried pancakes and piles of bread!" Lorenzo's arms were waving wildly and his face turned red. "While you're at it, tell her to control her workers! One of those boys was in the backyard last night poking the horses with a pin to see what they would do! Of all the nerve!"

Maya looked at him with her head cocked to one side, intrigued.

"Why do you look at me like that and say nothing?!" Lorenzo demanded.

"You always get like this before a show, don't you?" she asked innocently.

"How dare you! What are you saying?! That I'm out of control? That I'm LOSING IT! This is the best circus on the continent and it's all because of ME! Now get out of my sight or I'll leave you in this God-forsaken town!"

"Yes, Lorenzo!" Maya turned to leave and walked quickly out of the tent. She knew it was an empty threat, but he was a man who was used to people obeying without questioning him. As she exited the tent, she slowed down to enjoy the sights and sounds. With only two hours to show time, the grounds were full of townies getting their tickets, looking at the animals, playing games, and eating treats. She absorbed the sounds of the circus: children squealing, the elephants trumpeting, and the barkers offering wares and games to the wandering townies. She slowly made her way to the cookhouse. Lorenzo was full of hot air tonight, but Helen probably should know that one of her boys was pricking the horses.

Instead of getting in line for dinner, Maya went around the cookhouse and slipped in the back flaps. She spotted Helen as she wiped her forehead with a kitchen towel and tossed it over her shoulder. She turned and noticed Maya. Her focused stare softened into a welcoming smile.

"Maya! What a treat! We just got the first round out. What can I do for you?" Helen asked.

"Lorenzo sent me," Maya stated.

At that, Helen laughed in a short burst and shook her head.

"Opening night, huh? It's always something." Helen lowered herself onto one of the metal stools around the prep table and propped her elbow on the table. Maya padded up and slid onto the stool next to her.

"His highness requests more protein and fewer pancakes."

"Maybe he should tell his crews to skip the pancakes and eat the protein I put out at every meal. Anything else?" asked the older woman.

"He said he caught one of your boys poking the horses with a needle last night."

Helen's eyebrows arched and she sat up straight.

"Oh! That *is* an issue. I'll talk to them." She put a hand on Maya's forearm. "And how are you tonight, miss Maya? I haven't really seen you since the fight."

Maya was startled, not used to other people touching her, but she relaxed at the rays of warmth and caring coming from Helen.

"I'm good. Busy night getting ready for the show. And you know how Lorenzo is."

"I didn't ask about the show. How are you adjusting to being here?" Helen looked at Maya in a motherly way.

The question surprised Maya. Between recovering, hiding, getting used to her role, and making new friends, she'd barely had time to think about the drama of the last week and how her life had completely changed.

"The fight was scary and crazy, but most of the time being here is exciting. Though sometimes it's overwhelming. There are so many things to see and learn. And people to meet and I want to do a good job." she paused to reflect. "But… honestly, it's easy to focus on all the newness and forget that this is temporary. That this life isn't really for me, I don't think. The letter from my mother reminded me of that."

"You're one of the few. One of the lucky ones," Helen replied reassuringly.

Maya stared at her hands.

"I feel guilty that I have somewhere else to go to. It'll be different than it was now that it's just my mother and me. Tony and Bella and Bonkers don't have anyone. Boris has me and my mother, but that's it. And...do you have anyone?"

Maya sensed Helen's heart beating faster.

But the older woman didn't get out more than, "I..." before Tony and Billy barged into the kitchen, all energy and excitement.

From behind several boxes Billy began blathering, "You won't believe it! Cash! Tony! We had some money."

Tony punched him in the arm which caused the little boy to lose his grip on the boxes. Acting quickly, Tony caught the off-balance packages and helped Billy put everything on the table.

"Tony! Where on earth have you been!? You completely missed prep!" Helen cried through the commotion.

"We found Cash's grandfather!" Tony burst with pride.

"What?!" Helen and Maya both stared at him wide-eyed.

"We were at the train station and they called his name. They actually called his name!" Tony laughed.

"But then a train arrived and there were so many people in the waiting area! Tony jumped over a bench to try to get to him!" Billy added excitedly.

"Why were you at the train..." Helen began, confused.

"I tried to reach him but he got through the door. I got a really good look at him though! Definitely has Cash's eyes," Tony said confidently.

"And nose!" piped in Billy.

"You barely even saw him," Chided Tony.

"Well, that's what you said..."

"Look at this!" Tony reached into his back pocket and spread the train map on the table between Helen and Maya. He pointed to the three black circles. "He was going to one of these towns! Now Cash can find him and have a family again!"

"We have to tell him!" Maya stood up. "Where is he?"

"Wait!" Helen stood and paced. "Hold on. We should wait until after tonight's performance. There is so much depending on his first performance back. I'd hate to distract him."

Maya squealed with excitement. "Yay! Cash has a family!" She squeezed Helen's arm.

"Oh no! The performance! I almost forgot." Panic

briefly crossed Maya's face. "Helen, can I borrow Tony for a little bit? Please?"

Helen looked from Maya to Tony.

"Hmmm…" She glared at him lightheartedly. "Billy, you can get started on the popcorn for tonight so Tony can go with Maya."

"Great! Let's go!" Maya almost ran out of the cookhouse and paused to grab Tony by the lapel. They ran out of the tent and faded into the twilight.

CHAPTER 17

BACK ON THE TRAPS

Cash unconsciously fidgeted with his fingernails, clicking them together. He stood in a dark corner of the marquee tent that served as the main entrance into the ring. Though he had done this many times before, tonight he could barely keep his breath under control. The building murmur of the crowd of people buzzed in his ears. He watched as townies entered the big top and hustled to the best seats. Focusing on individual people helped calm his nerves. There was a father in a suit with a three-year-old daughter in a yellow dress. The father removed his hat, ran a hand through his hair, and returned his hat to his head as he watched his daughter squeal at one of the clowns wandering and interacting with the audience. The clown turned and Cash saw that it was Bonkers. Bonkers made eye contact with Cash, nodded, and then turned his attention back to the father and daughter. He bent over to say, "Hi," to her and when she reached for the flower on his jacket, he squirted her with water. Her giggles flowed on the airwaves to Cash and he smiled. He saw Tony and Billy across the tent with their trays of popcorn. Billy tripped on his own shoe almost upending the full tray, and Cash chuckled at the boy.

After a moment, he ducked into the changing area and put on his costume for the first time since the accident. He struggled into the half-gold, half-blue stretchy pants and then buttoned on the red and gold vest. He stepped behind the ring doors and heard the overwhelming wave of cheers from the crowd. A smile almost cracked his focused face. Adrenaline pushed through his body as he approached the ring. He took his place waiting next to Bella and bounced on his toes to release energy. Bella smiled and punched him jokingly in the arm.

They peeked through the ring door curtains and watched the clowns in the ring as they tumbled, flipped, and performed slapstick gags that had the crowd laughing. The clowns wrapped up their act by arranging themselves in a circle so they were facing the crowd and they all took their bows to cracking applause. That was the cue Cash and Bella were waiting for. They ran out of their tunnel at the same time the equestrians departed the tunnel across from them. The equestrians were next, but Cash and Bella needed to get in place during their routine to keep the acts rolling seamlessly. The spotlight swiveled from the clowns to the horses and riders.

Cash and Bella ran across the ring in semi-darkness and crossed paths with the clowns returning to the tunnel. Bonkers headed for Cash and tousled his hair with a laugh. Cash arrived at his ladder, put his hands on the side rails, and took a deep breath. He exhaled with a smile and bounded up the rungs. Jojo greeted him at the top of the ladder with a large grin. Below them the equestrians rode in circles around the ring, executing perfect summersaults and riding two at a time. Looking across the ring he saw Bella climb onto her platform.

Her red-trimmed gold bodice and fluttery skirt shimmered in the glints of spotlight. The equestrians began their final formation and Jojo took his pole and reached for Cash's bar. The lights, the noise, the full tent. Cash flashed back to his last performance and how everything seemed fine that time. He froze. Suddenly, he felt a poke in his ribs that knocked him back into the present.

"It's almost time," Jojo whispered fiercely at him. "Won't be like last time, hey?" The well-meaning joke made Cash's stomach roll.

The horses ran their final lap at full speed and headed for their tunnel to end their act. Soon the spotlights were swirling around the ring, teasing the crowd to look for the next act. Sweat broke out on his back and his arms got chills. As he reached for his trapeze, he noticed his arms shaking. As Cash grasped the metal bar, he heard cheering from the crowd. It sounded like his name. The spotlight, instead of highlighting him, cruised the crowd to see where the chanting was coming from. Cash managed a quick look down at the ringmaster who was also looking at the crowd and was, for once, speechless. The spotlight landed on one section of the crowd. Cash broke his focus to see what the ruckus was. An entire section of the crowd stood up and held up the posters Tony and the boys had been posting around town. Then, in unison, they all flipped them over.

When all of the posters flipped, painted words declared,"Go, Cash!" across the section. Cash gasped and staggered back while keeping one hand on his trap. He tried to figure out how this happened, so he looked around the stands. In front of the section, Tony and Maya were jumping up and down and waving at him.

Emotion grabbed at his throat and he blinked to prevent tears from falling. He was overwhelmed by the gesture. Happiness filled him from his toes to his head. Then like a spark in his chest lighting a stick of dynamite, Cash's insides erupted with courage.

The ringmaster focused again on the act and his voice bellowed, "It looks like Cash has some fans in the room!" A wave of noise and cheers rolled from the crowd. Elon paused as the crowd quieted down. He looked around, arms wide open, building anticipation. All of the spotlights focused on the ringmaster, leaving the rest of the tent in mysterious darkness.

"Ladies and gentlemen, friends and fiends... I'm excited- no - proud- to reintroduce our star- the Flying Phenom who defied death and a grueling recovery to fly for you here tonight. Put your hands together for the immaculate, the inconceivable, the incredible SOARING CASH CONNOR!" The rest of his speech fell silent beneath the screams and stomping from the audience as two spotlights darted to Cash and Bella. The rest of the lights swept the audience, creating a frenzy as they cheered.

Squinting in the bright light, Cash waved at the crowd with his free hand. He took a quick breath in and turned with confidence to face his bar and grabbed a firm hold of it. Across the ring, Bella smiled at him and nodded. He returned a nod of his own.

The ringmaster turned on his podium and played to each section of the crowd. And the excitement built to an uproar. Then the lights slowed and Elon indicated for the noise to die down.

Cash stood on the platform and locked his vision on Bella. He was vaguely aware of the noise dimming, but his focus was on the starting word and executing a perfect start.

"Hep!" Lorenzo called through his megaphone.

The word resonated in his brain as he pulled back, swung forward, and flew off of the platform, into the air, and over the yawning abyss below. He wasn't aware of the height or the nerves. He felt determined and his body moved by muscle memory. He barely had to think about the moves. The timing ran through his head like a favorite song. Out, back, release, flip, clasp hands with Bella, swing, return, trapeze is waiting. He perfectly executed the routine and landed back on the platform. It felt as though he had been in a daze or a trance. As he came out of it, his awareness of the tent returned.

At first, he was confused by the thundering noise, like an earthquake. Then it hit him that he had just pulled off the hardest routine of his life and the crowd was going crazy. Cash jumped to the guard rail on the platform, ecstatic with adrenaline. He bounced up and down, shouting at the crowd and waving at them. He turned to the next side and did the same thing, releasing a roar of pride. The spotlights moved from him, back over the audience that was on its feet, cheering and stomping.

The lights landed on the ringmaster, who attempted to close the show with reminders to buy souvenirs on the way out. In a lighthearted flurry, Cash bounded down his metal ladder where Boris immediately pummeled him with a bear hug. Bella ran up behind him, light as a fawn, and joined the hug. Looking over toward the crowd, he saw Maya standing with her hands behind her back, smiling knowingly and rocking on her toes.

His friends released him, grabbed his arms and headed

out the tunnel. Boris lifted the flap and Cash gasped as he took in the crowds of people lining each side of the tent exit. A cheer roared when they saw him. Shocked, Boris gave him a little shove to move down the line.

"Shake their hands," Bella said into his ear. Cash grabbed and shook the fist hand he saw, it belonged to a boy about his age. The boy's face lit up and his friends jockeyed and shoved him admiringly as Cash moved on. It all became a blur as Cash moved down the line. Smiles, shouts, handshakes, people patting his shoulder and congratulating him.

Waiting at the end of the line for him was the ringmaster. His green velvet jacket stretched across his broad shoulders and shimmered in the lights from the tent. He wore a grin with a hint of greed that made Cash pause.

"Well done, my boy, well done! Lorenzo thought you'd freeze, but I knew you'd be back on top!" The ringmaster wrapped an arm around Cash's shoulders as Cash considered how to respond. But Elon kept talking. "We have business to discuss." The ringmaster steered Cash toward the red wagon, a few yards past the crowd. His crowd.

"It's time we talk about your future, Cash," the broad man started his pitch as they walked. "We're on the cusp!" He raised his left fist with a flourish. "You saw the crowd tonight! They went crazy for you. You're the performer who escaped death... NO! cheated death! You think this is famous? It's only the beginning!" Elon ascended the stairs to the red wagon entrance and threw open the door.

There was a flurry of activity in the office. Nina and a team were counting tickets and receipts and there were piles of cash on all of the surfaces. The looming safe creaked as the open door swung slightly on its hinges. Nina paused her work and pushed her glasses back up her nose.

"Good evening, sir. This could be the best take we've had all year. We'll know soon," she commented.

"Thank you, Nina. Bring the figures to my office as soon as you have them. Cash and I have some things to discuss."

The ringmaster walked down the hallway to his office and settled into the chair behind his desk, leaning back into it. Elon stared at him, as though waiting for something. Awkwardly, Cash looked around the office. His eyes stopped on the front of the ringmaster's desk. It was a carved oak monstrosity with curls at the corners and a circus scene laid out in detail. Mostly animals, the scene depicted horses and elephants around the outside, a bear in the bottom left corner, and in the center, a ringmaster with a large roaring lion.

At the shuffle of paper, Cash snapped out of his examination of the desk. The ringmaster had pulled a stack of papers out of a drawer and dropped it on the desk in front of him.

The ringmaster leaned forward and clasped his hands together in an iron grip.

"I promised you more money if you performed again and I am always a man of my word. In front of you is a contract. It is a five-year contract with my circus, performing your aerial act. I think you'll find the compensation more than adequate."

Elon stood up and turned to look out the window behind his desk, at the lit tent and straggling attendees. "Read over the papers. You'll find it straightforward. We're simple people, really." He turned back to Cash and picked up a pen from the desk. Running his forefinger and thumb along the pen he continued. "Your housing is covered and of course your food. You'll have plenty of spending money to make your accommodations luxurious. Your own car, with your name painted on the outside."

Cash began to read over the contract. It was exactly as Elon said, but several things nagged at him.

Looking at the first page, he asked, "This says, 'aerial act with Cash Connor and partner'. Why isn't Bella mentioned?"

Elon set the pen down in front of Cash and straightened to his full height.

"Bella and I have our own contract. She isn't contracted to you nor you to her. She's replaceable. You're the star now, Cash. Sign the contract." Cash looked up at the ringmaster and shifted in his chair, then looked down to continue reading. His eyes widened and he sat straight up in the chair when he saw the pay. It was ten times his current wages.

"Generous, yes?" The ringmaster said slyly. "I have to take care of my star performer." He slowly pushed the pen closer to Cash.

Feeling more uncomfortable, Cash wriggled in his chair again and kept reading.

"I see housing, pay, food. What about time off?"

"Well, that is at my discretion. I plan to move us to warmer areas in the winters with larger crowds, so we won't have the usual winter time off. But think of the extra shows and the extra money." He tapped the area of the contract with Cash's new salary and bonus for each performance.

Cash thought of his grandfather. If he was going to find his grandfather, he'd need money to travel. But if his grandfather was out there, and if he had a home there, he didn't want to wait five years.

"What if I don't sign the contract?" Cash looked up at the ringmaster and saw a flash of annoyance across the older man's face.

"If you don't sign the contract, nothing changes. Same pay, same living quarters. I can change the show and the lineup at any time without a contract. Your job is only guaranteed as long as you make me money. If you freeze or get hurt again..."

Cash's insides wriggled. Other performers would kill for the deal in front of him, but his stomach tightened. If he had any chance to get back to a normal life, this contract suffocated the air from it.

"Thank you for the offer, but I would like to keep things as they are."

Elon stared at him fiercely. His right eye twitched. The swagger and showmanship disintegrated.

"Ok. The offer is off the table." The ringmaster quickly grabbed the contract and ripped it in half, throwing the pieces on his desk. "Leave! Now!"

Cash stood and, not knowing what else to say, left the office. He quickly escaped down the hall and exited the red wagon without a word to Nina or the other workers. He paused outside wondering if he had just thrown his future away. If he couldn't find his grandfather, then he just made the biggest mistake of his life. The thought made him nauseous. Realizing he was still in his costume, he made a beeline for the caboose. He thumped up the stairs and opened the door.

Helen, Maya, and Tony were sitting in the 'boose.

Tony spoke first. "We need to talk."

CHAPTER 18

THE BRIDGE IS OUT

Cash closed the door to the caboose and turned to face his friends.

"Tony found your grandfather!" Maya blurted out and then covered her mouth with her hands and looked at Tony. "Sorry, I got excited."

"It's OK," Tony murmured to her.

Cash's mind began to spin. He looked from Helen over to Maya and then to Tony in a confused way. The roar of the crowd from the performance still rang in his ears, and he was off-kilter from his conversation with Elon. Could this be the news he had been waiting for?

"Where?" Cash whispered in disbelief, sinking onto his bed.

Tony relayed the story from the train station then stood and pulled the map from his back pocket. Maya and Helen leaned back from the table as Tony unwrinkled it and spread it on the small table. Cash stood to take a closer look. Tony pointed to the map and Cash looked at the three black circles on the map.

"We're down here..." Tony located their current position,

"and your grandfather was heading north to one of these towns."

"We're heading north next." Hope and excitement rose in Cash as he realized the possibilities of what was happening. "We're heading towards my grandfather! What if I find him? What if he comes to the show? I could meet him tomorrow!"

Cash looked at his friends who were beaming at him.

"You very well could find your grandfather in the next few weeks," Helen looked at him like a proud mother.

Cash sat back down on his bed and put his head in his hands, having a hard time comprehending the news. He thought of his time at the circus. Close to half of his life had been spent on this train, in the tent, and with these people. But as much as he loved his friends, he thought back to the easy and relaxed days with his parents. More than anything he wanted family and a house that didn't move.

Cash looked up at his friends.

"Tell me again."

Tony relayed the story of seeing his grandfather once again.

"It could really be him," Cash pondered. Tony nodded slowly.

"This could be it!" Cash exclaimed and jumped up from his bed. He walked to the other side of the car and back. "What do I do? Should I pack? What about my act? Did he look nice?" Cash stopped and looked at his friends for answers.

"Take it a day at a time, Cash," Helen said. "We aren't heading north quite yet. Wait a little bit before you go and quit the circus."

"Yeah, yeah, yeah. Ok," he agreed, his head spinning.

"This is so exciting!" Maya almost squealed, and in her excitement grabbed Tony by the arm. He gave her a sad warning look and she released his arm.

"Cash has had quite a day between his performance and this news. Maya, let's leave the boys alone." Helen stood to leave and Maya obediently followed.

Helen gave Cash a kiss on the cheek and put a loving hand on his upper arm.

"I'm very proud of you, Cash." She squeezed his arm and went out the door. Maya gave him a quick wave and a sly grin as she slipped out the door and closed it behind her.

Cash fell back on his bed and started laughing in amazement at the timing of Tony's discovery. One week. In a week they would pull out and head north and closer to his grandfather.

———

The next morning Tony swept open the cookhouse entrance and bowed in jest before Cash, "After you, Mr. Star-of-the-Show."

As they entered, Cash noticed others looking at him admiringly. For years he had been completely ignored, but even circus vets were impressed with the daring performance he gave. As they got in line for breakfast, Cash briefly locked eyes with Elon on his platform at the front of the tent. The ringmaster shot daggers at him then curtly returned to his eggs.

The exchange didn't go unnoticed by Tony.

"Whoa. What'd you do? I thought you were his golden boy."

Cash started explaining the meeting in Elon's office, but before he got to his decision, the hair on the back of his neck stood up with a fluttering static feeling and he felt someone brush against his back. He grabbed his neck and whipped around to find Maya.

"Word has it that the ringmaster is upset because you turned him down," she stated factually.

"You said *no* to that much money!? What's wrong with you?" Tony's mouth dropped.

"He wanted a five-year contract. I just... can't. My grandfather is so close!" Cash looked at Tony in a desperate way. "Though it's risky, because if I get hurt again or Elon changes his mind, I'm out of a job. Then I'll really be in a bind."

"Yeah, but, but, the MONEY!" Tony blurted.

"It's not about that," Maya said quietly.

Cash turned to Tony.

"If you had a chance to see your family again, would any amount of money keep you here?"

Tony looked off over Cash's shoulder and fidgeted with his fingers. He shook his head sadly.

"No. I'd give anything," he said resolutely.

With trays loaded, Cash and Tony went to sit down at their usual table. Bonkers slid into the spot across from Cash.

"So what's the plan? You gonna find your grandfather at the next stop?" the clown asked, swiping a piece of bacon from Cash's tray.

Cash had stayed up most of the night planning how to go about finding his grandfather and needed his friends' help.

"Well, I'll definitely ask around at busy places in town: restaurants, banks, shops, pubs. I wish I knew more about him, but that's all I can do. Hopefully, someone will know of him," he replied.

"Yeah, hopefully he's not a hermit," added Bonkers.

Fear flashed in Cash's eyes as this new thought triggered panic in him.

"He's not a hermit," Maya glared at the clown. "Tony saw him out in public."

Bonkers shrugged and ate the rest of Cash's piece of bacon.

"Yeah. He wasn't dressed like a hermit. More like a professor or business owner." added Tony.

Turning to Cash, Maya asked, "With practices and shows, you barely have any time off. How are you going to get into town?"

"Well, that's where I wanted to ask you all for help," Cash began. Just then Boris and Bella joined them at the table and Cash filled them in on the plan.

"I figure I can get away the first day after we pull in and everyone is setting up. I'll get the lay of the town and ask around as much as I can. Then I'll divvy up the different parts of town and popular places. Will you all help me ask around?" Cash looked around at all of his friends. They all smiled, nodded, and otherwise showed their support.

"Of course, buddy," Tony slapped him on the back. "I'm obviously the best at this so far since I found him once."

"But you let him get away," Maya added snarkily.

"Well, yeah, but, at least I found him and where he was going…kind of," grinned Tony.

———

Seven Years Ago

Tony rambled up the path, swinging a stick at the over-growth along the way.

"You're so slow!" yelled Bella's brother Martín from up ahead. "Hurry up!"

"Your legs are longer." Tony hollered back.

"Maybe, but you're still walking slow!"

Tony huffed and stopped swinging his stick. He focused on the path and catching up to Martín. The trail led up a hill and Tony's progress slowed again as he navigated the rocks now dotting the way. Ahead of him, Martín scrambled up the boulders and toward the top of the waterfall. Tony was starkly aware of their age difference as he assessed the rocky path ahead. Martín was already 14 and strong and quick but allowed ten-year-old Tony to tag along on his adventures.

Halfway up the steep path, Tony watched Martín reach the top.

"This is amazing!" Martín shouted over the sound of the water. Tony scrambled quicker. As he neared the top a trickle of little stones came down around him. Martín was practically running down the stony path.

Reaching Tony, Martín pulled him up and turned him around.

"We have to go now. There's hail coming! I should have sensed it sooner, but I wasn't paying attention. There's nowhere to hide out here. We have to reach the town." Fear flooded the older boy's face and Tony immediately began descending the trail, stumbling as he went. Martín reached the bottom of the hill first and encouraged Tony along. As soon as Tony reached Martín, the crash of pelting ice started behind him. Tony glanced over his shoulder and panic washed over him at the apple-sized hail pounding the top of the hill where they had been a few minutes before. Martín grabbed his arm and they both ran as fast as they could.

The thrashing sound of hail ripping the leaves off of the thin trees behind them kept them both going at a grueling pace. At the rate the storm was catching up to them, they weren't going to make it to the town in time. Even though Tony ran as fast as he could, Martín got fifty yards ahead of Tony.

Tony reached into the depths of himself to find more energy to make his legs move faster. He suddenly felt a heat in his chest that was a different kind of energy. As he ran, he focused on the sensation in his chest. He kept up his pace, but it seemed that the world around him had slowed down. Before he knew it, he caught up to Martín.

As Tony approached, Martín looked at him in amazement. As he returned the look, Tony felt the energy in his chest reach out to Martín. Suddenly, they were running at the same pace through the slow-motion world.

The sound of the threatening hail began to recede and they eventually slowed their pace as they approached the town. The world around them went back to its normal speed.

They silently walked into town and paused in the doorway of a closed shop to catch their breath.

"There's no way we could have, or, should have outrun that storm," Martín said, looking intensely at Tony.

"I know. I-" Tony began.

"Excuse me." A quiet voice interrupted Tony and both boys jumped.

A blonde boy about his age stood on the sidewalk in front of them.

"I heard that the circus is in town. Can you tell me which direction it is?" the boy inquired politely.

"First show's not 'til tomorrow. You're a little early." Martín said, examining the boy, his backpack and dirty face, and clothes.

"I'm not here for the show. I want to, you know, work with them and travel with them," came the reply.

Martín raised his eyebrows and Tony looked closer at the boy.

"You a runaway?" Martín questioned him.

"Yes? Well, no. I'm not sure. My parents died and I left…"

Tony glanced at Martín, who nodded.

"You can follow us. We're going there now." Tony said invitingly.

The blonde boy's sad face transformed into a charming, hopeful smile.

"Are you from the circus? Do you live there? What do you do?" Tony and Martin chuckled at the torrent of questions and headed down the street, the boy falling in step next to Tony.

"I'm Martín and this is Tony."

"Nice to meet you. My name's Cash."

––––––––––

Present Day

After breakfast, they had an hour before practice, so Cash followed Tony to the caboose. Tony dug out a deck of cards and they sat on the platform behind the caboose to play in the sun.

"I win!" Cash smacked an ace down on the pile of cards. Tony groaned when he saw it and moved to gather and shuffle the deck. Tony paused and glanced at Cash with a strange look on his face.

"Did you hear that?"

"No, what?" Cash furrowed his brow as he asked.

"It sounded like-"

A train whistle sounded in the distance. Cash and Tony looked at each other confused. Then the whistle sounded again. Conversations between people milling around next to the train stopped and everyone began looking around. The train track was on miles of open land, but beyond a big curve, the track disappeared into a forest.

"Look!" One of the ballerinas yelled. She pointed her delicate finger to the woods. Everyone turned to look where she was pointing. Suddenly, another train came barreling out of the trees.

Cash grabbed Tony's arm when he realized what was happening.

"It's on our track! It's coming at us!" There was a commotion and all the bystanders scrambled for the closest car. Cash watched as the oncoming train continued to emerge from the woods. The black engine was followed by cars that were each painted in a different black and white pattern. Cash watched the conductor run for the engine while Elon leaned out of his doorway yelling and gesturing to the back end of the train. Cash and Tony both stumbled when their train jolted forward, then backward. Their train gained speed heading in reverse, the way they had come into town.

With the train running in reverse, Cash and Tony's caboose was at the front of the train.

"What is going on?" Cash asked loudly.

"I dunno! What about the circus!?" Tony shouted.

Cash looked at the big top and all of the tents and booths lining the midway.

"How long can we go in reverse like this?" The wind whipped in Cash's face and hair.

"I don't know! I think the track separates on the other side of the river."

Cash and Tony looked straight ahead as the landscape passed by faster and faster. The river slowly came into focus.

"Is there something on the track up ahead?" Tony squinted his eyes.

Cash looked down the track.

"It looks like a wooden wall, with writing on it."

"Huh. That's weird. What does it say?" asked Tony.

"Something about the bridge. Bridge… oat. Bridge… out? Bridge out! Tony! There's something wrong with the bridge!" He remembered the violent thunderstorm that had rolled in right after they arrived.

"What are we gonna do!?"

Cash's heart pounded and blood flooded to his head. His vision went out of focus as he realized they were heading toward the river without a functioning bridge.

"We have to get to the front of the train and warn the conductor!"

CHAPTER 19

TRAPPED

Tony turned without saying a word and grabbed onto the ladder on the side of the 'boose. With a grunt, he pulled himself up and over onto the ladder, then scrambled up. Cash followed. As his body made the leap from the platform to the ladder, he saw the brief moment when his feet were over the fleeting ground and he gasped. He shook himself out of it and looked up to see Tony pull himself up onto the roof of the caboose. Cash grabbed the rung above him and hurried to follow his friend. Pulling himself up to the roof, Cash paused on his hands and knees, looking forward. Tony pulled him up by his upper arm. "We have to run." The boys took off as fast as they could go with the wind blasting them and the slight sway of the train that made balancing more difficult.

As they neared the edge of the caboose Tony yelled, "Don't think about it, just jump!" Cash and Tony both launched themselves over the gap and landed on the roof of the first storage car. A splintering crash caused Cash to turn around. The train had barreled through the wooden wall. Cash saw another sign in the distance. Tony grabbed his arm.

"We're running out of time. Hurry!" Tony yelled.

The boys popped up and ran the length of the storage car and jumped onto the next one. This time, Cash barely lost any speed when he landed and kept running. Car after car they ran. With each step, Cash knew they were seconds closer to crashing into the river. Fields of trees and early-autumn grass zipped by in his periphery. They got past the other storage cars and landed on the ballerina's car. Their running on the roof caused the ladies to pop their heads out of the side windows to try and see what was going on. Cash heard the windows, but didn't slow down. He and Tony kept their pace, occasionally swerving to avoid a hatch and hop to the next car.

Past the residence cars, they hopped onto the first animal car. The lion roared, but Cash didn't even flinch, he was too focused on the engine which was only a few cars ahead. Over the elephant car and only two cars remained: Elon's car and the coal car. Their feet pounded the roof of the ringmaster's car. The hatch ahead of Cash popped open and the ringmaster emerged. Cash skidded to a stop and Tony kept going.

"The bridge! The bridge is out!" Cash gasped and watched Elon's eyes grow large. Out of the corner of his eye, Cash saw Tony jump onto the coal car and the pile of coal. His friend landed and quickly lost his balance on the shifting coals. Then he fell over the edge.

"Tony!" Cash scrambled toward the side of the ringmaster's car and looked over the edge. Tony was barely hanging onto the lip of the coal car. Cash put a foot on the lip and eased himself over, trying to keep his balance. Knowing the pile of coal was unstable, he crept along the side and lowered to his knees when he got to Tony. He felt a nudge at his side and looked back to see the ringmaster behind him. Elon pointed Cash forward. They both got into place and grabbed Tony's forearms. "1-2-3!" Elon yelled as they both heaved Tony up.

Tony climbed up the side of the car. As he came over the edge, the train heaved and they all landed against the pile of coal.

Relieved, Cash caught his breath, only to have Tony lightly shove him toward the engine, "Go!" he rasped. Cash felt a strange tug in his chest as he turned toward the front of the train. He walked quickly along the lip of the edge that was no wider than his feet, but it felt like the train wasn't moving as fast as it had been before. He leaned inward and kept a hand on the coal pile to help balance. He arrived at the far side of the car quicker than he thought he would. Steam billowed in his face, making his eyes water and he struggled to breathe. He leaned across the gap and wrapped an arm around the metal pole that served as the corner of the engine cab. With a jump, he swung his body around and into the cab, colliding with the conductor as he landed.

Cash reached out and grabbed the conductor by the front of his jumpsuit and pulled him up on his feet while yelling, "The bridge is out! We have to stop! We have to STOP!"

The conductor nervously leaned out the cab opening and looked toward the bridge, then at the train barreling towards them.

"THERE IS NO BRIDGE!" Cash cried desperately.

Frozen with fear, the conductor glanced at a lever in the corner attached to a valve. Cash let him go and turned to look at the cylinder. A metal tag read "Air Brake". Cash pushed the lever with all of his might. It pushed back against him, but he held steady and shoved it as far as it would go, holding it there with everything in him. A high-pitched screeching began that grew and grew until it was all he could hear. The sound of metal screeching on metal bore into his head, but he gritted his teeth and didn't let go.

He finally felt the momentum of the train begin to slow down. Cash pushed and pushed until the train finally came to a stop. He let go of the lever and his body collapsed into a heap in the corner of the cab. With all of his remaining energy, he turned himself over so he was leaning against the wall. The conductor stared at him. Behind the conductor, Elon swung himself into the cab.

"You did it, my boy!" Shoving aside the conductor, Elon stepped in front of Cash. "You saved us!"

Then Tony's head popped up alongside the ringmaster.

"You saved *me*, Cash, I couldn't have held on much longer!" his friend cried.

The ringmaster extended a hand and helped Cash up, then he slapped him on the back.

"An extra serving of dessert for you tonight for saving us," Elon exclaimed.

Realizing how cramped it was in the cab, Cash, Tony, Elon, and the conductor filed out of the small space. As Cash stepped down onto the grass, he watched the black and white train curve along the track ahead of them and slow down to a stop only 10 feet from their engine.

Elon watched the approach and then turned to Cash and Tony, his demeanor quickly changing from excitement and gratitude to concern.

"You boys head back to the caboose. I'll find out what in blazes is going on," the ringmaster said before heading toward the other train to find its conductor.

Cash and Tony began their trek toward the end of the train.

"What was all that racket? You two causing trouble?" Barnaby leaned out of the window of the car he shared with the other animal hands.

"The bridge behind us is out. We had to stop the train," Cash explained in his defense.

"Yeah," added Tony, "Cash saved us."

Barnaby looked toward the end of the train, then back to the front, and examined the black and white train. He looked back at the boys and grunted.

"Seems like trouble to me. You better get back to the 'boose. I imagine we'll be moving back toward the circus again soon. Looks like we're at least a mile away." With that, Barnaby retreated into his car and slid the window shut with a bang.

Cash and Tony continued their walk to the caboose in silence. Once inside, Cash laid down on his bed and reached for the adventure book he had been reading. Tony fiddled with their radio until he found a faint signal playing jazzy music. Time passed. Cash finished his book, sat up, and looked around. Across the caboose, Tony was picking at his nails in a bored way.

"How long is this going to take?" Cash said aloud.

Tony looked at him and sighed.

"Couldn't tell ya." Tony sat up, reached for something in the corner of his bed, and threw it at Cash. "Catch!"

Surprised, Cash caught the airborne object. It was one of the clowns' juggling balls. He threw it back to Tony, which began a long game of catch. As the game progressed, they attempted to bounce it off of the floor, walls, and ceiling. Only a mug and a book got knocked off of their shelves.

As they played, the sunlight from the window in the back door crept across the floor. Finally, Cash gently rolled the ball on the floor where it stopped in the middle of the floor.

"It has been hours. What could be taking so long?" he asked Tony.

Instead of replying, Tony hopped up and went to the window.

"Let's see," he said as he gazed out the window.

Cash joined him. The other train was at least as long as theirs. Each car was painted a different black-and-white pattern. It was somehow both simple and aggressive.

"Do you think they're another circus?" Cash wondered out loud.

"I dunno. Looks like it might be some sort of show. I don't see a name anywhere though," Tony replied.

A group of people from their circus, including Boris and Bella, was gathered near the front of the train.

"Let's go see what's going on," Cash hit Tony on the arm, turned, and headed for the door. Tony followed right behind. They walked quickly toward the crowd. Boris saw them coming and stepped a couple of paces away from the group. Cash jogged past the final car and stopped next to Boris.

"When are we leaving?" he asked the big man.

"No one knows anything," Boris answered. "Elon talked to the other train's conductor for a while and looked pretty angry. The conductor finally pointed him to that car there." Boris pointed toward a car farther down the line with white triangles painted along the top and bottom of the car, pointing towards the middle. The effect looked like two rows of pointy teeth. "He went in over an hour ago and hasn't come out."

Just then, the door slid open and Cash could see Elon in the doorway. Their ringmaster descended the steps, but another large figure loomed in the shadow of the doorway. Elon headed toward them. After a few moments, the other man emerged from the car and slowly strode down the steps. Cash couldn't believe what he was seeing. The man looked like a larger version of Elon.

Elon reached their group and, without a word, turned to face the approaching man. The tension in their ringmaster's body made it seem like he was braced for whatever was coming. The other man dominated Elon by at least a head. Dark curly hair brushed his shoulders. His very, very broad shoulders tapered down to a trim waist supported by legs like tree trunks. He wore black pants and a jacket over a black and white shirt. The domineering man smiled or maybe sneered, past Elon at the group that had gathered.

"Well, brother, it seems we are at an impasse!" The large man shouted, partly to Elon, but he made sure everyone in the group was paying attention. Elon's face appeared as stone and nothing gave away what he was thinking. Cash noticed another figure hiding in the doorway of the car with the teeth. Sacha emerged, walked over, and stood next to his father. Murmurs rose from the crowd along their train.

"It has been a long time since I have seen my brother," the big man continued. "A very long time." He stared down at Elon. "I thought it was time for a *reunion*. I keep hearing about the circus with the amazing acrobat. The circus that seemed to always stay one step ahead of me. But here we are." He took a step closer to Elon. "Where you can't get away." The last statement came out like a growl. Cash's heart began to race. *What did that mean?*

Elon's brother gave a quick nod in the direction of his engine, and the train's whistle blew. Doors slid open on more of the black and white cars and people emerged. At first, Cash couldn't tell if they were men or women. They all wore black pants and either a white, black, or striped shirt. Their hair was slicked back and many of them had their faces painted white. They swarmed together and formed a line behind Elon's brother and Sacha and stared menacingly at Elon and his circus. There must have been more than a hundred of them. Cash realized that Boris was no longer at his side. The big man had planted himself next to their ringmaster. Cash tugged Tony's sleeve and they confidently followed Boris to support their leader. Tension rose in the crowd as the brother continued his address to Elon's circus.

"In case my brother hasn't mentioned me, allow me to introduce myself. I am Louka, his older brother." The people in black and white crowded in behind Louka, and the brothers faced off. Louka continued in his reverberating baritone voice, "Since he and I have unfinished business, we'll be joining our circuses for the near future. While audiences adjust to my less traditional circus, we could benefit from your recent popularity and renown." With hawk eyes, Louka examined the crowd in front of him, starting with Boris. When he stopped in front of Cash, one side of his mouth raised in a scornful smile. "I'm particularly interested in getting to know you, my young star."

Louka walked along the front of their group, inspecting everyone. He then looped back to stand beside Sacha and addressed Elon's circus again.

"You all know my son Sacha and that he is intimately

familiar with your circus and routine. We spent the last week and a half planning an entirely new show that combines the greatest talents from both circuses. It's going to dazzle viewers with acts they never dreamed of! Tonight, the show will go on as you prepared. We will observe so we can finalize our plans and begin rehearsals for the new show tomorrow. Please, return to your regular schedules. For today, pretend like everything is normal. But now, head back to your cars, and we'll get these trains back to the circus."

Cash stood between Boris and Tony, dumbfounded. Glances at his friends showed that they were equally shocked. They stood silently as the crowd around them stirred and people slowly headed back to their cars. It didn't take too long to load everyone up, and for the conductors to move the trains back toward their setup.

As soon as the train stopped, Cash went out to the platform to see what would happen next. Two beefy men from Louka's circus approached Elon's car where they pounded on the door. When the ringmaster opened the door, one of the goons gestured to the red wagon. Cash watched as Elon followed them to the red wagon and went inside. The newly arrived circus began opening train car doors and unloading boxes and equipment. Then Cash spotted Lorenzo heading toward the big top and remembered that he had practice that afternoon. He yelled goodbye to Tony and hopped down. He was soon joined by Boris on the way to the tent.

As they passed the red wagon, they heard shouting from inside. Cash gestured toward the building and they crept to opposite sides of the front door to listen. The door flung open. One of Louka's bodyguards shoved Nina out of the door and she stumbled down the steps. She turned back toward the door with genuine surprise on her face.

The enormous man stared down at her and declared, "You no longer work here." He stepped back into the shadows of the red wagon and closed the door. Nina continued to stare at the door.

"Psst!" Cash tried to get her attention. "Nina," he whispered.

With a dazed expression, she looked at him.

"What is going on?" Cash's question didn't seem to register so he asked, "Why did they kick you out?"

"I don't know. Cash, I have no idea what's going on. They came in right behind me, then demanded that I open the safe. I wasn't going to, I never open it in front of people, but I looked at Elon and he nodded for me to do it. The brother looked at all the money and his eyes got really big and so greedy. Then they all went back to Elon's office. Except for the one who threw me out." Cash caught Boris' eye and gestured his head toward the back of the red wagon.

"Oh no! Do you think they meant I don't work in the red wagon anymore? Or at the circus anymore?" Fear danced across her eyes. "I don't have anywhere else to go. This has been my home for so long, I can't leave!"

"I'm sure it will be ok. Elon won't let anything happen to you," Cash reassured her. "Go back to your car and lay low for a while." Nina nodded and headed toward the train.

Cash snuck along the side of the red wagon, around the back, and rounded the far corner to where Boris was stationed under Elon's window. Boris cupped a hand around his ear and pointed up at the window with his other hand. Cash got as close as he could and breathed as quietly as possible to try and hear the conversation. He heard a low voice talking, then Elon exploded and Cash could clearly hear him yelling, but he couldn't understand the words.

He mouthed and barely whispered to Boris, "What language is that?"

Boris shook his head with a blank look and whispered his reply, "I'm not sure."

"But you can you understand it?" Cash asked. The big man nodded his affirmation and began whispering what he heard.

"Elon is saying 'You can't have my circus! I'll never work with you!'

Now Louka, 'I'm taking over your circus with or without you! You made your choice when you deserted me twenty years ago! Without you, my circus suffered. I suffered! You have a lot to pay back!'" This was followed by shuffling and the scrape of a chair on the wood floor. Chills of fear ran down Cash's arms and a pit formed in his stomach.

Louka's voice was quieter when he spoke again and Boris continued to translate.

"I was hoping we could come to an agreement, but it seems that you're being difficult, so we'll do this the difficult way." More indiscernible words and then Louka's final instructions. "Take him away. Lock him up! Make sure he can't leave." Cash and Boris looked at each other and crept back toward the front of the red wagon. Peering around Boris' big shoulders, Cash saw the goons leaving the building, each with an arm through Elon's, who was between them.

They half walked, half dragged Elon toward his car. He stumbled along with them. The larger lackey opened the door, pulled Elon up, and pushed him in. Then he leaned against the doorway and the other lackey left. He returned a couple of minutes later with a length of chain. Cash saw a glimpse of the ringmaster's shadow before the big flunkey slammed the door closed and took the chain. He ran the length through the handle, and then through one of the bars on the window. He took a padlock from his jacket pocket and hooked it through two chain links. He dropped the lock and it hit the side of the car with a thud. The guard descended the stairs and they both headed back toward the red wagon.

Boris grabbed Cash's arm and pulled him toward the bigtop.

"What just happened?" Cash whispered fiercely, looking back toward the goons to make sure they weren't being watched.

"I don't know. Elon didn't even put up a fight." Boris sped up his walk to get away quickly.

Cash's mind whirred as he tried to comprehend what was happening. Around him, the circus bustled on like normal and then they were at the entrance to the tent. He grabbed Boris' arm.

"Whatever is happening isn't good. We have to stick together. Tell everyone to meet in the kitchen after lunch."

"Ok. Have a good practice, Cash. And be careful," Boris replied with a stern look in his eyes.

"You too."

———

Cash's legs were throbbing as he sat down to lunch. During practice, everyone was on edge, which meant mistakes. For every mistake, Lorenzo made them run a lap around the ring. Cash stared down at his tray of food and wondered if he was more hungry or more tired. Boris, Bella, and Maya crumbled into their seats around him.

"How about that practice?" Bella commented quietly.

"Did you see everyone from Louka's circus? They were sitting in the stands watching your every move," Maya added and put a forkful of mashed potatoes into her mouth and closed her eyes.

"I saw them when we ran laps," Cash looked at Bella.

"There were a lot of laps," she said, meeting his gaze.

"Two of them looked right at me and started whispering and laughing at me when I ran by them." Cash finally decided he had enough energy to eat and took a giant bite of spaghetti.

"Well, at least they weren't whistling at you," Bella added. Boris finished a drink of his water and slammed his cup on the table so hard the contents splashed Cash and Maya.

"Sorry! I just can't believe what is going on- what is happening to *our* circus! Who do they think they are?" The big man exclaimed.

As if in reply, Louka stood up on the edge of the staff platform and addressed the crowd.

"Ladies! Gentlemen! Clowns and carnies! I know this change is a shock for many of you, half of you to be exact. My dear bother wishes he could join us, but he seems to have fallen ill shortly after my arrival."

Cash looked worriedly at Boris.

"Don't be concerned! You are in good hands - the best of hands! My circus is on the cutting edge of entertainment. We have acts that viewers - and performers - have never dreamed of. While my brother's acts are more...

traditional, the reputation of his show and the popularity of his acts are nothing to scoff at. Townies clearly like your predictable escapades."

A tray slammed down at the table behind Cash. A quick turn of his head revealed Lorenzo standing with his hands on the edges of his tray, looking like he wanted to murder someone.

Louka continued his monologue.

"Nonetheless, my innovative acts combined with your crowd-pleasing fodder will catapult our joined circus into worldwide fame! I would like for you all to be the first that I welcome to Louka Mastiff's World-Renowned Circus of the Future!" Louka's troupe clapped and cheered, while Elon's people rustled in their seats and looked around uncomfortably. Elon's absence made the announcement feel even more foreboding.

While half of the tent cheered, Cash leaned in to speak quietly to Bella and Maya.

"Elon isn't sick. When we were on our way to practice earlier, we heard an argument in the red wagon and then saw two of Louka's thugs drag Elon out and lock him in his car." Maya's eyebrows twitched with surprise and Bella looked shaken. With big eyes, she covered her mouth with her hand. Cash continued, "We can't talk here, but something very bad is happening."

Louka silenced the crowd and resumed his speech.

"The show tonight will go on as my brother intended. But starting tomorrow, we will close for a few days while we practice our new, combined acts and finalize the first show for the Circus of the Future." More cheers erupted, but Louka continued. "There will be changes. Many of you will find yourselves in new roles. If you are a headliner now, don't count on being a headliner tomorrow. With so many talented professionals, we can't keep everyone in the same positions. But don't worry, there will be a place for every one of you here at my circus." He gave a grotesque grin and bowed to his audience. "Return to your meals and enjoy your last show tonight. Check in at the red wagon tomorrow morning at 8 am to find out your new roles."

"I have a bad feeling about this," muttered Maya as she stabbed a carrot with her fork. She lifted it to eye level and stared at it. "A very bad feeling."

CHAPTER 20

A NEW PARTNER

Bella gasped awake at the sound of something thudding on the wood floor of her car. She quickly sat up and stared at her roommate in terror which was quickly followed by anger. Elena, her bunk-mate, was getting dressed as rapidly as possible by trying to pull on a sweater and put shoes on at the same time.

"What are you doing?!" A glance from Elena to Maya's bed told her that the younger girl had already left.

"It's 7:55. The new roles are being posted this morning. In five minutes! I don't want to be late," Elena said slightly breathless.

"Shoot! I don't either!" Bella threw off her sheets, stood up, and turned around looking for clothes. She found the sweater she had tossed on her trunk last night and a pair of pants. Getting dressed nearly as quickly as Elena, the two women exited their car to find most of Elon's circus flowing toward the red wagon.

"Do you think Louka's people already know what they're going to be doing?" Elena asked, looking around.

"Sure looks that way. I have a feeling this wasn't a

last-minute plan for them."

"I have no idea where I'm going to end up," interjected Elena. "I really don't. At least you don't have anything to worry about."

"Me? I'm super nervous. Who knows what's about to happen!"

"Are you kidding? You're in the most popular act with the star of the circus. I really don't think they're going to change that." Elena sounded confident.

"Yeah, I suppose that's possible," Bella responded, unconvinced.

They reached the edge of the crowd, but Bella spotted Cash, Boris, Maya, and Tony near the front.

"I'll see you back at the car," Bella squeezed Elena's arm and pushed her way through her fellow acrobats, clowns, and workers to take her spot next to Boris. He leaned down, wrapped an arm around her, and kissed the top of her head without saying anything. His eyes were fixed on the red wagon. The door opened and the crony who had ousted Nina the day before squinted at the light then grunted at the crowd. Without a word, he tramped down the stairs, raised a hammer, and nailed a long sheet to the side of the building. He retreated back up the stairs just as silently and the crowd pressed forward. Boris pushed back against the flux and pulled Maya, Bella, Cash, and Tony in front of him. Bella could see that the paper had a long column of names listed alphabetically on the left and their role, overseer, and call time on the right.

"Cookhouse? That's fine," Maya shrugged. "I'll get to hang out with Helen and Tony and not have to deal with Lorenzo all day."

Bella thought she noticed a blush on Maya's cheeks but looked for her name on the list instead of asking her about it.

"Strongman still. No change for me," Boris read the list from behind her.

"Me either. Kitchen like always," added Tony.

Bella scanned the first few lines until she saw her name just as Cash found his role and he said quietly, "Flying Trapeze finale with Coco…"

Bella's whole body froze momentarily. Then she looked at Cash whose face showed total shock.

"Aerial silk act? What is an aerial silk act?! I don't even know what that is!" she exclaimed.

"And who is Coco?!" Cash looked around at his friends and stopped on Bella. "I've only ever flown with you! They can't take you out!" His entire face turned red and he looked like he was going to speak a lot more of what was on his mind.

"Let's move out of the way," Boris corralled his friends to the edge of the crowd and out of the way of the rest of the circus finding out their new roles. The majority of the reactions they overheard were negative or at best neutral. It seemed that Elon's circus was getting demoted at a very rapid pace.

Cash and Bella stared at each other, both starting sentences and not finding the words to express their anger.

"This is ridiculous!" Bella whispered angrily. "They can't do this to me, to CASH. He hasn't even been back on the traps that long!"

"Yeah! And it takes time to get to know someone and trust them in the air! I don't want to be with this Coco person!" Cash added.

Bonkers interrupted and despite his drawn-on smiling face, Bella realized the clown was more sad than she had ever seen him.

"Bonkers, what happened?" Maya asked him, putting a hand on his arm.

"You're still a clown aren't you?" Bella whispered.

He shook his head and then dropped his chin toward his chest.

"Assistant to the animal keeper," Bonkers whispered.

Everyone stared at him in shock.

"Barnaby is going to *love* that. But even worse, it looks like all the clowns got reassigned. I don't think there are going to *be* any clowns." Bonkers added.

"What?!" Boris roared. "You can't have a circus without clowns!"

Maya put her other hand on Boris while he tried to stutter out another sentence in his anger.

"Let's all calm down. We're going to be OK," she intoned calmly then moved toward Cash and Bella. With a hand on each of their shoulders, she said, "Things will all work out."

Everyone took a deep breath to try and calm their racing emotions. It hardly helped.

"Yeah, you're right. We've gotten through a lot. We'll get through this. Maybe it won't be that bad," Cash said, now a bit more level-headed. He tried to smile but didn't feel that positive.

———

Cash headed to practice early to warm up and look for his new partner. He glanced over his shoulder as he scanned the other acrobats in the ring. Many of the new acrobats were men. In their tight black and white outfits, they stuck out from Elon's crew. The outfits were almost dizzying with all of the patterns. Some outfits were white with black lightning bolts all over. Others covered the acrobat in black and white squares like a chessboard while other ones were white on the left side of the body and black on the right. No two were exactly alike. He spotted a new blonde girl, but she was warming up with the tumblers. As he looked around, Bella wandered in looking uncomfortable. She traced the edge of the crowd before sitting on the front row of the bleachers. He tried to catch her eye, but she had her elbows on her knees and was staring at the dirt.

Lorenzo entered and took his usual place in his chair, but didn't address the crowd. Instead, he crossed his legs and tapped his knee impatiently. Suddenly, darkness engulfed the tent as the lights went out. A few surprised murmurs arose from the players on the floors. A single spotlight beamed next to Lorenzo's chair to illuminate Louka. In the dim edges of the light, Lorenzo rolled his eyes.

"Welcome to the first practice of our *new* circus!" he bellowed into the near darkness. He paused. After a few seconds of silence, he looked around expectantly. Someone near Cash started clapping. The crowd gave a half-hearted clap. "You might have noticed some changes already, some new additions and the removal of old, tired acts. Instead of clowns, we have the aerial silk act, trampoline athletes, and sand painters in our *cirque moderne.*" Cash shot Boris a confused look. The big man shrugged in response.

"However, there is one act from your old circus that I could never get rid of. But with my genius additions and changes, it will be more popular than ever. By taking your rising star and pairing him with the belle of my show, we will dazzle audiences with new wonders," Louka paused for dramatic effect. "I want to introduce you to our new headlining act: Cash and Coco!"

Louka's performers burst into applause. Before he knew it, people were pushing Cash forward toward Louka, who was waving him to the front. He scanned the crowd again for a sign of his new partner and the fate ahead. As he took his place next to Louka, Cash heard the quiet sounds of bells behind him and turned around. His heart stopped beating and the room grew silent as he took in the young woman walking toward him. She was the most beautiful girl he had ever seen. With confidence, she walked toward Cash and Louka while waving at the gathered crowd with a smile on her face.

"Cash, I'd like you to meet Coco Lovely," Louka said a little louder than necessary.

Cash's mouth stopped working because all the saliva had evaporated. Louka laughed and smacked him on the back.

Leaning his head toward Cash he said under his breath, "I see you have figured out why we call her Coco Lovely."

Louka leaned toward his star and asked her how she was finding the new location.

Cash came back to his senses and reached out his hand to introduce himself.

"Cash Connor. I look forward to working with you." Coco's hand pressed into his and she held on. "I've heard a lot about you, Cash." Her voice was clear and confident.

Was Cash imagining it, or did she have a knowing sparkle in her eyes? Her beautiful brown eyes. Looking down, he quickly realized the source of the bell sounds. She wore a wrist-to-ankle white leotard with a silver streak swirling around her that started at her chest and wound down her left leg. The silver streak was decorated with tiny bells, so she trailed music when she walked. Cash wondered if he'd be able to hear it in the air as they swung toward each other.

Across the crowd of onlookers, Cash caught Bella's eye. Her crossed arms and stern face snapped him out of the daze that Coco put him in. Louka put one arm around Cash and the other around Coco and turned them both towards Lorenzo.

"I'm sure you two will enjoy your first rehearsal. As long as Lorenzo sticks to the routine we discussed," the ringmaster directed his comment toward Lorenzo, not them. The old man grunted in reply and led them to the trampolines to begin their practice. Cash glanced over his shoulder to the rest of the acrobats. He saw Bella edging her way toward acrobats from Louka's circus that he assumed were on the aerial silks.

"Attention!" Lorenzo hissed at him to get his attention. "Now, I've never had so little time to get two acrobats ready for a new routine. You both must give *everything* over the next three days."

He led them through a grueling practice. Afterward, he addressed them.

"I don't think you'll be terrible," Lorenzo said reluctantly. "Drink water, get dinner, sleep well tonight. Tomorrow we start putting the sections together. Go!"

Cash and Coco headed toward the bleachers to get their things.

"Does he tend to be a little dramatic?" Coco nodded toward Lorenzo as she reached for her water.

"Little doesn't begin to cover it. Our routine is basically my old routine, with your section added in, which you clearly know. You seem super comfortable on the traps, so we'll nail it in no time."

"I loved your full-full, and your gazelles are perfect. You're so effortless in the air, I've never seen anything like it." Coco's face lit up as she spoke with him, but just as quickly the smile disappeared and she turned to block the view of the other acrobats. Cash looked over her shoulder and saw a tall, strikingly good-looking acrobat staring daggers at them.

"Who is the tall guy from the aerial silk act who looks like he wants to kill me?" Cash glanced back down at her as he asked quietly.

"That's Anders. My former partner. He is not happy about the change in lineup," Coco replied with a quick glance.

"I can see that."

"He's probably jealous too. You know how it is when you fly with someone and spend all day practicing together…" She risked another glance at Anders.

"Uh, sure." Cash muttered, but he didn't know what she meant. Bella had always seemed like an older sister. Even if she weren't dating Boris, he couldn't think of her any other way. "Bella is, or, was my partner. She's over with the aerial silk acrobats now." He pointed her out to Coco.

Bella was staring up at the tent. Cash could make out Jojo and other prop hands and riggers he didn't recognize in the scaffolding. Suddenly, they released long, silk ropes that unfurled and almost reached the ground. Bella and the other acrobats tugged on their silks. Bella, Cash, and Coco watched as Louka's acrobats deftly began scaling the silks. In synchrony, they wrapped various limbs in the silks and performed twists and flips. Never having seen anything like it, Cash was mesmerized by the grace with which they moved. It looked like they were dancing.

"I better go," Coco put her hand on his upper arm and whispered in his ear. Then she bounded off after Anders and Cash tried to ignore the heat on his cheeks.

———

Helen looked at the clock above the serving area. Only two hours and six minutes had passed since *Bertina* had entered her kitchen and taken over. She bit her lip in agitation as she watched Louka's chef saunter around her kitchen like an agitated bull, complaining about Helen's organization, about her team, about her *recipes*. The intruder stood nearly six feet tall and seemed nearly as wide as one of the elephants. Frizzy red hair stuck out from under her white chef's hat. Helen tapped her foot in annoyance as Bertina set a pot to boil without salting the water. She let out an exasperated sigh and turned to check the stock in the pantry. As she did, Louka entered the kitchen with hurricane-level force. He caught her eye and in two long strides was following and forcing her into the pantry. Helen turned to face him, but he kept coming until she was backed up against the wall between two metal storage shelves.

"If you have a problem with my workers and with my circus, you keep your mouth shut! How *dare* you question my choices to my workers! You think you know better than me?!" Louka towered over Helen as he yelled at her. "*Do not* try to poison my people against me."

"How dare *I*? How dare *you* show up here like nothing happened!" Helen stood up to her full height and took a step toward Louka. She yelled up at his face. "I can't believe your gall and your stupid, stupid PRIDE. Your own brother *died* and you didn't bother to show up to the funeral. How *dare you* not even reach out to me or to Elon. It has been thirteen years, Louka! What kind of disgusting, selfish person doesn't even acknowledge when his brother dies?!"

Helen's hands were balled in fists as the brother-in-law and sister-in-law fumed at each other. Louka reached his hand back and Helen braced for impact. With a roar, Louka swatted a bag of flour off the shelf toward Helen. The bag exploded on the floor and a white cloud of flour enveloped Helen. Even though she saw it coming, the flour invaded her nose and mouth and sent her into a fit of coughing.

As the cloud settled, Helen realized that Louka's face was an uncomfortable couple of inches from hers. Particles of flour dissolved into the beads of sweat on his cheeks.

"If you question me again," he whispered, "you're done." His eyes drilled into hers, and then he raised his eyebrows. "Do you understand?"

Helen coughed into her elbow one more time and nodded her head without looking at him. He took a couple steps back and brushed flour from his jacket.

"And Helen," he turned back to her. She looked at him with disdain, "I don't want any problems with Cash. Keep your little friends in check. I'll know if you're planning something." Without waiting for her to respond, Louka turned and exited the pantry. Helen dropped onto a bucket of pickles and put her head in her hands. She listened to Louka greet Bertina out in the kitchen and didn't begin to relax until she heard him exit out the back flaps. The well of pain in her chest cracked open and the familiar pangs of loss and grief from Henri's death made it hard to focus on anything else.

Her reminiscence was interrupted by a light voice.

"I've been reassigned to the kitchen!" the voice announced cheerfully.

Helen raised her head and Maya gasped.

"You look like a ghost!" Maya cried in surprise.

Helen chuckled and wiped at the flour on her face, but not before Maya noticed the tear-streaked paths on her cheeks.

"Well, looks like we've both been reassigned." The older woman replied. Maya looked quizzically at Helen.

Running a hand through her hair, Helen responded, "I've been demoted. Louka sent his own 'chef' in here and she just started bossing everyone around. Even me!"

Maya furrowed her brow, but Helen encouraged her.

"I'm glad you're here. We need more of us in the kitchen. I don't like that one of Louka's people is running the kitchen. This is the hub of the circus for the workers. We need as many eyes and ears as we can get. I'm pretty sure Louka's people are reporting back to him."

Maya's eyebrows raised in surprise and Helen told her about the interaction with Louka. "After Bertina showed up, I vented to Tony, but only him! Or so I thought," Helen reflected.

"Ok. We're going to have to be careful. I have bad feelings about how things are going," Maya responded.

"Me too. Louka is unhinged. He's likely to do anything to maintain his power," Helen confirmed.

"If you distract Bertina, I'll give Tony a heads up," Maya whispered.

"Ok."

The women left the pantry and Helen headed towards Bertina at the stove while Maya searched for Tony. She looked around the kitchen, glanced into the dining room, and finally found him out back organizing empty vegetable bins for the next shopping trip.

She suddenly appeared next to him, "Are we alone?"

Tony jumped, flushed, and responded, "Yeah, I think so." Maya still looked around to make sure and grabbed his arm to pull him away from the edge of the cookhouse.

"What's going on?" he shook her arm off, then looked around too, unsure what he was looking for.

"We have to be careful," Maya looked up at him with her big, confident blue eyes. He gave her a quizzical look. "Your conversation with Helen earlier got back to Louka. He just threatened her in the pantry."

"What?!"

"Shhh! Don't draw attention. Louka's people must be spying on us," she continued urgently.

"No way. That sounds totally paranoid," Tony insisted.

"He knew about your conversation and Helen didn't remember seeing anyone around. Someone must have been hiding so they could listen."

"Maybe it was a fluke," Tony replied half-heartedly.

"And maybe it's a fluke that he chose his people to lead every team and crew around here. It doesn't seem like Louka is combining our circuses. I'd say it's a hostile take-over." Maya filled him in on Elon's current situation. Tony shook his head while trying to comprehend the unbelievable changes.

One of Bertina's sous chefs popped his head out the back of the cookhouse.

"Oy! Team meetin'. Let's go!" he yelled in a thin British accent.

Maya and Tony looked at each other one last time and Tony led the way back in. The kitchen crew circled around the prep table. In unusual fashion, no one in the kitchen was speaking. Bertina bustled in and forced her large frame into the circle. She wiped her hands on her apron and addressed the crowd.

"As you might have noticed, there are some changes in the kitchen. I expect immediate obedience when I give a command. No games, no jokes, no complaining. You will not be late, you will not miss work. Any questions?" No one moved.

"Some of you worked with Helen. She is no longer in charge. She will be cooking and serving alongside you. Eric will oversee the shopping." Bertina nodded toward the gangly man who had called them into the meeting. "If we need something from town, you tell him. Where's Tony?" Tony raised a hand silently. Bertina looked him up and down with disgust. "You're on dishes now." Tony's heart started beating quicker.

"If you have questions, figure it out yourself. We're done here. Dinner's in an hour!" Bertina dismissed them.

Everyone scattered to their positions.

Tony leaned down and whispered to Maya, "It's like they don't want us to leave." She looked up at him and they exchanged concerned glances.

Cash woke from his nap to screams and thuds. Flinging off the blanket he ran to his window in a panic and pulled back the curtain. His heart raced as he watched people diving to the ground. Only as the fog of sleep lifted did he realize that the screams were laughs. The thuds were the sound of people hitting a ball over a net. His heart began to slow down as he observed what must be a game.

Curious, he stepped onto the back platform of the caboose and leaned on the railing in the dimming late afternoon sunlight to watch. A tall net was stretched between two poles and there was a group of Louka's people on each side. They swooped and swiped at a tan ball to get it over the net to the other team. The ball fell to the ground and the team on the opposite side cheered. His eyes fell on one of the girls at the back of the group cheering. His heart started beating faster again but for a different reason. Coco had traded her white leotard for black warmup pants and a black and white striped sweater. Her shiny black hair swung from the top of her head as she laughed and congratulated her teammates. Before they were ready, the ball came back over the net at them. It headed in Coco's direction and she casually swung at it but it was just out of reach. When she jogged to recover the ball, her eyes connected with Cash's. She grabbed the ball and continued in his direction.

"Hi." She said with a smile as she tucked the ball under her arm.

Cash blinked while his brain tried to compute the next normal thing to do.

"Hi again." He hoped he sounded more coherent than he felt.

"Do you want to join us?" she nodded toward her comrades. "We need one more."

"I've never played." In fact, he'd never even seen this game, but he didn't mention that.

"It's easy. Well, the idea is simple. Your team has three tries to get the ball over the net and if it hits the ground on the other side, your team gets a point. Come join us." She smiled at him and before he knew what he was doing, he was climbing down the stairs of the platform and walking beside her.

"I found our sixth!" She joyfully yelled at her teammates and skipped once. When they joined the other four, Coco gave quick introductions that Cash was certain he wouldn't remember. The others nodded at him. The ball started flying and players jumped and dove for the ball. Cash took a tumble and bumped the ball up to a burly-looking teammate. The burly guy tipped the ball over the net where it fell to the ground among the opposing players scrambling to get to it. The ball quickly came back over and Coco popped it up and over the net, only to have it returned aggressively and hit the ground out of reach.

"Game point!" A short red-headed girl on the other team yelled.

Cash and Coco were up by the net. She leaned in so their shoulders were touching and tilted her head towards the surly, thin acrobat across the net from them, "Watch this guy, he'll try to tip it, but you have a couple inches on him". The other team lobbed the ball over and their teammates in the back returned it over the net. Cash watched the ball pass from the redhead girl, to one of her teammates and finally toward the surly man in front of him. His opponent had his eye on the ball as it descended toward him.

Cash jumped right after the other man did. But instead of tapping the ball, his opponent swung down at the ball, right onto Cash's outstretched hands. Pain shot through his left hand and when he landed it took a moment to realize that his teammates were congratulating him. They won! Coco looked at him. Instead of the glowing congratulation he desperately hoped for, her eyes were angry and she grabbed his left wrist.

"What was that crack?" She hissed at him, pulling his wrist up to examine his hand. His middle finger was already swelling and turning a murky purple. Coco began pushing and pressing closer and closer to the center of the swelling until Cash retracted his hand in pain. She grabbed him by the elbow and turned before anyone else noticed what they were talking about.

"You go and break your finger on the first day of practice?" Coco said it quietly, but the anger behind her question made it feel like a scream to Cash. He didn't understand why she was so angry.

"You can't fly with a broken finger. You *have* to fly, Cash. You *have* to!"

"Why?" he asked her.

"Because if you don't, he will punish *both* of us!"

"What are you talking about?" He was still missing something.

"Louka is counting on you as the star act. And he takes everything personally. So, so personally. Even injuries. He'll see it as you trying to sabotage the new show, and," Her voice broke. "He'll make sure you remember not let it happen again."

Before he could respond, she pulled him behind the caboose and pulled up the sleeve of her warmup suit. On the inside of her bicep were a series of circular scars. Scars the size of a cigar. Cash's eyes grew wide and anger burned in his chest.

"Are you saying he did that to you?"

"It's never *him*, but always one of his men." Coco rolled down her sleeve. "Cash, he's going to punish me too since I got you to play in the first place." Tears filled her eyes as she looked up at him.

Guilt seared him. How had he been so stupid?! Thoughts flooded his brain, then he knew what he had to do.

He put a hand on her arm. "It's going to be OK."

"How? Your finger is clearly broken." The fear in her eyes gutted him.

He pulled her into a hug and reassured her, "I promise, Coco. Louka won't know that anything happened."

She was still stiff as she replied, "There's no way. He knows everything."

"Will you try to trust me?" he asked. She pulled away and looked up at him unsure.

"Ok."

He gave her one more squeeze with his good arm and left to find Helen.

———

As Cash approached the back of the cookhouse, Tony saw him and his friend's face transformed from his normal happy-go-lucky to looking like he had seen a ghost.

"Hey man, what's up?" Tony asked nervously.

"I need to see Helen," responded Cash.

"Nope. Not here." Tony hurriedly turned him around back the way he had come.

"Are you crazy? I *really* need to see her now."

Tony kept glancing around, then smiled nonchalantly at one of Louka's aerial silk acrobats heading for dinner.

When they were out of earshot, Tony whispered.

"Stuff went down in the kitchen. Helen's not in charge anymore. One of Louka's people is - *Bertina*." Tony scrunched his face as he said it. "His people are all over. They're like ants. They're spying on us, man. If you need Helen, the last place to talk to her is the kitchen. Go around into the cookhouse and I'll tell her to find you when she has a break."

What was happening at the circus?

"I can't go into the cookhouse. People will see my finger." Cash said in a low tone.

"What are *you* talking about?" Tony asked, confused.

"I broke my finger playing a game with Coco and I really can't *not* fly right now. I'll explain later. But I need Helen's you know… *ability* before anyone notices."

Tony muttered curses that Cash rarely heard his friend say.

"Ok. Go back to the 'boose. I'll tell Helen to meet you there after dinner. I have to get back before *Bertina* realizes I'm gone. Hopefully, no one notices you're not at dinner," Tony directed.

Cash turned to go, but before Tony let him go, he said with a serious tone to his voice, "And don't talk to anyone on the way." Cash nodded slightly and set off for the caboose.

Cash's stomach rumbled as he sat up on his bed and he regretted not having Tony grab him some dinner before he headed to the 'boose. He was examining his throbbing finger, which was twice its normal size when he heard a quiet knock on the door. He heaved himself off the bed and padded to the door. Quietly, he unlocked the door and opened it to reveal Helen. She gave him a tired smile and he noticed circles under her eyes and the pale color of her face.

"Long day?" He asked as he moved aside to let her in. Helen sighed a loaded sigh and brushed back some of the black and gray strands of hair that had fallen loose.

Helen seated herself at his table and he gingerly pulled out the chair opposite her and sat, resting his hands in his lap beneath the table.

"Very long day," she smiled weakly and propped her chin up on her fist. Cash noticed a tiredness in her face he hadn't seen before.

"Tony mentioned the changes in the kitchen," Cash offered.

"Mmmhmmm… he also mentioned you needed my help. And that you skipped dinner." Her eyes sharpened as she said this, examining him for clues.

Cash took his hands from his lap and rested them on the table.

"Cash! What happened?" The older woman slid her fingers under his forearm and gently raised his arm to inspect the wounded finger.

"I was playing a game with Coco and some of her friends." At that, Helen turned her gaze to him, her eyes suddenly piercing.

"What were you doing with them?" she whispered.

"Nothing. Just playing a game. It was harmless." Cash said the words casually, but his stomach pulled into a knot.

"Nothing is harmless with them, Cash. You have to be more careful. Not just because of this," she looked down at his finger. "But with *them*. You don't know Louka like I do. There isn't a good bone in his body, Cash. You *watched* what he did to Elon. His being here is very, very dangerous to us, and everyone like us. He will do anything for money and if you cross him, he will not forget it. Who knows about your hand? Is there any way it will get back to him?"

Cash felt ill. "I told Tony when I came to look for you."

Helen nodded.

"And Coco was there when it happened, but she pulled me away from everyone else quickly," Cash continued.

Helen grimaced at this information.

"You've put both of us in a bad position, Cash. If I heal you right now, she'll start asking questions and possibly tell Louka. If I don't, you'll suffer at his hands since you can't perform."

"Oh, saints. And Coco too."

"What do you mean?" Helen asked.

"She was really worried when she saw my hand. Seems to think that if I don't perform, she won't perform and then Louka will punish her too."

Helen stared off past Cash for a moment.

"That might work in our favor." Her focus shifted back to him. "I'm going to heal you, but you have to talk to Coco. No matter what she says, do not tell her how it got healed, and make sure she isn't going to say anything about this to anyone."

"Ok. I'll talk to her tomorrow at practice," Cash promised.

Helen put his wounded hand flat between her palms.

"Cash," she paused until he made eye contact. "That is if she hasn't told anyone already. Conversations from the kitchen got to Louka in a matter of hours. If she did rat you out, I imagine Louka will be looking for you in the morning. For your sake, I hope you can trust her. But I wouldn't count on it."

They sat in grim silence with Cash's injured hand sandwiched between Helen's hands. His finger grew warm. When the sensation shifted to cool and tingly, Helen pulled her hands away to reveal five normal fingers. He bent his fingers in awe. Though he had been at the receiving end of Helen's gift before, this was the first time he witnessed it.

"That's so amazing," he whispered.

Helen smiled at him.

"Do you really think Coco will tell Louka?" he asked, getting serious again.

"I don't trust any of them, Cash."

He groaned at her response.

CHAPTER 21

GETTING OUT

Cash was laughing so hard he could barely breathe. He grabbed his stomach as it started to cramp.

"And then the monkey threw the pie right in my face!" Boris bellowed as he finished a story about one of his early, and unsuccessful, acts. Everyone in the small group laughed at the recounting. Cash wiped water from his eyes with one hand and suddenly felt someone holding his right hand. Startled, Cash looked over to find that Coco had silently joined the group. Heat radiated from his face and his breath caught in his chest at the end of a laugh. He was shocked by her forwardness. Then she grabbed each of his fingers and he realized what she was doing. She looked up at him with an inscrutable face then dragged him by the wrist out of the arena and into the hallway leading to the dressing rooms.

She stopped and gaped at him.

"How? What?" She sputtered then pulled his hand toward her face and gestured at it incredulously. "Your finger was purple and swollen and definitely broken yesterday."

"Shhhhh. Not so loud." Cash panicked that someone would overhear them. "Don't worry about it?"

"Don't worry about it? That's *all* I'm going to do. Tell me how this is possible," Coco demanded.

"I can't tell you. But it's better, and we can go on with our routine like normal," Cash tried to end the conversation.

"But it doesn't make any sense."

"I'm sorry, Coco. Please don't ask me about it. I really can't say anything." Cash didn't want to beg, but he would to keep Helen's secret.

Coco stared at him, then her face softened and she exhaled.

"OK. I don't get it, but I'm so glad you can perform." She closed her eyes. "So glad," she whispered. She opened her eyes and examined his hand once more, gentler this time. "I can't believe it."

Cash's heartbeat slowed back down and he realized how close they were standing. Her smell reminded him of the flowers that were in his yard growing up. Were they lilies?

"Guess we should head to practice." Coco dropped his hand and snapped Cash out of his reminiscence. She turned to go.

"Yeah. Wait!" Cash suddenly remembered his conversation with Helen. Coco turned and looked at him, eyebrows up. "Could we… or… could you not tell anyone about this? About my finger?"

She looked at him and it seemed to Cash that she was having an internal debate.

Finally, she replied, "Sure. It's our secret." With a smile, she turned confidently and stepped out toward the arena for practice.

Practice went as smoothly as it could go. Cash's finger

felt completely normal. His grip was strong on the bar and when he supported Coco. He left practice feeling confident until he remembered his friends' doubts about his new partner. Suddenly, he felt exposed and nervous that she knew that something suspicious had happened. He wondered how bad it would be if word got back to Louka. Would his act get taken away? Would Helen get locked up like Elon? Cash bit his thumbnail as he headed to the cookhouse for dinner.

———

There was just enough warmth on the breeze to make Cash forget that fall would soon turn to winter. In a rare occasion, he and all of his friends had the day off and were heading into town. Tony and Maya were a few paces ahead of him. Boris, Bella, and Helen were having an animated conversation behind. And next to him, Coco radiated an intoxicating warmth, or was that his imagination? She was talking about some town she visited with her family when she was young, but Cash was more preoccupied with her presence than her words.

As they neared the exit of the circus, Tony turned around, walking backward, to address them. With a hilariously accurate impression of Elon, he chided, "Don't do anything to embarrass me, you miscreants!" Everyone, including Tony, laughed. Suddenly, the ground shook and Tony stumbled backward, hitting the ground hard. Everyone else managed to stay on their feet, but barely. A tearing sound filled the atmosphere so loud that Cash felt it in his chest. The grass under them rippled and suddenly a crack in the earth appeared under Tony and started spreading in opposite directions. Tony's eyes grew large and he scrambled backwards to get off the crack, but he wasn't fast enough.

The crack became a large gap as the two sides of the earth drew away from each other. With a scream, Tony tumbled down the newly formed cliff. Maya wavered on the edge which quickly collapsed as the crevice grew into a small canyon and she fell in after Tony. As the earth continued to part, Cash watched as Bella, Boris, and Helen all plunged, crashed, and tumbled into the depths of the earth. Fear locked Cash's body and he felt a hand grasp his wrist as the earth crumbled beneath his feet. He fell, then jerked to a halt as Coco's grip stopped his descent. Hanging on the side of the cliff he looked up at her strained face.

"I'm sorry, I can't, I can't!" she cried.

He felt his wrist slipping under her trembling fingers as she tried to desperately hold on. He was acutely aware of a burning sensation as her nails dug into his flesh, trying to keep him from dropping.

Tears trailed down her cheeks as she let out a cry. Their fingers connected for one more second and then they weren't. Cash was plummeting. His head was light and it felt like his stomach floated out of his body. Echoing laughter started quietly and then bounced all around, surrounding him. Next to Coco's weeping frame, Louka stood laughing… laughing… laughing.

Cash awoke with a jump, his heart pounding, turning quickly in his bed to make sure he wasn't actually falling to his death. Reality settled in and he realized the darkness was the familiar darkness of the caboose. He wiped sweat from his forehead as he tried to catch his breath. Once the sound of his heart quieted in his ears he heard the subtle hard-breathing of Tony sleeping across the room. He took a few breaths and got up. Quietly, he walked to the window and looked out at the moon-doused circus. No cracks or canyons. It was only a dream, but the most real-feeling dream he had ever had. He got back in bed but stayed wide awake until the moon turned to faint lights of morning and Tony began to stir.

A few leaves crunched as Cash quietly left the 'boose in the early light of the morning, trying to shake off the intensity of the dream. He stood on the platform looking out over the circus. Sadness spread in his chest as he gazed at the spot where Magda's tent would have been. He thought about her book with dream interpretation notes. His dream from the night before seemed more real, more literal than his other dreams. He doubted that the earth was going to open up under his feet, but he had a dreadful feeling that he and his friends were in danger now that Louka was at the circus. The days since his arrival had been weird, but he hadn't sensed any real danger. Now, he would be on alert.

Normally, when he woke early, he'd head to the cookhouse to hang out with Helen and her boys, but that didn't seem as fun with Bertina now in charge. He still had an hour until breakfast. Cash wandered past the animals and stopped to say good morning to Major and Flora. Quickly climbing over the wooden fence that contained the elephants when they weren't traveling, Cash sat on the top beam and clicked his tongue. Major turned his big head and sauntered over. Cash gave him a scratch along the ears. Across the pen, Flora drank from the water trough with one eye on Cash.

"What? Don't want any pets this morning?" Cash directed at the female elephant. As if she understood, she shook her head and sprayed water from her trunk in Cash's direction. Laughing at the snarky animal, Cash hopped back off the fence.

With nowhere else to go, Cash headed toward the big top. The tent was now a combination of Louka and Elon's tents. The red top remained, but during the night, Louka's tent master and crew replaced the sidewalls with the ones from their tent. Giant black and white triangles on the sidewalls interlocked and gave the impression of large teeth or daggers emerging from the ground.

He slipped in the back door and walked through the dressing area. Mirrors and vanities lined the walls and costumes hung on racks for easy access. The silence in such a normally busy place made him uncomfortable. He moved into the main ring. It was so similar to Elon's, and yet strange and unfamiliar. The bleachers remained the same, but the black and white pattern from the outside was repeated inside which made it dizzying to look around too quickly. Mercifully, the rigging for his act was the same. Familiar. Comfortable.

"Up early, aren't we?" Cash whipped around to find the source of the voice. Sacha. He hadn't heard anyone come in and didn't like the feeling of someone sneaking up on him.

"Just visualizing the routine to get ready for dress rehearsal. It's an acrobat thing," Cash hoped he sounded casual.

"Uh-huh." Sacha stepped forward and looked Cash up and down. "Sure you're feeling up to it since your injury?"

Cash's mind went momentarily blank with fear. How did Sacha know about his finger? Then he quickly felt lightheaded as he realized Coco must have told someone.

"I saw it, remember," Sacha continued. "Never seen an acrobat fall from that height before. And unconscious too. You really cheated death on that one."

Cash felt his blood flow return as he realized which injury Sacha was talking about.

"Doc patched me up good. Once I realized it was a freak accident and the likelihood of it happening again to me is so low, I didn't have a problem flying again." Cash turned to look at Sacha. The look on Sacha's face told Cash that he clearly did not believe him.

Sacha turned away to look out over the ring again.

"The new changes are better, aren't they? My father really knows how to run a circus."

"Hard to tell since we haven't performed in front of an audience yet," Cash replied, sending the conversation back to Sacha.

"Yeah. And it's too bad we'll only have one show here. So much work," Sacha casually mentioned.

Cash whipped his head to the side and looked at Sacha, shocked. "What do you mean we're only doing one show?"

"My father doesn't think the weather will hold. We're going to do one big, all-out performance and then head south for the winter. He's calling it a 'VIP Experience'. Very important people, that is. With all the decision-makers of this God-forsaken town, the mayor, the city council, the police chief, all of them. We'll give them a taste of the new show so they beg us to come back next year." Sacha replied smugly.

Cash's heart sank into his stomach at this revelation. He couldn't head south. He was so close to finding his grandfather and couldn't wait another year to possibly come back and then head north. In a fog, he turned and left without saying anything else to Sacha. Once he stepped out into the crisp morning air, his surroundings returned. An uncomfortable feeling nagged at him. He was going to have to choose between the circus and his family very soon.

————

"Ouch!" Coco shook her fingers, then examined her pointer finger to see if it was bleeding. "This stupid outfit is so annoying!" She swatted at her costume, making it jingle and chime. That morning as she was getting ready for dress rehearsal, she noticed that some of the bells were loose. The old seamstress had shown her how to sew, but she had never quite mastered the needle and thread.

"Better be careful, wouldn't want to hurt one of your *fingers*." Coco jumped and looked up to find Anders, lurking in the shadows, leaning against the entry to the dressing room. He pushed off from the wall and walked toward where she was sitting, working on her costume. He grabbed the stool from the dressing table next to hers and sat down so their knees touched.

Leaning an arm on her table he continued, "How does it feel to be in the star act? Must be nice to know that Louka trusts you so much."

"I haven't had time to think about it with learning Cash's act and everything." Coco kept focusing on her costume, trying to hide her annoyance at his presence.

"You've been spending a lot of time with him. Have you learned anything useful?"

"I don't know what you mean," Coco said coolly.

"Oh, but you know as well as anyone how Louka likes to ensure that his talent will stick around."

She slowly sat up and gave him a stony stare.

"No, I haven't learned anything," Coco replied and looked him in the eye.

"I'm just saying. If you do find out anything of interest, you can always tell me. I'll make sure it's worth the effort if you know what I mean." He flashed a cunning grin.

"I have to finish my costume," she spat.

He stood and walked toward the exit, but paused and turned back toward her.

"Coco, don't forget whose circus this is. And the agreement you made." All the humor and arrogance had left his voice and Coco felt the threat reverberate through her. After he left, she kicked the stool where he had been sitting and didn't flinch when it tumbled over and clattered on the ground.

———

Maya sighed as she shoveled a scoopful of mashed potatoes onto the plate of another one of Louka's ungrateful *artistes*.

"You're welcome," she said to the acrobat's back. Looking toward the next person in line, she was startled to see Coco. Maya was intrigued by Cash's new partner.

"Ready for dress?" Maya queried as she heaped potatoes onto the lithe acrobat's plate.

"Yeah. I've got the routine down and Cash is a great partner."

"Hmm… great friend too."

"Yeah… I mean, I guess. You all seem super close," Coco replied hesitantly.

"We've been through a lot, even in my short time here. Makes you loyal, *I guess*."

"Well, see you later," Coco said then moved down the line. She turned back to Maya. "And thank you," she said, lifting her tray and giving a small head nod. Maya stared at her retreating form with narrow eyes.

The trickle of people coming in finally slowed enough that Bertina told her to take her dinner break. Maya went through the line and headed over to her friends. She sat down next to Bella and shoved a hunk of bread into her mouth. They stopped their whispered conversation and all looked at her.

"What's going on?" Maya muttered through the bread.

Cash shifted uncomfortably on the bench across from her.

"Cash had an interesting conversation with Sacha today," Bonkers said, leaning forward from the other side of Bella. She stared at him for a moment, still unused to seeing him without his face paint.

"Oh?" Maya looked toward Cash.

"He said we're only doing one show in this city," Cash informed her.

"That's great! You'll get to your grandfather even sooner!" Maya exclaimed.

Uncle Boris shook his head as Cash replied, "Then we're heading south."

Maya's jaw dropped.

"Louka thinks it will be an early winter," added Cash.

"Oh no! What are you going to do?" Maya asked.

"That's what we were just talking about."

"I think he should leave tonight after dress and get out of here," whispered her uncle.

"I think he should wait until we're about to leave town so he has a longer time before anyone realizes he's gone. It's three days to the performance, so it's not that long to wait." Bella countered.

"I don't want to leave tonight. I have people to say good-bye to." Cash stared at his food for a minute. "Maybe tomorrow after morning practice. If you all cover for me for evening practice that will give me almost 24 hours to get away. Then they will have a day to figure out what to do for my act."

"You're thinking about the show right now?" Maya asked, exasperated.

"Well, Coco will be the most affected. I don't want anyone to get hurt when I go, and she'll definitely take some heat. I know people are counting on me and I hate letting her down, but I can't lose this chance. For almost ten years, I didn't have blood family. I want that more than anything…" he trailed off and stabbed a piece of chicken.

Maya thought about the letter from her mother. Her mother had found a safe place to live, far away from her father. Was Maya ready to leave the circus? She had ended up there by accident. Her previous life was a nightmare, but she wondered what it would be like with just her and her mother. She could go to school and maybe get a job in the little town where her mother settled. Live in one place again.

"So tomorrow morning after practice?" Boris asked.

"Tomorrow," Cash confirmed.

CHAPTER 22

WHAT COCO DID

Boris brooded in the tunnel, letting the frantic rehearsal prep zip around him, managing to hide his large frame in the shadows so he could concentrate. A blond tumbler in a solid black leotard limped toward the dressing room, not bothering to cast a glance at him. The big man watched his friends and the strangers of Louka's circus run back and forth, yelling at each other. He closed his eyes and listened to the hum. Suddenly, he felt the subtle static of his gift activating. Sorting through the sounds drifting toward him, he picked out a quiet conversation in a western dialect.

"Do you think she'll do it?" asked the first voice, a male.

"I'm not sure she'll want to, but being placed in the headlining act comes with a certain exchange and expectations. And now we have more leverage. She'll do it," the second voice, also a male, replied.

The conversation ended and a few moments later, a blonde aerial silk acrobat brushed past him. Boris didn't know his name but remembered him being very angry when the new assignments were posted. An uneasy feeling dropped into his stomach and even though he didn't have details, he knew he needed to warn Cash to be careful around Coco.

———

Cash bounced on the balls of his feet. His eyesight was unfocused as he stared out at the ring, but his mind focused sharply on his routine. Swing out, back-end hocks off with a demi followed by Coco's forward under. Then the finale. He aimed his chin left and then right to stretch his neck. His shoulders and arms got a turn. He stretched and loosened up from head to foot, all the while tuning out the pre-rehearsal sounds around him. His new costume wasn't too different from his old one, thankfully. Instead of his blue, gold and red outfit, his vest was pure white. The pants were black with a white stripe going down each side that twisted around each calf, mimicking the pattern of the bells on Coco's leggings. Dress rehearsal progressed without too many issues. Boris took his place on one of the podiums in the center of the ring. Tumblers next to him launched one of the female acrobats straight up in the air and over his head. Boris grasped her feet so she was standing over his head. He moved her to one hand and the tumblers launched another acrobat up. He grabbed the second acrobat's foot with one hand so she was also hoisted over his head.

The two acrobats joined arms and each extended their free leg and caught the ankle with their free hand. This was Boris' finale, and Cash's cue to get to the bottom of his ladder. He jogged to his place while the spotlight was on Boris's act. Boris squatted, then pushed up and flipped one acrobat so she did a somersault in the air and the tumblers caught her. With the second acrobat, he launched her with both arms and she flipped two somersaults before landing with ease in the tumblers' outstretched arms. Cash shook his head, amazed at his friend's strength.

Then Boris took his bow and the spotlight found Louka, who was on the ringmaster's podium. Louka used his megaphone to address the stands and the groundsmen, foodies, kitchen workers, and carnies watching rehearsal. The spotlight split and found Coco and Cash, each standing at the bottom of their ladders. Cash waved at the somewhat imaginary crowd and bounced up the ladder, full of energy. At the top, he paused at the edge of the platform, waiting for the new prop hand to hook his trap for him. Louka continued his introduction and Cash imagined the crowd roaring in excitement. Everything momentarily faded as he focused in on Coco standing ready on the opposite platform. Cash gripped the trap and waited for his cue.

From the side of the arena, Lorenzo yelled, "Hep!" and Cash was swinging.

———

"Great job, Cash!" Coco breathlessly gushed after dress rehearsal.

"You too!" Ecstatic, Cash pulled her in for a sweaty hug, which she returned.

"Really, so good! We even hit the forward-under timing perfectly! I can't believe it." She shook her head, still smiling. Cash looked back to the arena where Louka and Lorenzo were gesturing for everyone to come closer.

"We should probably join," he said, nodding toward the gathering.

"Yeah, I'm sure Lorenzo will notice if we aren't there." Coco walked alongside Cash toward the group where they lingered at the back.

"Ladies and gentlemen, young and old, flyers and freaks, I have one thing to say to you," Louka said as he looked across the small crowd intensely. "We are ready! I demand the highest excellence at my shows and you all met those expectations tonight. I anticipate as we continue to gel and mesh, that the show will become better, more daring, more exciting! We are at the beginning of something very special. And I want to highlight the fearless flying of the new prince and princess of our *cirque moderne* — Cash and Coco!" Louka raised both arms toward where Cash and Coco were standing. Everyone turned and clapped at them. Blushing, Coco didn't know where to look. She saw Louka clasp his hands at his chest and bow in their direction. Despite the cheering crowd, the spotlight, and the kind words, a chill ran down her spine. After a moment, Louka resumed his speech and then handed the spotlight back to Lorenzo who, as usual, had plenty of critiques of the rehearsal.

Afterwards, she said goodbye to Cash and they headed toward different exits. Coco stopped in the dressing room to change back into her warmup outfit and out of her performance costume. As she exited the back flap into the cool night air, someone grabbed her by the elbow and pulled her roughly to the side.

"Get your hands off of me!" Coco shook free. "Don't ever handle me like that again." She stared into Anders' stony face.

"I need you to do something," he stated without responding to her.

"Oh really? I don't need to do anything for you." Coco couldn't believe his audacity.

"It's a direct request from the ringmaster." With that, Anders handed her a knapsack.

It weighed more than it seemed, and she almost dropped it.

"What does he want me to do?" she sighed.

Anders raised his eyebrows and nodded to the bag.

Coco looked inside and saw a length of chain.

Disappointment and fear commingled as she asked, "What is this for?"

"It's very simple. Stop by the caboose and chat with Cash about dress rehearsal. When you leave, chain the door so he can't leave. Then security will get him in the morning, keep an eye on him, and lock him up in the evening. Your part is simple," Anders instructed.

Coco continued to stare at the chain in the bag. "Why are you doing this?" she whispered.

"The *ringmaster* is doing this to protect his assets. Especially after your rehearsal tonight, he thinks your act is going to bring in droves of people." Anders shrugged.

Coco sighed. "When do I have to do this?"

"Tonight. Better get going," he said before turning to go.

Coco slowly walked off in a daze in the general direction of the back of the train. A few cars away from the caboose she stopped, slipped between the cars, and took a seat on the coupler. With the bag on her lap, she closed her eyes to think. She knew too well the feeling of being a prisoner in Louka's circus. She liked Cash and his friends and envied their camaraderie, but she also knew it would be a huge risk to defy the ringmaster. As she sat, assurance grew that she could delay a day and make up an excuse for Anders tomorrow. She could give Cash one more day of freedom. She *would* give him that. Nervous, but resolute, she took one look at the caboose and turned toward her car. When she got inside, she hid the bag under her bed and went to sleep.

———

Cash's heart beat quickly. Today was the day. Standing in the middle of the 'boose in the morning light, he slowly turned to take in everything there. He began to mentally visualize which things he could take and which he couldn't. There were mementos from their travels, postcards he collected but never had anyone to send them to, a red and white yarn sweater from the first town where he performed on the trapeze, and so much more. This wooden car held his whole life.

Cash sighed, knowing he couldn't take it all with him. Suddenly, there was a knock at the door and he slid gracefully across the car to open it.

Maya was on the platform, arms pulled in close and hands buried in pockets. "Got a minute?" she inquired, looking up at him with her big eyes.

"Yeah, sure. Come on in." Cash moved aside to let her in. She stepped inside and looked around.

"Have you decided what you're going to take with you?"

"Not yet. I really need to get packing." Cash picked up one of the few photos he had. It was of him and Tony in front of a waterfall from one of their rare summer breaks a few years back. They were both in shorts and soaking wet, and Cash had an arm around Tony's shoulders. Tony made a goofy face and Cash looked happy. He was happy.

"I'm all packed," she stated.

"What?" Cash looked up from the picture to Maya, who had sat down on his bed.

"I'm coming too," she said nonchalantly.

"What?!" Cash repeated.

Maya reached into her cardigan pocket and pulled out a letter. It looked like the one from his birthday.

"My mother isn't too far away. If things here are going to be as bad as you say, then this might be my only chance to leave too."

"Oh." Cash sat down next to her and held his hand out for the letter. Maya handed it to him and he opened it, skimming the swirly writing.

"If I can just get to a train station, I'm sure I can find my way there," Maya said while Cash was still reading.

He finished the letter and looked at her, still holding on to it.

"You're lucky, you know. To have a mum."

She nodded, holding his gaze. "Yeah. I know now," she whispered.

"OK, you can come," Cash stated decidedly, handing the letter back to her.

Maya turned up one side of her mouth in a half smile.

"I wasn't asking." She half laughed and half scoffed, her normal confident attitude back as quickly as it had left.

"Whatever. Meet me here after practice. I'll pick up my bag and we'll go," Cash said.

"I'll be here." With a hop, Maya stood up and left. Cash heard her whistling as she headed back toward the circus.

———

Coco brushed into the cookhouse, looking much more assertive than she felt. She kept her back straight and head up as she went through the line to collect her breakfast, barely acknowledging what the kitchen team put on her tray. A knot of regret turned over in her stomach. She knew she shouldn't have disobeyed Anders and Louka, so why did she? As she grabbed an orange juice and turned to head toward a table, someone ran into her shoulder and pushed her. The drink went flying and she scrambled to stay on her feet. Whoever it was kept shoving and she had to backtrack behind the serving line and into the kitchen.

Anders swatted her tray out of her hands and gave Coco another shove. As her plates and bowls went crashing, she tripped over a broom and fell to the ground. Anders slowly dropped to a crouch in front of her.

"You're lucky you're performing in two days," he whispered menacingly. "Because I can't hurt you. But I came across some interesting information recently. About your half-sister, and the school she's attending."

Coco's anger turned to fear.

"You wouldn't…" she whispered, knowing full well that he and Louka would.

"It's really up to you. Do what I ask and you don't have to worry about it. And you had better do it after morning practice."

Anders stood up and laughed. To the kitchen staff who had stopped to see what happened, he joked, "For a graceful acrobat, she sure has clumsy moments." Then he extended a hand. Without thinking, Coco grabbed his hand and let him help her up. He slapped her on the shoulder in a friendly way and walked off, leaving Coco in the mess of her breakfast with the kitchen staff staring at her.

Her eyes got hot as she tried to shove away the tears that were welling up. Suddenly, a gentle arm was around her and a woman spoke.

"Let's give you a moment to compose yourself." Coco looked over at an older woman with dark hair with sparkles of gray. Helen ushered her into one of the storage rooms. The cook gently turned Coco so they were face to face. The woman's kind visage displayed worry. She reached out and put her hands on Coco's shoulders.

"Are you ok? I saw the whole thing and know you didn't trip. At least not until that troll shoved you at the broom," Helen said reassuringly.

Fear braced Coco as she realized she might be hurt. She grabbed her opposite arms and checked her elbows and wrists, then shook each leg.

"I'm, I think I'm OK. Yeah," Coco replied weakly.

"How do you know that man?"

"He used to be my partner. In an act." Coco relinquished.

"Doesn't seem very nice, now does he?" Helen asked.

"You have no idea," Coco remembered Anders' threat, and the tears finally broke through and flowed down her cheeks.

"Oh. Uh oh. It's OK. Let it out." The older woman wrapped Coco in an embrace.

For the first time in years, Coco felt like she could relax. After a couple of minutes, Coco slowly pulled away and wiped her tears, first with her hands, then on her sleeves.

After a big inhale and exhale she said, "Thank you, uhh... I'm sorry I don't know your name."

"I'm Helen." The woman replied with a warm smile.

"Coco." She extended her hand, which Helen took.

"I know who you are. Better take good care of my Cash," Helen winked at Coco.

"I will," Coco chuckled.

"I'll fix you another breakfast tray since yours is all over the ground."

"Thank you." Coco followed Helen back to the line. Guilt rose in her, knowing what she had to do to Cash after practice.

After sending Coco on her way, Helen loaded dishes on her own tray and made eye contact with Tony. He nodded and reached under the counter for a small box wrapped in twine. They both made their way toward their usual table and joined Cash, Maya, Boris, Bella, and Bonkers. She sat down next to Cash, and Tony took the seat across from her.

She leaned over and whispered in Cash's ear, "We got you a little something." Tony pushed the red box toward Cash. He reached for the twine and Helen continued in a hushed voice. "I know you can't take much with you, so we got you something you can eat now. But we also didn't want to draw attention to us."

Cash opened the top to find a cupcake shaped and decorated like a circus tent. In that moment, Cash felt his heart tear in two. With the sudden nature of his departure, he hadn't fully processed yet that he had to say goodbye to his friends today. His stomach dropped as he realized that this was his going-away meal. Emotion overcame him and he wrapped an arm around Helen.

"Thank you, Helen. Thank you for everything," he whispered into her hair.

Cash made eye contact with Tony and said, "Thanks,

buddy." Tony nodded. Cash grabbed a knife and cut a bite for everyone while Tony told the story about the time Cash thought the caboose was haunted, but it was Boris and Bonkers making noises to scare them at night. Everyone in the group laughed. Cash looked around at his friends and tried to freeze the moment in his mind to remember it forever.

———

By the end of practice, Cash had said his goodbyes. He walked back to the 'boose with a lighter heart as he thought through his plan to find his grandfather. Hopping up the steps, he barged through the door. His knapsack was packed on his bed. As he reached for it, he paused and looked at the books on the shelf built into the base of his bed. Magda's dream journal caught his eye and he couldn't believe he almost forgot it. As he crouched to pull it out, he heard light footsteps on the platform.

"Come on in, Maya!" he called as he shoved the book into his already full bag.

Instead of the door opening, he heard a chain rattling. It took him a second to realize what he was hearing.

"Nooo!" Cash cried and ran to the door. When he tried to open it, it only budged an inch. Through the small window on the door, he could see Coco standing on the platform with tears on her cheeks.

"Coco! Why are you doing this?!" Cash desperately tried the door again. The shaking knocked the picture of him and Tony off of its shelf. "I have to get out. Please, Coco!"

"Security will be by to take you to lunch. I'm so sorry," she replied dejectedly.

Cash barely heard her apology, then she turned to leave and was quickly out of his sight.

In disbelief, Cash leaned on the door and ran a hand through his hair. He sank to the floor and stared unfocused across the caboose. His chance to escape was gone.

CHAPTER 23

CHANGING COURSE

Footsteps thumped on the platform. Cash jumped up and peered through the small window in the caboose door. He could just see Maya's face and her brow furrowing as confusion set in. She looked up.

"Cash! What's going on?" Maya hurried to the window in the door and stood on tip toes to look in. "Why is the door locked?!" She pulled at the door and chain.

"I don't know! Coco locked me in!" Cash yelled through the door.

"What?! Why? When are you getting out?" she exclaimed.

"I...I don't think I am."

Maya jiggled the door again and looked around for another way in or out of the 'boose. Then reality set in. "We're not going."

"No, it doesn't look like we're going," Cash conceded.

Maya dropped her knapsack on the platform.

"What do we do?" She looked at him, a hopeless expression on her face.

"I don't know." Cash could barely believe what was happening. "Can you tell the crew what happened?"

Nodding, Maya replied, "Yeah. It's not too long 'til lunch. I'll see if I can find them before there are too many people around."

Cash watched her turn away and walked over to his bed where he sat down hard. The silence of the caboose felt like it was crushing him, and he felt totally alone.

————

Loud footsteps pounded on the platform. Cash sat up. He must have dozed off. The chain rattled and two of Louka's security men came in without asking.

Cash couldn't tell if it was the ones who locked up Elon since they all looked similar. They stepped to each side of the door and then Louka's hulking silhouette filled the doorway. He ducked to get through the door with his top hat on. The big man looked around and disgust briefly flashed across his face. When his eyes fell on Cash, his scowl turned into a sinister grin.

"You underestimated me, boy. Clearly, you think that I'm as naive as my brother and that I don't know what's going on at my circus," Louka drawled as he slowly approached Cash. "You were wrong," he growled. Cash backed up, his legs hitting the edge of Tony's bed.

"Since I can't have my new star running off, I made some changes to your living situation." Louka gestured to the goons by the door. "Aldo and Francesco will be watching over you. If you try to run away or pull anything, your friends will find themselves in similar accommodations. If I run out of cars to lock them in, I have plenty of animal cages we don't use anymore." He took two more, large steps toward Cash. With no more space behind him, Cash sat quickly on the bed to get away from Louka. "Can you imagine poor Boris and Bella unable to see each other? They seem so in love." Louka glared at Cash. "Do you understand our arrangement?" Louka whispered.

"Yes," Cash said. Louka narrowed his eyes to slits. "Yes, ringmaster," Cash added.

"Good," Louka spat, turned, and walked decidedly out the door. The two goons remained.

"Time for lunch," the slightly bigger one announced while grinning at Cash. He stood well over six feet tall, wore a black bowler hat, and had biceps almost as large as Boris'.

Cash grunted as he stood and followed Aldo and Francesco to the cookhouse. He hoped they would give him space once he was inside, but the large men followed Cash through the line and sat a table away from him, within ear and eyeshot. His friends joined him, but Louka's men looming over them squashed any real conversation. Instead, Bonkers told old stories and tried to make everyone laugh.

When he had finished eating, Aldo and Francesco made a show of escorting him out in front of everyone. Before exiting the tent, Cash glanced over his shoulder to the ringmaster's platform. Louka was looking at him with a rigid face, then the edge of his mouth lifted in an evil grin.

Cash sat alone in the dim caboose. Normally, Tony would be talking about what happened in the kitchen, or they'd be laughing about some joke. Once again, he heard steps on the platform. He felt excited until he got to the door and saw his guards through the window. The chain rattled and

Cash anxiously waited to see what was in store for him. When the door opened, Tony was standing between Aldo and Francesco.

"This guy says he lives here. Is that true?" Francesco's gruff voice sounded like it had a hard time getting out of his throat.

"I already told you, *Fran...*" Tony struggled to break free while Francesco stared icily at him.

"Yes. Tony is my roommate." Cash stood and looked from Francesco to Tony.

"Not anymore." Aldo gave Tony a shove on the back and Tony stumbled into his former home. "You have five minutes to collect your things."

Tony looked at Cash in a panic.

"What? Where am I supposed to go?" Though he was looking at Cash, Aldo answered.

"Dunno. Don't care. Just can't be here. Yer boy is too precious for roommates." The guards exchanged a look and snickered.

"Grab your bag. I'll help you with your things," Cash scooted past the guards, toward Tony's side of the 'boose. Whispering, he added, "Go stay with Boris. He has room."

"Yeah, ok. Good idea." Tony began grabbing clothes out of his drawers and toiletries from next to the mirror. After a moment he added, "This is crazy, Cash."

"I know. All I can think about is how close I was..." Cash gritted his teeth and grabbed a crate they had been using as a footrest. Then he snagged Tony's extra boots and loaded them in the crate. "I need your help."

"Yeah, anything," Tony briefly looked up at Cash from his almost full bag.

"Tell the gang to meet on the platform tomorrow night

after dinner. Make sure it's dark. I'm going to come up with a plan."

Tony's eyes went wide.

"You're still gonna…"

Cash nodded.

"Time's up!" Aldo yelled at them.

As Aldo crossed the 'boose, Tony whispered, "We'll be here."

Aldo yanked Tony by the elbow and half dragged him across the caboose. Once they exited, Fran locked the door leaving Cash alone. The wind whipped around the corners of the caboose and the old car creaked on the tracks. Waves of fear washed over Cash dotted by the occasional glimmer of hope.

———

The next morning, Cash paced the 'boose. He hadn't slept much. All of his ideas to get himself and Maya away from the circus were unachievable or too risky.

He had to figure this out. Sitting down at the table, he grabbed a notebook, lit a lantern, and began to write everything he knew about Louka, his workers, and the new show. After several pages of writing, Cash slammed his fist on the table.

"This isn't helping," he yelled to the empty caboose.

He put his head down on the table in frustration and prayed that an idea would come to him, but nothing happened. Then everything faded to black.

———

Cash hurried across the circus grounds toward the big top when he suddenly crashed to the ground. His ankle throbbed. He pushed himself up to sitting and examined his ankle, slowly moving it to make sure it wasn't broken. It would be fine. He noticed a hole in the ground. Curious, he got closer and heard faint cooing. Befuddled and wondering if he hit his head, he reached his hand into the hole and touched feathers. Gingerly, he wrapped his hand around as much of the animal's body as he could. He pulled it out to find a bird in his hand. It looked like a cuckoo, but instead of gray or brown feathers, they were a mix of black and gold. A chain dangled from the bird's leg. With a firm tug, he realized the chain was attached to something in the hole. Cash pulled harder. The chain released from the hole and at the same time, the manacle fell from the bird's foot. Immediately, the bird flapped its wings and took off. Cash squinted and watched it perch on top of the tent.

Cash peeled his face off of the table, pulling a page of notebook paper up with it. He forced his eyes open and swiped at the page. A dream! Taking the paper from his face, he grabbed his pen and wrote it down. As he wrote, three things stood out: the bird, the colors of the bird, and that it landed on the big top. He got up and went to retrieve Magda's notebook from his bag. Returning to the paper with the dream, he began flipping through Magda's notebook looking for animals, colors, or items from the circus.

"If the dream is about me, it must mean that I'm going to get away," Cash muttered to himself. With excitement rising, he found a page with swatches of colored ink. Each rough square of color had words scattered around it. The black swatch noted, "Night, secrecy, and authority." Next to gold, Cash found, "fortune, wealth, and glory."

"Huh. That doesn't sound like me." Cash stood to his feet and began to pace the caboose. "Someone with authority, wealth, secrecy. The bird landed on the tent." The pieces fell into place and Cash knew what the dream meant. He laughed to himself and punched the table. "It's not about me, it's about what I need to do!"

———

Helen was the last to arrive for the meeting Cash called. Bella, Boris, Bonkers, Maya, and Tony were already sitting on the platform. The door was propped open as much as the chain allowed, which was two inches at the most.

"Ok, what is going on?" Helen asked as she took a seat on the platform next to Boris.

"Apparently I'm so valuable, that Louka feels like he needs to make sure I don't run off," Cash's slightly muffled reply came through the crack in the door.

"The timing is dubious," Bonkers muttered.

"What can we do?" asked Bella. "The performance is tomorrow and then we head South. If you want to find your grandfather, we have to do something now."

"I know. I don't have the money to get back up here if I were to escape down South. Who knows, maybe you all will be locked up by that time too." Cash heard several whispers from his friends. They clearly hadn't thought of that. Confidence rose as he prepared to share his plan. "Here's the thing. If I manage to get away, you all will still be here with Louka the psychopath, and who knows what he is going to do next. I can't leave knowing you all are in danger."

"But, Cash, you have to go. This is your chance!" Helen leaned in front of Boris to look at him pleadingly through the gap.

"I know, but I don't want to escape. I want to take back the circus," Cash stated. Gasps echoed from his friends and then they all started talking at once.

"Are you out of your mind?" yelled Bonkers.

"What?!" bellowed Boris.

"Yes!" Cheered Helen.

"I knew you'd have something good!" Tony encouraged.

Cash continued, "I'll be free during meals, practice, and the performance. The performance will have everyone busy and distracted, so that's our best option. We have to get Elon out of his car, and we need to get the police here and convince them that Louka is a monster!"

"Oh! The performance! The police constable is going to be there," Tony piped in.

Bella shivered with excitement. "I'm in the finale and Louka is planning to come out in the middle of our act and address the audience. You all could get Elon, bring him out at that end, and interrupt Louka with accusations of all the nasty things he has done. The constable will hear it and will have to arrest Louka."

"So how do we get Elon out? A couple of us could overpower a guard and make them unlock his car," Tony suggested.

"That would draw too much attention, and one of us could get hurt. I don't think they'd hesitate to use force." Cash replied.

"Surely someone else has access. We just need to find out who," Maya added.

"We need someone on the inside to find out. One of Louka's people," Bonkers said, his tone not indicating confidence.

"Coco," Cash softly suggested.

"Are you crazy! She locked you in here!" Tony shouted.

"Shhh!" Maya grabbed Tony's arm.

"She hasn't really spoken to me since, but she had tears on her face. I don't think she wanted to do it," Cash added, almost pleading.

"I'll vouch for Coco," Helen spoke up. "There was an incident in the kitchen the other day. I overheard her old partner threaten her. Something must be going on."

"Me too," Boris interjected. "I overheard that guy talking to one of the other aerial silk acrobats. I didn't know who they were talking about, but if it was Coco, then she didn't have much of a choice."

"So we're going to ask the girl who locked you up to help us?" Tony looked around at the group. "I just want to be clear that I think it's a bad idea."

"It has to be Coco," Cash confirmed. "She'll let us know who has the key. Then, Maya and Bonkers, since you're not working during the show, you can go get the key as soon as the first act begins. Bring it backstage and hand it off to Boris after his act. Then he can go get Elon during my performance."

"Aye, aye," Bonkers confirmed with a salute.

"Ok," Maya agreed.

"Once you get him, bring him to the dressing room," Cash added.

"But there will probably still be people in there mingling after the acts before mine," said Bella.

Cash paused to think.

"The animal staging area!" Bonkers interjected. "The handlers will all be in the ring for the finale. It should be empty."

"Perfect!" Cash was getting excited. "Bring him to the staging area. I'll run over after my performance. Once Louka goes out to address the crowd, we'll all take Elon into the ring. Together."

"Helen and I will be in the stands selling our last few snacks," noted Tony.

"And I'll already be in the ring," added Bella.

Cash paused to see if they missed anything. He grinned.

"I think we have a plan," Cash tried to hide the excitement in his voice.

"We have a plan," Helen whispered back.

"Haha. We have a plan," Tony echoed.

"We just need Coco to tell us who has the key for Elon," Maya confirmed.

"And the rest of the plan is locked in as tight as the chain on Cash's door," Bonkers chimed in and laughed. He reached up and gave the chain a hard shake so it rattled.

Once the chuckles died down, Bella piped in.

"Wait, what happens after we bring out Elon?"

"Louka goes to jail, the circus goes back to normal with Elon at the helm and Maya and I can leave whenever we want." Cash clarified. "It should be pretty straightforward as long as there are no surprises between now and then." He peered through the crack and looked around the group, finding looks of determination on each face.

———

"Coco is avoiding me." Cash took a swig of water from his canteen.

"How can that be? You're partners." Boris asked, reaching for a towel to address the sweat from their conditioning run.

"Every time we break, she runs off. And we can't exactly have a conversation in the air."

Boris scanned the big top. The equestrians, tumblers, and acrobats were all in various positions of recovering from the run. Lorenzo walked around the ring, examining his artists, looking for weaknesses before the big show that evening. Coco was missing.

"We have to find out who has the key. The whole plan depends on it." Cash sighed, then looked directly at Boris. "I might need you to stall her after we run through our act."

"I can do that," the big man nodded as he continued to look out over the arena.

"Attention!" Lorenzo yelled from in front of his chair as he clapped three times for emphasis. "The run-through begins now! Places!"

A wave of nerves flowed over Cash. He tried to stay focused and act like everything was normal. He and Boris watched the first few acts from the bleachers. Soon, thoughts of their plan and his imminent escape disappeared from his mind as he got sucked into the show. This was the first time Cash had seen all of Louka's acts. They really were impressive. Different, but impressive. Highly choreographed, the tumbling acts utilized props and machines that catapulted tumblers and acrobats into the air. Some of the acts had so many people in the ring, that it was almost dizzying attempting to follow all of the action.

Soon, Boris took his place for his act and Cash's thoughts returned to their plan and the timing of everything. They just needed to get the key.

Cash landed on his platform with a thud and turned to wave and bow to the empty stands. Then he turned and repeated his waves to the other side. He glanced across the arena and saw that Coco was already near the bottom of her ladder. Cash scrambled down his and ran across the ring just as Coco disappeared into the tunnel.

"Please let Boris be there," Cash silently prayed as he ran.

Into the tunnel he flew, and almost ran right into Boris talking to Coco. He seemed to be going on about his mother's pheasant stew recipe. Then Boris' eyes caught Cash's and Coco turned around to face him, her eyes wide at the sight of him.

"We need to talk," Cash said in a low voice.

"I have to go." Coco turned back around and tried to sneak around Boris, but he stepped in front of her.

"This way." Cash looped his arm in hers and led them down the hall toward the changing stalls, Boris trailing behind them.

A few feet down the hall, Coco became nearly hysterical and tried to get away from Cash.

"Don't hurt me. Please, I didn't have a choice!" she begged.

The desperate look on her face frightened Cash and he let go of her.

"What are you talking about?" He addressed Coco, then looked quizzically at Boris. "We're not going to hurt you."

She stopped moving, but her body was still tense.

"You're not?"

"No," Cash nodded to one of the changing stalls. "In here."

Then he turned to Boris and added, "Keep an eye out

for Aldo and Fran. I'm sure they saw me run off." Boris nodded in reply.

The door swung and creaked shut. Turning to Coco, he began in a low voice.

"We need your help."

Now Coco looked at him skeptically.

"What with?"

"I just need to know everyone who has a key to Elon's car," Cash replied casually.

"What? Why!" She hissed and backed up against the stall wall. "That's all you need. Just a little, *dangerous* piece of information." She mimicked him. "You must have really done damage to your brain when you fell."

"Hey! It's *your* fault I'm a prisoner in this circus. You can at least hear me out!" He whispered aggressively at her.

Her body language softened slightly as she replied with a "Fine."

"We're going to break him out tonight and we just need to know who has keys," Cash explained.

"Oh no. I'm not going to be part of this. Louka will make things worse for me," Coco shook her head.

"If our plan works, you won't have to worry about Louka anymore."

Coco gasped. "You're going to kill him?"

"What? No! We're going to have the constable arrest him at the show."

"Oh. But if you fail, I'll get in trouble," Coco replied with fear in her voice.

"How will they know it's you? Surely there are other people who know where to find the key. If anyone needs to worry about failing, it's me," Cash searched her eyes.

Coco crossed her arms and bit her lower lip. Cash

moved closer until he was right in front of her.

He put his hands on her upper arms and whispered. "Please, Coco."

She closed her eyes. "Sacha."

"Ok, who else?"

She opened her eyes and met his gaze.

"No one else, he has the only key. The guards get it from him when they deliver meals," Maya said quietly.

"Haaaa!" The door to the stall flew open to reveal Aldo. He yelled over his shoulder, "Got'em!" Then turning back to Cash and Coco he smirked, "We're always finding you young'un's back here bein' all romantic." Cash's face flushed crimson as he realized how close they were standing and quickly backed away. Aldo grabbed him roughly by the arm. "Gotta get this one back before he causes any trouble."

As he was being dragged off, Cash looked over his shoulder and mouthed, "Thank you".

Boris gave an apologetic shrug to Cash as he passed. He followed the trio back to the caboose, keeping his distance. Once the guards locked Cash in and were a decent distance away, he crept up the platform and knocked gently. Cash appeared in the window almost immediately.

"Sacha! Sacha has the key! Tell Maya and Bonkers," Cash yelled at Boris.

"Got it! I'll find them now." Boris deftly hopped over the banister and strode along the backside of the train to avoid being seen and headed toward the cookhouse to find Maya.

CHAPTER 24

THE SHOWDOWN

The circus grounds buzzed. The sun had fallen below the horizon, offering a slight pink glow against the dark silhouettes of the trees. Torches lit the entrance to the circus, each booth on the midway, and the towering black and white tent. The torchlight flickered as people walked by. Whispering couples darted from the red wagon with their tickets in hand to excitedly visit the caramel corn stand or enter the tent of mysteries.

Maya kept her head down as she slipped through the sea of people flooding into the circus grounds for the show. She deftly dodged a mother dragging her young child by the coat as the child cried about wanting a candy apple. She passed an illusionist on a stage, wowing the crowd with silent card tricks and exaggerated expressions. Despite all of the changes Louka had made, the smells of the circus stayed the same. Popcorn, fried dough, straw, and mud mingled with the occasional whiff of perfume. Every few moments she glanced up at her destination. She passed twin contortionists bending their bodies in ways that made the crowd gasp. Turning right just after the frozen woman, Maya dashed for the train in darkness. Once she reached the train, she hopped over the coupler between two cards and paused for a moment when she was out of view. Her heart beat with excitement as much as with danger. A few deep breaths later, she was jogging down the train. She slowed as she reached Major and Flora's car.

SPLAT! A large pile of dung hit the ground a few feet ahead of her.

"Ugh!" Maya shivered and shook, examining herself to ensure it didn't splash on her. "Hey! You could have hit me."

From the open car, Bonkers pulled down the handkerchief covering his mouth and nose and rested on his shovel handle with a grin.

"Yeah. But I didn't," he smirked with a raise of his eyebrows. "It's easier when the elephants aren't in here if you know what I mean."

Maya cringed. She wasn't sure what he meant but could imagine.

"You ready? Or do you want to keep shoveling dung," she questioned. Bonkers looked down at the shovel considering it, then threw it down and hopped from the car.

"Let's get this crazy plan going."

They walked silently along the train until they got as close to the red wagon as they could.

Bonkers stuck his head around the side of the train car and whispered, "You sure he's in there?"

"Well, I didn't see him, but there was still a line when I passed by, so he *should* still be in there."

"Ok. Only one way to find out." Bonkers said, and they crossed over the train and walked casually toward the back of the red wagon, then they skirted along the side toward the front.

"Think anyone will stop us?" Maya whispered.

"Nope. Just walk in like you own the place. Follow me."

Maya followed right behind Bonkers as they turned the corner to the front of the red wagon. Bonkers smiled at the few people still in line, strode up the steps, and opened the door. He entered first and Maya quickly followed, shutting the door behind her and sliding the bolt lock into place.

Sacha turned from the ticket window as soon as they entered. Alarmed, he stood and crossed the small room, heading toward them. As Sacha approached, Bonkers grabbed his arm, whirled them both around, and shoved Sacha against the large safe.

Maya stared with wide-open eyes at the strength, speed, and ease with which Bonkers handled Sacha.

"Maya!" he whispered forcefully. It snapped Maya back to her senses and she squeezed past Bonkers and put a hand on Sacha's shoulder.

They waited.

"What is this?" Sacha said, getting louder and trying to break free of Bonkers' grasp. Bonkers clasped a hand over Sacha's mouth and looked at Maya. She had her eyes closed, then put her other hand on Sacha's forearm. Sacha wriggled, tried to move, tried to speak. After a few more moments, Maya opened her eyes.

"Give me the key to Elon's car," she said calmly, keeping one hand on his shoulder.

Sacha drew his right arm up and Bonkers loosened his grip on that arm. Putting his hand in his front pocket, Sacha's eyes grew wide enough to see the whites all the way around. He shook his head in disbelief as much as he could with Bonkers' hand still over his mouth. When he drew his hand out of his pocket, there was a small ring with only a few keys on it. He grabbed one by the end and held it up to Maya who grabbed it.

"Thank you, Sacha. That wasn't so hard." She grinned and put the key in her own pocket.

"Grab me the chair he was sitting in. And some rope or adhesive tape," Bonkers directed Maya. She ran a few paces to the other side of the room and grabbed the chair.

"Hey, we want to buy tickets," a boy's voice carried in through the ticket window. Maya turned with the chair in her arms and flashed him a charming smile.

"We'll be right with you." She left the chair by Bonkers and dug through the hall closet until she found a roll of tape, which she took to Bonkers. He already had Sacha in the chair and she pulled the end of the tape off the roll and handed it to Bonkers. When Sacha was secure, Bonkers nodded at Maya, then planted himself in front of the ticket window with a big smile.

"Who is ready for the best night of their life!"

Once the customers were engaged, Maya slipped out the front door but not without taking one last look at Sacha. Rage radiated from his dark eyes. She couldn't keep a grin from forming on her face.

Darkness shrouded the nearly empty circus grounds, but the lights from the show made the tent glow like an otherworldly form. Applause reached her ears as she approached the artist's entrance. She slowed down and let her heart rate return to normal. Inside, she walked through as she always did, trying not to stick out, yet intentional in her destination. There were still several acts before Boris's so she planted herself with a few other workers watching the show from along the tunnel by the back door. A dressage rider she didn't recognize gushed to her about the new acts. Maya mumbled an inaudible reply.

Then her spine contracted and a chill ran down her arms. She casually looked over her shoulder to see Aldo and Fran standing behind her. Heat and panic pulsed in her body as she wondered why they were standing there. They were talking just low enough that she couldn't make out the words. One act ended and another began, but Maya wasn't paying attention. She imagined the guards stopping her just as she was about to make the handoff to Uncle Boris. Her armpits were wet. Before she knew it, the act was over and Uncle Boris was on his podium with the spotlight on him. Though his act remained mostly unchanged, she was always impressed by it. He took on a different personality in front of the crowd and seemed bigger than life. Casually, she tugged at her hair and managed a glance over her shoulder only to find the guards still there.

Maya slid her hand into her pocket and wrapped her fingers around the key ring. The crowd cheered. Uncle Boris bowed to the crowd, turned, and bowed again. Then he was off his podium and running toward the tunnel. She joined the excitement of her fellow carnies as Uncle Boris approached and she lifted her fist holding the key-ring in the air in celebration. They locked eyes and Boris gave a big smile while clasping her raised hand in both of his. He shook her hand as they celebrated. As he quickly kissed her forehead, he grabbed the key from her palm and jogged off down the tunnel. Maya looked after him, praying to the saints that everything went as planned.

Then she headed to the animal holding area to wait for him to return with Elon.

———

Boris still felt the buzz of the crowd as he walked down the tunnel. More importantly, he felt the keys that his niece had handed to him. He turned into the dressing rooms so he wouldn't look suspicious by leaving straight after his act. After chugging some water from the canteen at his dressing station, Boris left the dressing area and headed toward the exit. Once outside, the tent muted the audience noise and the silence of the dim circus grounds collapsed in on him. He began a jog across the grounds and headed for the train, stopping briefly outside the red wagon. Bonkers' voice reached him through the walls.

"And then you'll never believe what happened... I had grabbed the wrong monkey!" The punchline of the story was followed by Bonkers' deep laugh. Boris assumed that no one had disturbed Bonkers and Sacha since the clown was telling stories. He turned and ran straight for Elon's red car and slipped between it and the one ahead of it. Any moonlight was blocked by the tall cars, so Boris pulled the keys from his pocket and felt them.

There were three keys of different lengths. He grasped them so the longest one pointed out. Boris crouched and quickly rounded the corner. He found the chain and felt for the lock, which he discovered near the handle. The first key went in but didn't turn. He felt for the second longest one and tried it in the lock. Again no luck. The last key was so small that the ring dropped out of Boris' hand and hit the metal step with a clang.

"Hey, who's there? I can hear you. Have you come to gloat again, brother?" The ringmaster's baritone voice startled Boris.

The strongman reached down and felt for the step, then scanned the area with his hands for the key. He found the ring, navigated to the smallest one, and quickly, but precisely inserted it into the lock and twisted. He was awarded with a click as the lock fell loose. He hurried to detach it from the chains and then unloop the chain from the handle. Once the door was free, Boris slid it open to find his ringmaster in the doorway with a chair above his head, ready to slam it down on his Boris' head. Boris reacted quickly and reached up to grab the chair.

"It's Boris!" He whispered ferociously, his heart pounding even harder than it had been. "We have to go *now*." Elon's face shifted from anger to surprise. Boris let go of the chair and Elon lowered it to the ground. Without a word, Elon exited the car and Boris slid the door closed and followed Elon down to the grass.

"What's the plan?" Elon whispered.

"We have to get to the tent. I'll explain on the way."

Maya listened to the progress of the show from an empty horse stall. Barnaby and Peter, his young assistant, were about to move Major and Flora back to their car.

"I can't believe that clown isn't anywhere to be found," Barnaby muttered as he prodded Major, the elephant, to move.

"He musta had something important to do," Peter replied.

"Ha! Not likely. He's probably watchin' the show

or sneakin' food from the cookhouse. Once a clown, always a clown."

They eventually led the elephants out of the prep area and Maya relaxed. The crowd erupted in cheers. Cash and Coco must have hit the new full-twisting forward over, which meant they were almost at their finale. Maya's stomach tightened, wondering where her uncle was. She jumped when the stall door next to her crashed into the dividing wall with a bang.

"Finally," she said as she opened the door to her stall and stepped out. Her eyes peeled wide.

It was not her uncle.

———

Coco let go and Cash flew through the air in two perfect pirouettes. He saw his trapeze and seized it firmly. It swung him back to his platform where he added a somersault and landed on his feet. The intense concentration from performing faded and he became aware of a noise so loud he felt it in his chest. He looked out over the audience and realized they were on their feet and roaring. Glancing across the ring he saw Coco beaming and bowing to the crowd. She turned and sent him a huge smile.

Cash bowed to each side, then pumped his fist. Heart pounding and full of energy, he bounded down his ladder and headed toward the tunnel. The gravity of the situation slammed down on him when he saw Aldo and Fran standing at the end of the tunnel, waiting for him. He momentarily felt lightheaded, but then noticed the fans by the tunnel, leaning over the rail to wave at him.

Cash stopped to shake hands and sign autographs.

When the guards looked away, he ducked under the canvas drape that created the tunnel walls and separated it from the underside of the bleachers. In the semi-dark, Cash ran under the bleachers as fast as he could toward the other side of the tent where the others were gathering. He prayed that the guards wouldn't quickly figure out where he went. As he neared the other side, he took a quick glance through the bleachers and the audience's feet to catch a glance of Bella's act.

————————

Boris stuck his head through the side entrance to the tent. Seeing a clear hallway, he opened the flap for himself and Elon and they barreled down the hallway toward the holding area.

Suddenly, the canvas wall ahead of them drew up and someone emerged 50 feet in front of them. They both slid to a halt, hoping the person wouldn't turn around, but the person turned and looked right at them.

"Cash!" Elon whispered forcedly.

Cash's face flicked from fear to relief. "Let's go!" Cash said quietly, but strained.

Boris, Elon and Cash ran the rest of the way to the holding area.

————————

Bella's arms burned. Despite all of the practice, the silk routine was grueling. They entered into the second act of their performance and sweat fell in her eyes as she glanced down. Louka wasn't in his spot. She climbed to the top of her rope and wrapped one leg in the fabric and lowered her torso so she was hanging upside down. Still no Louka. The acrobat on the silk next to her was just a little bit lower on his rope.

"Hey! Where's Louka?" she yelled over the crowd and music.

"He's going to be late," Anders replied with a nasty grin.

Bella's heart skipped a beat. She had to warn her friends.

———

Helen and Tony nervously watched the aerial silk act from their position in the stands alongside the VIP box. They took turns watching the constable, to ensure that he stayed in his seat for Elon's grand return. The acrobats climbed their ropes and hung upside down. Suddenly, Bella broke the routine. She hoisted her torso upright, released her leg, and began a quick descent.

Helen grabbed Tony's arm.

"Something is wrong! Get the constable now! I'm going back there." She spoke up over the noise of the crowd.

———

Cash flew into the holding area and stopped suddenly, digging his heels into the floor. Boris and Elon jostled him as they tried to adjust their speed.

He couldn't believe his eyes. Louka stood in front of him. *Why was he here?* His mouth went dry as the big man stared at him. A glint of light. Cash briefly looked down and saw the silver revolver in Louka's hand.

Louka took a couple slow paces toward Cash, not breaking eye contact.

"My star. The dream acrobat. But I knew I couldn't trust you," Louka whispered menacingly.

"Where's Maya?" Cash demanded through clenched teeth.

"Oh, your little friend?!" Louka practically yelled with wild eyes. Then he looked over Cash's shoulder and added, "Your niece?" The two men stared at each other until Louka took two big steps back and to the side with a revealing flourish of his arm. "Here's your precious Maya!"

Three gasps. Maya was locked inside the vacated lion cage. Strips of white fabric bound her hands and wrapped across her mouth, keeping her from speaking.

"You thought you could outsmart me?!" Louka shouted wildly, then slammed the cage with the butt of the revolver. Everyone else cringed at the sound. "You thought you could take MY CIRCUS?"

"Go right," Elon quickly whispered to Cash and Boris, barely moving his mouth.

Elon moved left and put his hands up as he addressed his brother, "I just wanted to see your genius new show. These boys were kind enough to let me out."

"LIES! I know you want my circus. You've always wanted it. You've always been jealous of my ideas!" Louka flailed with hair flapping and gun flinging.

"Let's talk about this. You're right. You do have amazing ideas. Maybe we can work together again," Elon kept his hands raised and spoke in a calm voice.

As Elon preoccupied Louka, he continued moving to the left so Boris and Cash could sneak up behind Louka.

"No. You failed me once and now this. It's clear there's only one way for me to have everything," Louka's tone shifted and his demeanor became focused. He raised the gun and pointed it directly at Elon's chest.

Cash's heart felt like it stopped. His hearing dimmed like there was a pillow over his head and it seemed like time slowed down. From behind him, Boris made his move, but he was too late.

Someone else was running in from the doorway.

"Nooooo!" screamed Helen. She lunged in front of Elon as the shot rang out. Helen fell to the ground.

Time stopped with Louka braced against the pushback from the gun, a bewildered look on Elon's face, Boris about to pounce on Louka from behind, the constable running toward Louka, and Maya in a cage screaming despite the gag.

When the world snapped back into motion, Cash's ears rang from the shot. The pandemonium of screams was overwhelming.

Boris crashed into Louka, and the constable bowled into both of them, knocking them into the cage. Elon crumbled next to Helen.

Red. He saw red. It was spreading across Helen's front.

"Get the doctor!" Elon yelled at the doorway. Cash glanced over to see Tony, with an unbelieving look on his face. Tony turned and ran.

The sound of flesh cracking against bone captured Cash's attention. Boris, Louka and the constable were scuffling by the cage. Louka's nose was pouring blood down his mouth and onto his shirt from what Cash could only assume was a punch from Boris. The constable pinned Louka to the cage and was trying to push Boris off of them both. Boris pulled his arm back and landed an uppercut on Louka's jaw. Louka's head slammed against the bars and he slumped into the constable's arms as three police officers pulled Boris away from Louka, the big man fighting and kicking as he went.

Cash dove to his knees next to Helen. Elon had her head in his lap. "Where's the doctor?! Where's Keller?" Elon screamed to the panicked room.

"She can heal herself." Cash said frantically. So much blood. He grabbed Helen's hand and put it over the wound in her abdomen. "She can heal herself. Come on, Helen!"

Elon shook his head in disbelief and said, "Not when she's unconscious." The ringmaster took off his jacket, moved Helen's hands, and pressed the coat over her abdomen.

"What do we do?" Tears slipped down Cash's face as he realized his friend was fading away. "We have to do something!"

"We wait," Elon replied helplessly. "We wait for the doctor."

Cash wept and whispered prayers and commanded Helen to wake up. It felt like the doctor would never arrive, but finally, he did. Dr. Keller shoved Cash away and knelt next to Helen. Cash stood and took in the scene. He was shocked by how much blood there was. The doctor looked at the wound, then took Helen's hand and placed two fingers along her wrist. He didn't move. Cash didn't move. Slowly, the doctor laid Helen's hand on her chest and shook his head. Elon looked away and his body began to shake.

Suddenly, there was an arm around Cash. Boris was moving him away from the scene. Someone had let Maya out of the cage and they met in a hug that was desperate for comfort. She buried her head in Cash's chest and he rested his chin on her head. Boris wrapped his arms around both of them and they sobbed. A police officer led Louka out in handcuffs. The constable, Elon, and the doctor were huddled in the corner talking. Elon kept look-ing down at Helen's body, now covered in a grey blanket.

Tony joined Cash and Maya. Cash mindlessly watched the conversations and the people coming in and out. This was the point where Helen would wrangle them, wrap an arm around them, and lead them out. She would take them to the kitchen, sit them on stools around the prep table, and pour mugs of hot cocoa. Cash could almost feel her hand on his forearm. Then the feeling vanished. Helen was gone.

CHAPTER 25

GOODBYES

A dense quiet settled over the circus in the aftermath of the show. Even the following day, everyone talked in low tones about Helen, Louka, and how Sascha had vanished during the chaos surrounding his father's arrest. They glanced at Cash when he walked by, but quickly averted their eyes and returned to their tasks. Cash felt antsy. He had been answering questions, trying not to remember even though he had to. Wondering when he could get away. Dusk descended.

Cash slowly headed toward the red wagon, hands jammed in his pockets and collar up to guard against the bitter wind. Louka was right about one thing — winter came early. He climbed the steps and paused before knocking softly. Somehow it felt wrong to barge in. Nina opened the door. Cash suddenly was reminded of the younger woman who opened the door the first day he came to the circus. Back then, he could barely speak because he was so scared. Nina welcomed him in and made him feel calm. Today, pain was evident on her kind face and redness rimmed her eyes.

"Is Elon in his office?" Cash asked.

"No, I'm sorry, I don't know where he is," Nina replied.

"Ok," Cash didn't know what to do or say. He looked around the red wagon. Everything felt final. His eyes landed on Nina again. "How are you?" He asked.

She closed her eyes and brushed a strand of dark hair off of her forehead and let out a sigh before looking at Cash. "I can't believe everything that has happened. And Helen…"

"Yeah," Cash added, uncomfortable that he brought it up. He tried a different conversation. "Thank you for everything, Nina. Thank you for taking a chance on me."

"You're welcome," She returned with a gentle smile. "I can't believe how much you've grown, Cash, and not just because you're taller than me now." They both laughed.

"Goodbye, Nina," Cash said simply.

"Bye, Cash," she said casually like he'd be there again tomorrow or the next day. Cash took in the moment with one last glance around the small room: the ticket window, the giant safe, the chair where he sat next to Nina's desk, though she replaced it at some point in the last eight years. He exited and walked down the steps. When he got a few paces away, he looked back over his shoulder. Nina stood in the doorway, watching him. He waved. She smiled, then stepped back and closed the door. Cash redirected toward Elon's car. The chain still hung from the window, and the door was slightly ajar. He knocked and waited… nothing. Sliding open the door, Cash peeked his head in.

"Elon?" Cash stepped in and looked around at the green walls and gold accents. The room was dark. He stood for a moment then saw a slight glow coming from the small window. Cash exited the car, climbed over the coupler, and turned the corner. Elon sat in a wooden chair, lean-ing forward and puffing on a cigar. At the sound of Cash approaching, he leaned back.

"Have a seat," the ringmaster gestured to the empty chair on the other side of the table without even looking at Cash. Cash walked over to the chair, leaves crunching under his feet as he approached. He sat.

"My car feels a bit claustrophobic right now. Can't quite stomach being in there," Elon confessed.

"I don't blame you," Cash stared into the trees in front of them. A squirrel ran across a bare branch, sending a few more leaves to the ground.

They sat in silence and stared into the forest. The weight of what they needed to say hovered like a cloud.

"I'm going to be gone for a few days," the ringmaster finally said. Elon took a puff of his cigar and turned his head to meet Cash's gaze. Cash gave him a surprised look. "I'm taking Helen home to bury her by her husband. By my brother…" Elon leaned forward and rested his elbows on his knees, then looked at Cash again. "Did you know she was my sister-in-law?" Cash nodded a yes in reply.

"She told me a couple of years ago. I don't think many people knew," Cash replied.

"You were close with her. You know, she thought of you like a son. Henri died when they were young. She should have remarried, but she came to the circus and never did." Elon sighed a sigh loaded with years of regret.

"You're not going to be here when I get back, are you?" Elon asked as he looked at Cash and caught a flash of shock.

"How did you…"

"Doesn't matter," Elon interrupted. "Who is going with you?"

"Maya," Cash whispered.

Elon nodded.

"Are you mad?" Cash braced for the response, but they both leaned into the tense stillness. A twig snapped in the distance.

Finally the ringmaster growled in a low voice, "I'm so angry it feels like my skin is going to burst into flame. But am I upset with you? No."

Cash relaxed and asked, "What are you going to do?"

Elon gestured with his hands. "What I always do. Rebuild the show. Figure out what to do with two circuses. Maybe Lorenzo will take one on the road."

"He'd love that!" Both men laughed, then Elon took another puff of his cigar. He blew out the smoke in a thin circle.

"I'll have a new star acrobat very soon," Elon said secretively. Cash looked at him questioningly. "Coco Lovely! Can't you see her on posters? She'll be a smash!" This brought a smile to Cash's face since he really could picture Coco on a poster.

Silence settled between them.

"Sure you don't want to stay?" Elon asked as he stole a glance at Cash. A smile tugged at one side of his mouth.

"I'm sure," Cash added, confident in his decision.

The conversation descended into stillness that was almost comfortable as memories from the past bubbled up. Cash had endured Elon's fury as an incompetent cook, clown and animal wrangler, and again when he refused to sign the last contract. Yet this man provided work and shelter for him and gave him opportunities. Elon always surprised him when it came to generously celebrating Christmas and birthdays. No one could replace his own father, but this man had provided for him and guided him into adulthood in many ways. Cash's breath caught short as he realized he was going to miss Elon.

Cash stood to leave and Elon pushed himself up from his chair as well.

"Cash," the ringmaster looked square at him. "I know you're going to do great things wherever you end up. I've never met anyone as determined as you. It has been an adventure having you at the circus." He extended his hand. Cash clasped it and they shook. Neither acknowledged it, but this was goodbye.

Elon and Helen left before the circus woke up the next morning.

———

Cash entered the silent caboose and closed the door. His hand lingered against the old wood as he realized this would be his last time in this room. He paused for a second to honor the moment, but he had things to do. Since he wasn't fleeing, he wanted to bring more of his things. Cash pulled two canvas bags out of his trunk and put them on the rickety table. More of his memories went into the bags: his costume from Elon's circus, the hat Helen gave him last Christmas, and some warm weather clothes for when spring and summer finally returned. He had just finished fastening the buckles on the first bag when the door flew open.

"Here he is!" Tony yelled. His friend stood in the doorway with a box tucked under his arm.

Bonkers came into view, dropped bags on the platform, then stumbled into the 'boose. He was followed by Boris, Bella and Maya who also dropped bags on the platform.

Cash looked from the platform to Maya quizzically. "Why do you have so many bags?"

Boris replied at an unnecessarily loud volume, "Bella and I are coming too!"

"You are?" Cash asked, surprised.

"With Elon gone for a few days, we decided to go with Maya so I can meet their sister," Bella added with a coy smile. Boris looked down at her and smiled.

Tony squeezed his way past Cash and dropped the box he was carrying on his bed.

"I forgot a few things in Boris' car," Tony said. The lid popped off the box as it landed on the bed and the contents caught Cash's eye.

"Hey! Is that my book about waterfalls?" Cash turned his back on the door and went over to look at Tony's box. He grabbed a small hardbound book with a white cover from the box. "It is!" He flipped through the book and looked at the black and white photos.

"What was it doing in your box? What else of mine is in here?" Cash began to dig through the box. Then the sound of more footsteps on the platform caught his attention and he felt the caboose fall into a tense silence. He heard his friends shuffling around and then next to him, Tony gasped, then whispered, "I saw you at the station…"

Disbelief seized Cash. He gripped the book in his hands and stared at the wall, afraid to grasp the hope of the situation. Slow footsteps came closer behind him. Tony began rapidly nudging him in the ribs.

"Turn around, man," Tony urgently whispered.

"I was told I could find Cash Connor here," an old, yet solid voice announced.

Cash turned slowly. First, he looked at Tony's astonished face, then his eyes fell on an old man a couple of inches shorter than himself. He was mostly bald with a trim beard, was dressed in a sharp beige overcoat and wore academic-looking glasses. His father's eyes stared back at him.

"I'm Cash," came the whispered response.

The old man's serious face morphed into relief and radiated kindness.

"Of course you are," the old man smiled. "Cash, my boy."

"You're my… you're my…" Cash stuttered. *What was he supposed to call him?*

"Grandfather," Cash's grandfather let out a hearty laugh. "I'm your grandfather, Cash." James Connor put his hands on Cash's shoulders and inspected him. "You have your mother's smile."

For a moment no one knew what to say.

"Maybe you two want to talk for a few minutes?" Bella piped up from near the door.

"Yes, that would be lovely," Cash's grandfather turned toward her and responded with a grateful smile.

Cash's friends worked to file out of the small space, and Cash moved his bags from the table.

He and his grandfather each took a seat.

"Are you going somewhere?" James asked, gesturing to the bags now on the ground.

"Believe it or not, I was going to find you," Cash replied with half of a chuckle of disbelief.

Cash's grandfather sat back in surprise.

"You were coming to find *me*? I wasn't even sure you knew I existed." Sadness briefly overshadowed his face, but James continued. "I have been looking for you for years, Cash. It took a long time for me to hear about your parents. That was devastating, but when the officials said they had lost track of you as well, I almost couldn't take it. I knew you would need me, so I packed up my belongings on the other side of the world and moved back. I talked to everyone who knew you. Finally, it seemed like you might have joined the circus. I can't tell you how many circus shows I have been to during my search." He let out a vivacious laugh.

Cash digested this information, then gave a shy grin and gestured to their surroundings. "You heard right. I was even the star acrobat."

Getting serious, his grandfather asked, "Oh! Sounds like you are quite successful. Do you plan on staying?"

Cash shook his head. "No. Things have changed. That's why I was leaving to find you. I wanted…" Tears choked the words he wants to say. Memories of his friends, his routines, Magda's funeral, and Helen's death washed over him and he let out pent-up tears. His grandfather didn't try to stop him, only rested a reassuring hand on his forearm. Eventually, those feelings ebbed away and a new one began to sprout: hope.

Cash attempted to speak again. "I hoped I would find you. And that we could be, if I found you and if you wanted me…I hoped we could be a family." There— he said it. He turned his red-rimmed eyes to his grandfather, his future hanging on the next words he would hear.

"That's what I've been praying for all these years. I can't tell you how sorry I am that it has taken this long to find each other, but please know that I never stopped looking for you." His grandfather spoke and looked into his eyes, and Cash nodded his understanding, then wiped at his nose with his shirt sleeve.

His grandfather continued, "I've been renting a little place several towns north. There's an extra bedroom. You can stay there with me until I can make arrangements to travel back to England. If you like, of course."

"Yeah, that sounds perfect." Cash smiled.

Their conversation was interrupted by a quiet tapping noise, like a nail on glass. Cash looked toward the door to find Tony and Maya enthusiastically peering through the window.

"It appears that your friends are eager to find out what we discussed," James observed with a laugh. Cash waved them in and the door banged open.

James leaned over to Cash and said quietly, "I'd like to meet your friends, but perhaps we move the introductions outside where it's less cramped."

"Good idea," Cash affirmed, then stood and addressed his friends, "We'll come out there." Cash put the waterfall book in one of the canvas bags and quickly buckled it, then picked up both bags. His grandfather immediately took one from him, and Cash grabbed his backpack that was next to the door. As his grandfather moved, Cash caught the scent of cloves, orange and old books. Grandson and grandfather exited the caboose and followed Cash's friends off of the platform. They all gathered on the grass next to the 'boose.

Cash went around the circle and introduced his grandfather to each of his friends. James looked everyone in the eye and shook their hands as Cash looked on in wonder. After the introduction, James added with a hitch in his voice, "Thank you for watching out for my grandson. It means more to me than you could ever know, that he has been surrounded by friends who clearly care about him."

As soon as introductions were over, goodbyes began, and a leaden weight landed in Cash's stomach.

Tony turned toward Cash, slapped him on the back and said, "I'm going to miss you, man. I don't think I'll ever find a best friend like you again."

"Me too. We can still be friends! We just won't live together. Or see each other as much." As he said it, Cash's heart sank, knowing their relationship would never be the same.

"Well, at least I won't have to deal with your morning breath and gross snacks," Tony joked.

"Hey! Pickles, cheese, and apples are normal snacks!" Cash defended himself

"Yeah, but not all together!"

"Ew!" Chimed in Maya and everyone chuckled.

Bonkers approached Cash and extended his hand.

"Cash, I always loved working with you. And I don't envy all those years you spent working with the elephants." They both laughed and Bonkers squeezed his hand in a solid shake.

Cash turned back to the group as Maya and Tony embraced. She wrapped her arms around his waist and leaned her head on his chest. He pulled her in close.

"Don't forget to write me," she whispered.

"I won't," Tony promised. Just as quickly they released the embrace and acted like nothing had happened, except that Cash caught a quick flick of Maya's hand as she wiped away a tear.

In that moment, Cash looked around their little circle of friends to Bonkers, Tony, Maya, Boris and Bella, and for a few seconds, he sensed Helen's presence with them, sending him off.

Before he could become more emotional he said, "Guess we better get going." Cash glanced at his grandfather and stooped to pick up his bags.

"Let's go!" shouted Boris. Boris, Bella, and Maya grabbed their bags and started on their way. Bonkers and Tony walked with them across the grounds. As they approached the exit, Cash heard someone softly running behind them and turned around. Coco came to a stop a couple of feet in front of him, slightly out of breath. His heart started beating faster.

"Cash! I wanted to say goodbye," Coco fidgeted with the edge of her oversized cream-colored jacket, "and I'm sorry. I'm so sorry for what I did—"

"I forgive you," Cash interrupted, "and I understand. There's no reason for you to apologize."

"I'm sorry about Helen," Coco whispered, looking away. "She was a good woman."

Cash nodded his head quickly in acknowledgment, then cleared his throat and put a smile on his face. "Enough apologies, I hear that congratulations are in order!"

Coco beamed, then gushed. "I signed a contract yesterday! It was so generous. I mean, when you compare it to Louka's."

"I'm really happy for you. You're going to be amazing." Cash said, and meant it. Impulsively, he grabbed her hand. "I'll come see one of your shows," he promised.

Coco squeezed his hand in return and gazed up at him with bittersweet eyes. "I'm going to miss you, Cash," she said so only he could hear it. "Meeting you and seeing the strength of your friendships inspired me to stay. Maybe

I can have that too."

"I'm going to miss you too, Coco," Cash said, smiling fondly at her.

"Goodbye, Cash"

"Bye, Coco."

Coco Lovely rocked onto her tiptoes, leaned in, and gave Cash a kiss on the cheek. With a final squeeze of his hand, she headed toward the circus.

Cash turned back to the exit and blushed as he realized that his friends had stopped to watch them. His grandfather had a delighted grin on his face. Then the five of them began their journey into town. They walked together and talked. Boris told stories of Cash's early days at the circus, much to James' delight.

Eventually, Cash and his grandfather fell a few paces behind Bella, Boris, and Maya. They spoke quietly.

"Back in England, I own a bookstore. It's a busy shop on the main street. People of all ages come to buy books, I take special orders for professors, and we host events. It's not as exciting as being an acrobat, but there will always be a job there for you." James explained.

"Oh wow. Thank you," Cash was overwhelmed for a moment, then added, "You know, it was partly because of a book that I even started looking for you."

James looked over at Cash inquisitively. Cash dropped the canvas bag he was carrying and swung his knapsack off his back. Reaching in, he withdrew the orange circus book and handed it to his grandfather. A look of awe overtook James' face as he gingerly took the book from Cash.

"I haven't seen this in at least 30 years," James laughed in disbelief at the book in his hands. "My father gave this to me for my tenth birthday. I passed it on to your father." The old man opened the cover and smiled when he saw Cash's name. "I see that your father passed it on to you."

"Yeah. He gave it to me for my tenth birthday. We were reading it when he and mum… you know. It was one of the only things I took when I left."

"And then you found the circus," his grandfather concluded.

Cash nodded.

James handed the book back to Cash which he tucked away while discreetly wiping tears from his eyes.

"Cash, I can't pretend to imagine how sad and terrified you must have been when your parents died. It is the greatest regret of my life that I was not there for you." James pulled a small red handkerchief from his pocket and pressed it against his eyes.

Images of what life growing up with his grandfather would have been like paraded through Cash's mind. But then he thought of everything he would have missed at the circus.

Cash addressed his grandfather, "I wish I hadn't gone through their deaths alone, but I have amazing friends and memories from the last eight years. Still, I always hoped and dreamed for a family and a permanent home. Hopefully, we can have that now?" Cash glanced at his grandfather looking for a reaction.

"Yes, my boy. We can have that now." James reached out and squeezed Cash's arm before continuing, "Let's go home."

Cash smiled a small relieved smile that grew into a big enthusiastic grin, then energetically picked his canvas bag up off the ground. Cash and his grandfather continued their journey into town and toward their new future. Together.

The End.

ABOUT THE AUTHOR

Sarah "S.A." Bastedo's passion for storytelling has been a lifelong pursuit. Born and raised in St. Louis, MO, Sarah spent her early years lost in the *Chronicles of Narnia*, *Nancy Drew*, and *Little Women*. Though her professional career led her toward different creative pursuits including graphic design, video production, and marketing, she never lost her love for reading and writing. One of her articles was included in the online magazine *Still Standing*, her marketing research was published in the *Journal of Brand Strategy*, and she was a contributing screenwriter on the *100 Pages* film. A firm believer in the power of stories to inspire, Sarah often explores themes of hope and perseverance in her work, aiming to resonate with readers on a personal level. When not immersed in a writing project, Sarah enjoys live music, getting absorbed in a TV show, and exploring new cities. She and her husband live in Nashville, TN.